AT HER SERVICE

ANNA STONE

BOOKS BY ANNA STONE

CLUB VELVET SERIES

Boss of Her

At Her Service

IRRESISTIBLY BOUND SERIES

Being Hers

Her Surrender

Hers to Keep

Freeing Her

MISTRESS SERIES

Tangled Vows

Ensnared Hearts

Forever Theirs

Guarded Desires

BLACK DIAMOND SERIES (WITH HILDRED BILLINGS)

The Girlfriend Arrangement

The Executive Liaison

The Bodyguard Affair

QUEENS SERIES

Capturing Tess

Saving Mia

CHAPTER 1

"Abby." Erin's expression grew serious on the phone screen. "I say this with love. You need to quit your job."

"Not this again." Abby propped her phone against her bag on the picnic table in front of her. "I can't quit. Do you know how hard it is to find a stable nannying gig in LA? Or anywhere? Unless you want to pay my half of the rent." Her job barely even covered that, let alone anything else.

"Okay, maybe not. But this job of yours is ridiculous. You're always working. I hardly get to see you, and we live together."

"Yeah, because you're always at your boyfriend's place," Abby murmured.

"But seriously, when was the last time you had a day off?"

"I don't know, last month maybe?"

"*Last month?* That family is turning you into their servant."

"Maybe. But the Hendersons need me. The boys, they have no one."

Abby looked across the park to where the two boys were kicking around a soccer ball. At 12 and 13, Connor and Owen barely needed watching. They barely needed a nanny at all. But their mom and dad were rarely around, so Abby was their only source of adult supervision. They were lucky if they saw their parents for more than a couple of hours a week.

But that was the reality of being a nanny in Los Angeles. The only people who could afford nannies in such an expensive city were outrageously wealthy types who had better things to do with their time than look after their kids. And it was always the wealthiest parents who tried to stiff her on pay or treated her like a maid, despite living in multimillion-dollar mansions and driving cars that were worth more than Abby's salary.

"If they need you so badly, they can afford to give you a day off now and then," Erin said. "I don't know why you care so much about them in the first place. You're always saying that the parents are a nightmare and the kids are brats."

Abby crossed her arms. "I never said that. I was just venting about my job, that's all. They're good kids." Sure, they misbehaved sometimes. But that was only because their parents threw money and expensive toys at them instead of giving them the love and attention they needed. "I can't just abandon them. Yeah, their parents are awful, but that's all the more reason they need someone looking out for them." Abby knew what it was like to have no one. No kid deserved that.

"Look, I get it," Erin said. "And I understand why that's important to you—"

"Then you understand why I can't quit. So can we just drop this?"

"Sure. I'm sorry, I just miss getting to hang out with you."

"I do too," Abby said. "But hey, I'll see you for your birthday thing next week. I've already told the Hendersons I need the night off."

"Good, because I have a big night planned. And guess who's going to be there?"

Abby sighed. "Who are you trying to set me up with this time?"

Erin crossed her arms. "I'm not trying to set you up with anyone. I'm just letting you know that Amanda is coming. You know, the new girl from work? We were talking, and the reason she moved to LA is because she broke up with her girlfriend. And she keeps going on and on about how hard it is to meet women in LA. The two of you should talk."

"Uh-huh."

"She's not the only one who's single. There are a few single guys coming too."

"I don't think so." While Abby dated men sometimes, Erin's frat bro friends were *not* her type. She had a very specific type, one that had nothing to do with looks or gender.

"I just don't get it. You have twice the options, but you're chronically single."

Abby resisted the urge to roll her eyes. "That's not how it works. And it's still not funny." It wasn't the first time her friend had made that joke.

Erin shrugged. "I'm just saying, I don't get it."

"I know you've been with Dan since we were in middle school, but being single isn't the worst thing in the world. I'm just waiting for the right person."

And if the right person would hurry up, that would be great.

"Well, if you change your mind, I'm here to help. I have tons of single friends. Or I could help you set up a profile on the apps. A hottie like you will get so many matches."

Abby murmured noncommittally, glancing up from her screen to check on the boys. They'd stopped kicking the ball around and were now throwing it at each other as hard as they could. Erin was right. They *were* brats.

But it was hard to look at them and not see her younger brothers. They were around the same age as Connor and Owen. It had been years since she saw them in person, but her mom and stepdad posted photos with them on social media every day. They were the picture-perfect family. Minus Abby.

She gazed around the park. Nearby, a mom pushed her daughter on the swing set, the young girl screaming with glee. Abby felt a pang of envy. Her mom had only ever taken her to the park to get her off her back for a few—

Huh?

Abby zeroed in on the path nearby, where a girl around 2 or 3 years old sat clutching her knee, silent tears streaking down her cheeks. There were no other adults nearby. She was all alone.

"Hello?" Erin said. "Are you even listening to me?"

"Yeah, sorry." Abby glanced at the phone again. "Look, I have to go. Talk to you later."

She ended the call and looked around the park. None of the adults nearby resembled the bronze-skinned, curly-haired girl, but not all children looked like their parents. And in a well-off neighborhood like this, half the kids were at the park with nannies and babysitters.

Keeping Connor and Owen in her eyeline, Abby got up from the picnic table and walked over to the little girl.

"Hey," she said softly, crouching down in front of her. "Are you all right?"

The girl sniffled and shook her head, her tiny ringlets bouncing.

"Is it your knee?"

The girl nodded, shifting her hands from her leg to rub her eyes. She had a nasty graze on her knee, and it was oozing blood.

"Ouch, that must hurt," Abby said. "How about I fix that up for you and we go find your mommy or daddy? Is that okay?"

The girl looked up at her, her doe-brown eyes wide. "I want Mommy," she said quietly.

"Okay, I'll help you find her. Can you tell me your name?"

The girl's lip trembled, but she managed to whisper her name. "Hazel."

"Okay, Hazel. I'll fix your knee right up, and then we'll go find your mom." With luck, her mom would come to them. The toddler couldn't have gotten far.

Abby took Hazel's hand and led her over to the picnic table where she'd left her bag, then began pulling things out of it until she found the first aid kit right at the bottom. Kneeling on the grass in front of her, Abby set about cleaning Hazel's knee, distracting her with soothing words and questions. *How old are you? What's your favorite color? What's your favorite animal?* It was easy to make kids forget they were hurt if their attention was elsewhere.

Hazel's tears were soon replaced by chatter. By the time Abby stuck a bright green band-aid on Hazel's knee, the toddler was babbling animatedly.

"All done," Abby said. "Now, let's see if we can find your mommy."

She looked around the park with narrowed eyes.

Where was this kid's mom?

CHAPTER 2

"Valerie Kane." The woman's voice rang clear through Valerie's earbud. "Writer and producer powerhouse, and owner of Kane Productions, the hottest film and television studio in Hollywood. And all before the age of 40. You're a hard woman to pin down, Valerie. I appreciate you taking the time to talk to me."

"The pleasure is mine." The response was practically a reflex. This was far from Valerie's first interview. But it was the first interview she'd done in the middle of a park with her daughter in tow and a Bluetooth earbud in her ear while she fielded an endless stream of emails and messages on her phone.

She peered into Hazel's stroller. Her daughter was strapped in securely, sleeping like an angel. It was hard to believe she'd spent the hour before screaming up a storm while Valerie desperately tried to get her down for a nap.

The babysitter couldn't have chosen a worse day to cancel. Valerie had had meetings all day leading up to the interview, which she'd already postponed three times. So she'd gone into her office with Hazel, but her daughter had been too restless, so they'd come to the park. Being outdoors had always calmed her down when she was a newborn. And thankfully, it still worked. Because Valerie had her hands full, literally and figuratively.

"Let's refresh our readers' memories," the journalist said. "You started out as a screenwriter on a popular daytime soap and climbed the ladder with astonishing speed. Between your television and film work, you've become the most influential woman in Hollywood. What do you attribute your success to?"

Valerie rattled off a carefully prepared answer, courtesy of her publicist. She was the one who suggested that Valerie accept the interview request in the first place. It was for some magazine or another. *The New Yorker, Harper's Bazaar, Mistress Magazine*—Valerie couldn't remember which. But her publicist had told her it was important, so she'd deferred to the woman's judgment. She didn't have the time to make those kinds of decisions herself.

As Hazel began to stir, Valerie rocked the stroller back and forth. Once her daughter settled again, she opened her inbox on her phone. Her stylist had sent not one, but three increasingly frantic emails about her look for an upcoming movie premiere.

Valerie skimmed the attached photos and shot him a quick reply. *Yes to the Balenciaga but swap out the black shoes for the ivory.*

"You've certainly ruffled some feathers on your way to the top," the journalist continued. "Some describe you as an interloper to Hollywood. How do you deal with the critics?"

Another predictable question, one Valerie was asked

some variation of in almost every interview. It was fuel for the narrative that was her rise up the ranks in Hollywood. A gay Black woman whose films and career success represented a challenge to Hollywood's old guard in the wake of the #MeToo movement? That was a story. And Valerie of all people knew the importance of a story.

"Quite simply, I don't give my critics a second thought," she said. "Grown men throwing tantrums because they have to share their toys? They don't deserve my attention."

Her phone buzzed. She glanced at the screen. Her ex-wife was calling her. That was someone else who didn't deserve her attention.

Still rocking Hazel's stroller, Valerie silenced the call and returned to her emails. The next was from the private kindergarten she'd applied to for Hazel, confirming that her daughter had been accepted. Hazel still had a few years before starting school, but Valerie needed to secure her place early. It was one of the few schools in Los Angeles that had the security required to keep children from high-profile families safe from the paparazzi, and worse.

Valerie glanced around from behind her sunglasses, one hand on the top of her wide-brimmed hat to keep it from blowing away in the wind. There were plenty of high-profile families living in the neighborhood, and now and then, unscrupulous paparazzi would stake out the park in the hope of snapping a photo of a celebrity out with their children.

The paparazzi didn't bother Valerie. But she needed to give Hazel as normal a childhood as possible, which meant shielding her from the spotlight. Whenever a photo of Hazel got out, Valerie would call her people and make it disappear. But it was simpler to keep her from being photographed in the first place.

As she rocked Hazel's stroller, she realized that the journalist had gone silent. Valerie asked her to repeat the question. It was yet another trite question about motherhood.

"I was under the impression that this interview was about my career, not my family," Valerie said. "Would you ask a man in my position the same thing?"

She could almost hear the journalist grimace through the phone. "Point taken. Why don't we move on?"

As she asked the next question, a notification popped up on Valerie's phone. It was a message from her assistant about a minor emergency on set. The young star who had the lead role in her sapphic historical drama series had gotten into an argument with the makeup artist, who was now threatening to quit. An actor behaving badly? That was just another day for her.

Valerie gave her response to the journalist's question, then texted her assistant back with instructions. His reply came a few seconds later. She was so focused on it that she almost missed the journalist's next question.

"You were previously married to Hollywood darling Francesca Moreno. She's certainly been busy in the years since you separated. Just recently, she was the subject of a scandal involving not one, but two members of the hot new indie rock band Sappho and the Poets. Do you have any comments about that?"

"No," Valerie said firmly. "I don't."

"Are the two of you still in touch? You both presented your divorce as amicable, but there are rumors that—"

"Rumors? And here I thought I was speaking to a journalist from a reputable publication, not some gossip rag."

"Let me assure you," the journalist said, "we are not a gossip rag. But our readers, they're curious—"

"Your readers will have to satisfy their curiosity elsewhere. My publicist made it clear that my previous relationship with Francesca is off-limits, did she not?"

"Yes, but—"

"Then this interview is over."

Valerie hung up the call. Her publicist wouldn't be happy. But Valerie would only play nice with the press if the press played nice with her.

As she took out her earbud, she noticed a text message on her phone that she'd missed earlier. It was from her friend Simone.

Ashton wants to meet tonight to talk about investing in the club. Can you make it?

Valerie rubbed her temples with her fingertips. She didn't have space in her schedule for yet another meeting. Simone could easily handle it on her own, but it deserved Valerie's attention. Club Velvet was a passion project she'd started with a few friends. It had only been open for a couple of months, but between Hazel and her job, she barely had time for it.

And the stress of it all was beginning to take its toll on her. She was no stranger to hard work, but even she had her limits. Right now, she was running on empty.

She sent a reply to Simone, letting her know that she had to look after Hazel so she wouldn't be attending the meeting. She needed to hire a new nanny, and soon. The last one had run off to Europe with her boyfriend and had no intention of ever returning. Valerie had been relying on sitters ever since, but she needed to find someone permanent.

However, finding a nanny was no easy feat. Hazel was a shy, anxious child, especially around strangers. She'd started talking late, and even now, she barely spoke more than a few words, never to anyone other than Valerie. Finding a nanny who Hazel felt comfortable with was proving impossible.

On top of that, Valerie needed a nanny she could trust to be discreet, someone who would respect the privacy she insisted upon, both for herself and for her daughter. The intimate details of their lives were valuable fodder to the tabloids and gossip sites. She hadn't forgotten the circus the media had created when she and her ex-wife divorced a few years ago. It had been a housekeeper who spilled the news of their break-up to the press.

That had been bad enough. If the press knew what Valerie Kane got up to behind closed doors? That would be a real scandal.

She peered into the stroller to check on Hazel. It took her a moment to register what she saw.

Hazel wasn't sleeping soundly.

She wasn't in her stroller at all.

Panic flooded Valerie's body. She looked around her, but Hazel was nowhere in sight. She'd been asleep in her stroller just a minute ago. How had she gotten out? Where had she gone?

Had someone taken her?

"Hazel? Hazel!" She looked around the park frantically, her pulse pounding. How could she have lost her daughter? She'd spread herself too thin for too long, and now she was paying the price. Now *Hazel* was paying the price—

No time to panic. Find her, now. Valerie steeled herself, every muscle in her body springing into action. As adrenaline filled her veins, she looked around the park again, her eyes narrowed with focus. Hazel couldn't have gotten far. She was barely two and a half, and Valerie had only taken her eyes off her for a moment. She had to be here somewhere...

There. Relief surged through Valerie's body. At the other side of the playground, Hazel stood beside a picnic table, a young woman with a mane of copper red hair kneeling before her.

As Valerie rushed toward them, Hazel giggled, then spotted her mother and beamed.

"Mommy!"

CHAPTER 3

"Oh, sweetheart, there you are!"

Abby turned to see a woman dashing toward them, tall and lithe with deep bronze skin and long dark curls. Her arms outstretched, she swept Hazel up into an embrace, holding her tightly as she let out a deep sigh.

"I thought I lost you." She looked Hazel up and down, her eyes falling on the band-aid on the toddler's knee. "Are you all right? Are you hurt?"

Hazel shook her head. Abby glanced at the woman, who was so focused on her daughter that she barely seemed to notice Abby at all. The resemblance between her and Hazel was undeniable. She had the same rich brown skin and dark curls, which cascaded down her shoulders from under a wide-brimmed hat. Large sunglasses adorned her face, and she wore a fitted black dress and heels that were far too glamorous for a trip to the park.

But Abby couldn't deny how striking the look was. It was like the dress had been stitched around each and every curve on her body. It was just short enough to accentuate her long legs while still looking professional, and the wide V neckline showed off her smooth, bronze shoulders and chest, allowing a glimpse of her full, luscious—

Abby glanced away. But it was too late. The woman had noticed her.

She peered down at Abby. "And you are?"

Abby's cheeks burned. Had the woman caught her staring? Her eyes were hidden behind her sunglasses, revealing nothing.

"Uh, hi," Abby said. "I found her just over there. She'd fallen over and was crying, and she was all alone, so I figured she was lost. I just finished cleaning up her knee when you came over. Oh, I'm Abby, by the way. I'm a nanny. The kids I'm looking after are playing soccer over there…"

Abby clamped her mouth shut. She was rambling. The woman was so mesmerizing that she couldn't help it. While her dark glasses hid her eyes, Abby could somehow feel the woman's gaze on her.

Finally, the woman took off her sunglasses, folded them up, and slipped them into the V-neck of her dress. "I'm Valerie."

Valerie. The way her name rolled off her tongue, melodic and firm and *sensual*, sent heat rising through Abby's body.

"Would you like to get up?" Valerie said.

Abby glanced down at herself. She was still on her knees. Why was she still on her knees? No wonder Valerie was staring at her.

Valerie held out her hand. "Let me help you."

Abby took her hand and rose to her feet, a shiver trickling down her back. Valerie's skin was soft as silk, her fingernails short but manicured. This was a woman who was meticulous about her appearance. Her nails, her clothes, her deep red lips and perfect curls, not a single strand out of place. Even the perfume she wore, velvet smooth and honey sweet, was subtle but intoxicating.

Valerie released her hand. Abby hadn't realized she was still holding it. She turned to the table and began packing up her first aid kit to give herself something to do.

"Thank you for finding my daughter," Valerie said. "I can't tell you how much I appreciate it. I don't know how she got out of her stroller. She's never done anything like this before."

"It happens," Abby replied. "They're little escape artists at that age. All that matters is that Hazel is okay."

Valerie tensed. "Hazel?"

"Yeah, isn't that her name?"

"Yes, it is." Suddenly, Valerie's voice was cold as frost. "But I didn't tell you that."

"No, she did. We had a nice little chat." Abby pointed at Hazel's knee. "She told me green is her favorite color, so I gave her a green band-aid."

Valerie's eyes narrowed. "She told you that? She spoke to you?"

Abby nodded. "It took a minute to get her talking, but once she got started, she wouldn't stop. She's a smart kid. Why?"

Valerie looked Abby up and down. "No reason."

Silence fell over them. Still in her mother's arms, Hazel reached out and grabbed Valerie's sunglasses, clutching them in her small fists as she tried to put the oversized glasses on her face. But Valerie barely seemed to notice. Her eyes were locked on Abby again.

Abby's heart thumped. *Why does she keep looking at me like that?*

Finally, Valerie broke the silence. "You're a nanny?"

Abby nodded. "Yes." Was that why Valerie was staring at her? Because she was suspicious of the strange woman lurking in the park who had found her child? "Here, let me show you."

She pulled out her phone and brought up her profile on the Nanny Finder app. All the parents in Los Angeles used it to find nannies and sitters. The app verified nannies' identities and credentials, so it was an easy way for Abby to prove that she was who she said she was.

She held her phone out to Valerie, who skimmed the screen, then nodded. But as Abby put her phone away, Valerie spoke again.

"What would it take for you to come work for me?"

Abby blinked. "What do you mean?"

"You're a nanny. I need a nanny. Rather, Hazel does."

"Are you… Are you offering me a job?"

"I am. There will be an interview, of course, and I'll need to look into your qualifications and experience. But Hazel likes you. And she *spoke* to you, a complete stranger." Valerie nodded at the first aid kit and other items from Abby's bag, which were still scattered on the table. "You're well prepared, which tells me you take your job seriously. And most importantly, you were the only person in the entire park to notice that Hazel was lost. You took the initiative, not just to help her, but to get to know her. That shows you care. And that's exactly what I'm looking for in a nanny."

"Wow," Abby said. "I'm flattered. Hazel seems like a sweet kid, and you're—"

Beautiful? Commanding? Hotter than sin?

"—you seem like a great mom. But I…" Abby shook her head. "I already have a job."

But her tone must have betrayed her.

"Are you happy with your job?" Valerie asked.

"I'll be honest. It's… not great. But I've been with the family for a few years now. I wouldn't feel good about leaving them without a nanny."

"Then I won't try to poach you from a family who so sorely needs you. But if you decide you'd like a change, my offer stands. Come work for me, and I'll make sure you don't regret it. A full-time position, with benefits, generous paid vacation time and sick leave, your own room, use of the rest of the house, everything."

Time off, and *paid* at that? Plus, her own room? She wouldn't have to pay rent on the shoebox apartment she shared with Erin anymore.

"And whatever salary you're on now?" Valerie said. "I'll double it."

Abby's eyes widened. "Double? But you don't even know how much I'm getting paid."

"I don't need to."

"But that's…" *Ridiculous? This is ridiculous, right?*

"Listen, Abby. My daughter is the most important thing in the world to me. So whoever I choose to help me take care of her will be well looked after. A good nanny is more precious than gold. When I find one, I'll do whatever it takes to keep her happy. Come work for me, and

I'll make sure your every need is taken care of. Come work for me, and I'll make sure you're treated right, just like you deserve."

Abby's breath caught in her chest. There was something captivating about the way Valerie spoke, her scarlet lips, her dark, piercing eyes, that compelled Abby to say *yes*...

She tore her eyes away, glancing at Connor and Owen. That was all it took to break the spell. She couldn't quit her job. She couldn't abandon them.

And there was no way she could work for Valerie when just being in her presence made her heart race.

"I'm sorry," she said. "I can't."

If Valerie was disappointed, she didn't show it. "I understand. Let me give you my number just in case." She shifted Hazel onto one hip and reached into her purse, withdrawing a small black business card. "It's the number for my personal cell. If you change your mind, give me a call."

Abby took the card from her. Hazel chose that moment to throw Valerie's sunglasses to the ground. Then, realizing they were now out of her reach, she began to wail.

"Looks like it's time to get Hazel home." Valerie leaned down and picked up the sunglasses, handing them back to her daughter. "Thank you again for everything."

Abby shook her head. "It was nothing. Really."

Valerie gave her a nod of farewell and walked away.

It was only once she was out of sight that Abby realized she'd been staring again. She looked down at the business card in her hand. It was matte black and inscribed with gold text.

She traced her fingers over the gold lettering. *Valerie Kane,* the card read, followed by a phone number. Otherwise, it was bare.

Wait, Valerie Kane? As in, the *Valerie Kane?*

Abby's hand flew to her mouth. She looked up again.

But Valerie was long gone.

She collapsed onto the bench behind her. She'd been talking to *Valerie Kane,* and she hadn't had a clue. She should have guessed the woman was someone famous. She was stunning. Magnetic. And oh so commanding in a way that made Abby's whole body sizzle.

And she'd made a fool of herself, getting all flustered and rambling about her job. Not that it mattered. There was no way someone like Valerie Kane would ever be interested in her. She was so far out of Abby's league that she was playing a completely different game. That had been obvious even before Abby realized who she was.

But as she replayed their conversation in her mind, all she could think about was the way Valerie looked down at her when she was on her knees.

And the way the woman's eyes smoldered as she did.

Valerie glanced out the tinted car window from her place in the back passenger seat. It was late, but the streets of West Hollywood were packed with traffic. At this rate, it would be faster to get out and walk, but she was wearing stilettos, and she'd been on her feet the whole day. No, the whole week.

But the week was finally over. It was Friday night. And for the first time in an eternity, she had a night to herself. She'd called in a favor and found a sitter for Hazel, all so she could have a chance to unwind somewhere there weren't toys scattered all over the floor and a mountain of scripts for her to review on the coffee table. For just one night, she needed to not be Valerie Kane.

And her destination was the perfect place for that.

But tonight was only a temporary reprieve. What she really needed was someone to help her with Hazel long-term.

As the traffic started moving again, she opened up the Nanny Finder app on her phone and began scrolling through the listings. Finding and screening potential nannies was her assistant's job, but none of the candidates he'd chosen had been suitable. Valerie had high standards, and she didn't compromise them. Not at work, not in her personal life, and especially not when it came to her daughter.

Even those who met her standards hadn't worked out, all because Hazel hadn't clicked with them. But there was one nanny Hazel liked. One nanny she'd instantly felt comfortable with. One nanny Hazel still remembered, even though they'd only spent minutes together.

And that was the nanny they'd met at the park a week ago.

Valerie typed her name into the search bar. *Abigail Peters*. Valerie had glimpsed her full name when she'd shown her credentials on the very same app.

Sure enough, Abby's profile appeared. Valerie skimmed the page. While it indicated that Abby wasn't looking for work, just like she'd said, she met all of Valerie's requirements except one. She was only 23, which wasn't old enough for her to have the level of experience Valerie wanted. Still, she'd been nannying for five years.

She scrolled back up to Abby's photo at the top of the page. Her copper hair flowed down her shoulders, and a sprinkling of freckles, the same shade of reddish brown as her hair, dotted her pale face. Her eyes were a vibrant green, and her lush pink lips seemed to tease Valerie through the screen. Even in the photo, she could feel the same eager warmth that had radiated from Abby that day at the park. She was everything Valerie desired in a nanny.

She was everything Valerie desired in a woman.

But no matter how perfect Abby was, she'd already

turned down the job. And that was for the best. Having a woman she was undeniably attracted to working for her, *living with her*, in her own home? That was a recipe for disaster.

As Valerie swiped the profile away, an image flashed across her mind. Of Abby at the park that day, on her knees, her long, floaty sundress fanned out beneath her, the thin straps and low-cut neckline framing her breasts. It was almost seductive, the way Abby knelt before her, peering up at her from under long dark eyelashes, a look in her eyes that stirred something deep within Valerie's body.

Valerie wanted her. And the way Abby had blushed at her every word made one thing clear—Abby wanted her too.

She pushed the thought from her mind. Obviously, the only reason she felt so intensely toward Abby was because it had been too long since she'd had any kind of intimacy. The last woman she'd been with had been her ex-wife, who she'd divorced years ago, but their relationship had been over long before it ended on paper. And while Valerie had moved on, she wasn't interested in entering into another relationship.

Her phone began to buzz. *Speak of the devil.* Because if anyone could be called that, it was Francesca.

She silenced the call. She was in no mood for her ex-wife. Not tonight. As she slipped her phone back into her purse, the car came to a stop. She'd arrived.

Her driver got out and opened her door, holding it for her as she stepped out of the car. She gave him a nod of thanks, informing him she'd be a few hours, and stepped onto the sidewalk.

Breezing past the queue of women lined up to enter the club, she nodded to the bouncer at the front, who unclipped the red velvet rope across the doorway and gestured her inside. She entered the lobby and checked her coat and purse, but she kept her phone with her.

Then, she stepped into the club.

She gazed around, taking it all in. The music, the lights, the buzz of the crowd. Despite appearances, Club Velvet wasn't a nightclub. No, she and the other owners had brought Club Velvet into being for a very different purpose.

It was a sanctuary. A temple of pleasure and self-discovery, of sensuality and sin. A place for women to explore their wildest, darkest desires. This was Valerie's world.

This was her empire.

She strode to the bar and ordered a martini. It was quicker than waiting for a server to come to her, and after the week she'd had, she needed a strong drink, fast. As the bartender mixed her martini, she drew a few glances. At Club Velvet, she was famous.

But not because she was Valerie Kane.

"I see Madame V has graced us with her presence," a voice said dryly.

Valerie turned as her friend Elle appeared beside her, gesturing to the bartender for another drink. She too drew stares, but that was because of her outfit. It was the definition of "little black dress," low-cut and devilishly short and tight on her curvy figure. She'd have women lining up to go home with her tonight, which, knowing Elle, was exactly what she wanted.

"Hello to you too," Valerie said, as the bartender

returned with their drinks. "I finally had a night off, so I decided to drop in. Are the others here tonight?"

"Just me," Elle replied. "As usual, it falls to yours truly to hold down the fort."

Like Valerie, she was one of the owners of Club Velvet, alongside Simone and Olivia. While all four partners played a role in managing the club, Elle's experience running nightclubs as CEO of her own entertainment company meant that much of the day-to-day management fell to her. But she made just as much time for play as she did for work.

She flicked her strawberry blonde hair over one shoulder. "It's good to see you here tonight. And it's good to see you letting Madame V out to play."

"It's been a long week," Valerie said. "I felt the need for an escape."

Her phone buzzed. Someone was calling her. The sitter?

So much for an escape. She glanced at the screen. It wasn't the sitter. It was her ex-wife. *Again.*

As she silenced the call, a message from Francesca that she'd missed earlier appeared on her screen. *I just want to talk. Can you call me back?*

Valerie took a long sip of her martini.

"Let me guess," Elle said. "Francesca?"

"Is it that obvious?"

"She's the only person in the world who can make that steely mask of yours crack. Not that I blame you. That woman is a real piece of work."

"You're telling me," Valerie murmured. "She's started contacting me again out of nowhere. I don't know why, but she's being very persistent about it."

Elle swirled her drink around in her glass. "So why even entertain her? Just let your lawyers handle it."

"It's not that simple."

"Why not? I just don't understand it. It's like she has this hold on you."

If only you knew. But the truth about Francesca and what she was capable of was something neither Elle nor anyone else would understand.

"Look, I get it," Elle said. "You were together for what, six years? She got her claws into you good. But it's time to move on."

Valerie's jaw tensed. "I *have* moved on."

"Then why haven't you taken a sub since Francesca?"

"Quite simply, I don't have the time to devote to a submissive. I have too much else going on. There's my job, to start with. On top of my historical drama series, I have a new film in development that has the potential to be my biggest yet. There's Club Velvet, which is still in its infancy, so we need to make sure it succeeds. And there's Hazel. She's my number one priority." At least she was supposed to be. But that day in the park had proven that Valerie was spread too thin to juggle taking care of her daughter with everything else. "I don't have room in my life for anyone new."

Elle set her glass down on the bar. "Just look around you. Look at all these women. Do you have any idea how many of them would give anything to kneel before Madame V?"

Valerie looked out over the club. All around them, women mingled and touched and kissed. And many were doing far more. Some were in pairs. Some were in groups. And some were alone, watching, waiting, *wanting.*

Elle was right. With just a look, Valerie could have an eager woman at her command. That was why she'd come here tonight.

But that wasn't what she truly desired.

"You need to find someone new. Someone who will worship at your feet. Someone to spoil and lavish with all kinds of wicked pleasures in exchange for her undying devotion." Elle's ruby-red lips curled into a smile. "That's the kind of thing you like, isn't it?"

For the second time that night, an image arose in Valerie's mind. Of Abby, kneeling before her like she had that day at the park, eyes down, pink lips and dark freckles tempting her, inviting her.

But this time, she wasn't at the park in that ethereal sundress. No, she was kneeling at Valerie's feet on the marble floors in that hidden room in her house, dressed in pure white lingerie, her red hair spilling down bare shoulders…

Valerie pushed the thought aside. She needed to put Abby out of her mind, along with any thoughts of finding a submissive, both tonight and any other night.

Because everything she'd told Elle was the truth. She didn't have room in her life for someone new.

Or in her heart.

CHAPTER 5

Oh my god, you met Valerie Kane? Where? When? Tell me everything!

Abby sighed. She knew that telling Erin about her run-in with Valerie would mean she'd want to know every single detail.

Abby didn't care about celebrities. Erin, on the other hand? She was obsessed. She scoured gossip sites daily, and she knew everything there was to know about every famous person in the city. If she found out that Valerie Kane had given Abby her number, she'd never hear the end of it.

It's no big deal, Abby sent back. *It was last week, at the park. She was there with her kid and we kind of ran into each other.*

She'd spent the days since trying desperately not to think about their encounter, and about Valerie herself. But that wasn't easy when she had a job that left her with plenty of time to daydream. Like right now.

She stretched out across the couch. It was Friday

night, and Connor and Owen were asleep upstairs, their parents out at a party. They'd been due home hours ago, but Abby hadn't heard from them, and they weren't answering her calls. That was nothing new. They came home late more often than not. It wouldn't be so bad if she didn't have to argue with them about getting paid for the extra hours every time it happened.

Her phone vibrated again. Erin had replied.

Last week? And you're only telling me now?

I guess I forgot, Abby lied. *Like I said, it was no big deal.*

It's a huge deal. This is Valerie Kane we're talking about. What was she like?

She was... Abby paused in thought. *A little intimidating. I got kinda tongue-tied. She's just so successful and talented.*

Uh-huh. I'm sure it's her "talent" that had you all hot and bothered.

Abby's cheeks flushed. *Ok, so she's gorgeous too.*

There was no point denying that to Erin or herself. The moment she laid eyes on Valerie, she'd forgotten how to breathe.

You have to tell me more when you get home, Erin sent. *Weren't you supposed to finish an hour ago?*

Two hours, actually. Abby erased the message without sending it. She didn't need Erin on her back about quitting her job again.

But the idea was starting to seem appealing. Especially now that Valerie had offered her a job. The pay and benefits were far better than her current job. And the conditions? They definitely sounded better.

Come work for me, and I'll make sure your every need is taken care of. Come work for me, and I'll make sure you're treated right, just like you deserve.

Heat trickled down Abby's back. Why did her body react that way to Valerie's words? Everything about her had that effect on Abby. Her dark, smoldering eyes. Her full red lips. Her luscious curves…

Abby shook her head. She'd made the right choice in turning Valerie down. She couldn't risk quitting her job for one offered to her on a whim by a stranger, let alone a stranger who made her body weak and sent her mind racing with all kinds of naughty thoughts.

Besides, Connor and Owen needed her. Their parents saw them as a nuisance and had no interest in raising them. Abby of all people knew what that was like. She couldn't abandon them.

It would be like abandoning her brothers all over again.

The sound of a key in a lock broke through Abby's thoughts. As she slipped her phone into her purse and sat up, the front door opened and a middle-aged man, red-faced, stumbled inside, a thin, blonde woman far younger than him clinging to his arm as she swayed atop sky-high heels. She kicked her shoes off, one after the other, almost tripping over her own feet. But she managed to stop herself from falling by grabbing onto the hall table next to her, the keys and trinkets on top of it clattering to the floor.

Her husband hurled a curse, slumping heavily against the wall beside him.

The Hendersons were home. And they were drunk.

Abby got up from the couch and cleared her throat.

Mrs. Henderson, as she insisted on being called, blinked as if surprised to see her there. "Abby, darling," she drawled. "I hope the boys weren't any trouble tonight."

"They were fine." Abby slung her purse over her shoulder. There was no point now in bringing up the fact that they were late. It was past 11 p.m. She was tired. And the Hendersons were too drunk for her to have a serious conversation with them.

"You can go home now," Mrs. Henderson said. "But remember to be here at six tomorrow morning. My sister is coming, so you'll need to clean the house."

Abby gritted her teeth. She was a nanny, not a maid. That was so far outside of her job description that it was in another zip code.

But before she could object, Mrs. Henderson spoke again. "We'll need you to work tomorrow night too. The Fairchilds are holding a gala, so you'll need to look after the boys."

Anger simmered in Abby's stomach. Tomorrow was Erin's birthday. She had to be there. She'd promised.

Abby shook her head. "I can't work tomorrow night," she said calmly. "I told you that weeks ago. I have plans."

"Well, you'll have to cancel them," Mrs. Henderson replied. "We simply can't miss this gala."

"I can't cancel this." And even if she could, she didn't want to. "I'm sorry, but you'll have to find someone else."

"Abby, darling." Mrs. Henderson leaned in close, her botox-frozen face inches from Abby's, her breath sharp with the smell of wine. "You seem to be under the impression this is up for negotiation." She jabbed her finger into Abby's chest. "*You* work for *me*. *You* do what *I* say."

"No, not this time." Abby's hands tightened into fists. "I'm not letting you walk all over me. I'm not letting you push me around. I'm not working overtime again just so you can stiff me on pay—"

"How dare you talk to my wife that way," Mr. Henderson shouted. "You're lucky to even have this job."

"No, *you're* lucky to have someone who cares about your kids enough that they're willing to put up with both of you." Abby crossed her arms. "Not anymore. It's been three years of this. I'm done."

Mrs. Henderson scoffed. "Excuse me?"

"You heard me. I'm done. Consider this my resignation."

The woman recoiled as if she'd been slapped. "You're quitting? Over this?"

"Yes. And I should have quit a long time ago."

"You ungrateful brat," Mr. Henderson snarled. "Go on, then. Leave. But good luck finding another job. If you walk out that door, we'll have you blacklisted. No one will hire you. You'll never work as a nanny in this city again!"

"Yeah, I've heard that before." His threats weren't going to work on her this time.

She picked up her jacket from the arm of the couch and headed for the door.

"Get out!" Mrs. Henderson yelled behind her. "Get out of our house. And don't think we're paying you for tonight after this stunt!"

Abby didn't break her stride as she left the house and marched down the driveway to where her car was parked on the street. It wasn't until she was safely inside that she realized she was shaking.

Oh my god. I can't believe I did that. What am I going to do now? Will the boys be okay without me? How am I going to make rent this month? What if the Hendersons weren't bluffing? What if they really can have me blacklisted?

She took a deep breath, then another. Connor and Owen were old enough now to take care of themselves. Despite their parents, they'd be fine without her.

As for finding a new job? Abby already had another offer, one that had fallen right into her lap.

She rummaged around in her purse and pulled out the matte black business card. She'd kept it all this time, even though she'd had no intention of ever using it. But now that she was unemployed, she'd be a fool to pass on Valerie's offer. That was if Valerie even remembered her.

Abby pulled out her phone and dialed the number on the card. As the phone rang, she realized it was almost midnight.

I shouldn't be calling her so late. But before she could hang up, Valerie picked up the call.

"Hello? Who's this?"

"Hi," Abby stammered. Valerie's voice was muffled, and there was a buzzing in the background. Was it music? "I'm sorry for calling this late. It's Abby. The nanny. From the park."

"Ah, yes. How could I forget? Give me a minute, Abby. I'll go somewhere quieter."

Abby waited silently. As seconds passed, the buzz in the background faded.

Finally, Valerie spoke again. "All right, Abby. Go ahead."

"Well, I've been thinking," she said. "About your job offer. Are you still looking for a nanny?"

She held her breath. Had she missed her chance? She'd

already turned the job down. Surely Valerie had moved on and found another nanny by now.

"Yes," Valerie said. "I'm still looking. Why don't you come by on Tuesday evening for an interview?"

"I'd love to." Abby cleared her throat. She'd sounded a little too eager. "I mean, Tuesday works for me."

"Good. I'll have my assistant send you the details. See you then."

Abby said goodbye and hung up the phone. But her relief was quickly replaced by anxiety.

Because her livelihood now depended on a woman who rendered her breathless every time she said Abby's name.

CHAPTER 6

Abby stared up at the Hollywood Hills mansion in the distance as she turned into the driveway, stopping before the ornate iron gates. The sprawling two-story house sat at the top of a hill, rising above everything else.

Abby grabbed her phone and checked the address again. *Yep, this is Valerie's house. Here goes nothing.*

She rolled down her window and pressed a button on the intercom next to the gate, glancing at the camera above it. A few seconds later, the gate rolled open.

Taking a deep breath, she put her car in drive and made her way up to the mansion. Why was she so nervous? Valerie wasn't the first wealthy parent she'd worked for. But she was the only one who made Abby's heart stop with just a look and had a voice that made her whole body burn.

She parked her car in the driveway. The enormous mansion was even more impressive up close. The sun was setting, the orange sky reflecting in the glass windows that made up every wall of the house, and it was high enough in the hills that even this far inland Abby could see the ocean stretching out beyond the Los Angeles cityscape.

She stepped out of the car, trying not to think about how out of place her old junker looked in front of the opulent mansion. When she reached the front door, she took a moment to compose herself, then rang the doorbell.

A few seconds passed. Then, the door opened and Valerie appeared, dressed in a light tan pantsuit and black heels that made her long legs look even longer. Her hair hung loose over her shoulders in tight curls, and her lips were a deep, rich crimson. She looked just as tantalizing as she had in the park that day.

And like that day, she sent Abby's heart racing.

"Abby. I've been waiting for you." Valerie looked her up and down. "Why don't you come in?"

Abby followed her into the wide-open living space. The inside of the house was much like the outside, all crisp edges and glass, with marble floors and modern art. But it didn't feel harsh or sterile. The evening sun streamed through the floor-to-ceiling windows, which gave the mansion a cozy warmth and brightness. So did the fluffy oversized cushions on the couch and the luxuriously soft rug on the floor that Abby longed to sink her bare feet into.

And there were plenty of signs of Hazel's presence, from the high chair at the dining table to the brightly colored wooden toy chest beside the couch and the discreet baby gate at the bottom of the stairs. The entire mansion, inside and out, had been meticulously designed, every element intentionally curated.

Abby turned back to Valerie. She'd been gawking for too long. "You have a beautiful home."

"It's only a few years old," Valerie said. "I had it built just before Hazel was born so she could have a place of her own to grow up in, something truly unique and special."

She led Abby over to the couch and gestured for her to sit. Abby sat down obediently.

"I've just put Hazel to bed, so let's get down to it." Valerie took a seat in the armchair across from her. "As you know, I'm looking to hire a new nanny. It's a full-time, live-in position. You'll work for me and only me."

"That's not a problem. I quit my old job, so I'm completely free." Abby would have to talk to Erin about it, but it wouldn't be hard for her to find a new roommate to take over half the lease.

"Good, because there's one thing I need you to understand." Valerie crossed one leg over the other, folding her hands neatly on her lap. "My daughter is my world. I'm entrusting her to you with the expectation that you give her, and your work for me, your undivided attention. That you put your job first."

Abby nodded. Unlike that day at the park, Valerie was all business this evening. But that only made her more enticing.

"While I may have high standards, I'm not an unreasonable woman. In return for your service, you can expect generous compensation. Double your old salary, as agreed. Full benefits, your own room, all food and meals included, ample time off. If you're going to be responsible for my child, I need you well-rested and at your best. You'll work no more than 40 hours a week, however, I expect some flexibility in terms of when you work. Do you have any other commitments? Family, regular engagements or appointments?"

Abby shook her head. "I can be available whenever you need me."

"Oh?" Valerie swept her eyes down Abby's body, then back up again. "Surely a young woman like you has plenty to do with her time. No boyfriend or girlfriend to keep you busy?"

"Nope. I'm all yours."

Valerie's lips curled up slightly. "Good to know."

Abby's cheeks grew hot. But Valerie's smile soon disappeared.

"Let me be honest. I've already vetted you—called your references, verified your credentials, run a background check—and I'm satisfied with what I found. And we already know Hazel likes you. With that in mind, I'd like to take you on for a trial. One week, starting next Monday. How does that sound?"

"That sounds great," Abby said.

"Do you have any questions for me? Any reservations or issues you'd like to discuss?"

"No, nothing comes to mind."

Valerie studied Abby's face. "You seem nervous. Is something the matter?"

"Not at all."

Valerie leaned forward in her chair. "Now, Abby, we don't want to start our working relationship off on a lie, do we?"

A shiver rolled down Abby's body. Was it that obvious how hot and bothered she was?

Was it obvious *why*?

"I…" She glanced away for a moment. "I guess I'm just a little intimidated by you."

"Oh? And why is that?"

"Well, you're so famous and talented, and—" Abby held up her hands. "Don't get me wrong. I'm not some obsessed fan. I didn't even know who you were until after you left the park and I looked at your business card…"

Abby cringed. With every word she spoke, she was making things worse.

"But I *do* know your work," she said. "I've seen most of your movies. And I've watched every single episode of *LA Legal*."

"I'm impressed," Valerie said. "*LA Legal* was my first production gig, and not my best work. The network had far too much control over it."

"It's a bit of a guilty pleasure for me. It has been since I was a teenager. I had the biggest crush on Monica."

Valerie raised an eyebrow. "Is that so?"

Way to out yourself to your boss. The last thing Abby needed was for it to be even more obvious that she was into Valerie.

But judging by the look in her eye, Valerie already knew.

"You're not the first woman who has told me as much," she said. "A strong, confident lawyer like Monica has a certain appeal. My one regret is that I didn't fight harder to have her end up in a relationship with the detective."

"You mean Evelyn? I always thought they were supposed to be a couple."

Valerie nodded. "But the network wouldn't allow it back then, so the best I could do was hint at their relationship by having them drive off into the sunset together at the end of the finale." She sat back in her seat. "Back to the topic at hand. Let me reassure you that you have no reason to feel intimidated by me. If you're going to work for me, live here with me, I want you to feel comfortable around me. Just pretend you're babysitting for the mom next door."

"Right. Sure." But thinking of Valerie as the mom next door didn't make her any less alluring.

She rose to her feet. "Let me show you around."

Abby got up and followed, Valerie's heels clicking on the marble floors as she led her to the stairs. The second floor was a labyrinth of halls and rooms, each of which Valerie described as they passed. There was a playroom for Hazel, stocked to the brim with books, crafts, and toys. Her bedroom, a forest of green filled with bespoke toddler-sized furniture, a magical woodland mural flowing across every wall. A guest suite and several spare bedrooms, each with their own spacious bathroom. A theater room and a cozy reading room. And the main bedroom, Valerie's room. All were meticulously neat and tidy. There was none of the usual chaos caused by a toddler.

Valerie stopped at a door midway between Hazel's bedroom and her own. "This will be your room."

Abby peered inside. The "room" was more like a full-sized hotel suite. In the center was a plush king-sized bed, a spacious sitting area off to the side. A loveseat sat by the large window, which provided a picture-perfect view of the sun setting over the city. At the other end of the room were two doors, one leading to a generously sized ensuite bathroom furnished with marble counters, gold fixtures, and a vast bathtub. The other led to a walk-in closet that was twice as big as her apartment bedroom.

Abby blinked. She was gawking again. "This looks great."

"I'm glad you like it," Valerie said. "I want you to feel at home here. You're free to make use of the rest of the house, aside from my bedroom and my study. It's downstairs. I'll show you."

Valerie led her back downstairs and over to a door just off the living room. It had a keypad next to it.

"My study stays locked at all times," she said. "It isn't safe for a child, and I keep sensitive material inside, so it's off-limits to both you and Hazel, understand?"

"Yes, of course." Valerie was a Hollywood executive. She probably had unreleased movie scripts and other top-secret material to protect.

They moved on to the home gym and the rest of the downstairs rooms before Valerie led her outside to show her the deck and crystal-clear pool. Then they headed back inside and into the kitchen.

"Help yourself to anything in the fridge at any time," Valerie said. "Emergency contacts are here. If you can't get a hold of me, try Simone first, then go down the list."

Abby nodded. Valerie was far better prepared than most of the parents she'd worked for before.

"That's the tour done. But there's one last thing we need to discuss." Valerie's expression grew serious. "I value my privacy, and Hazel's even more so. As a woman in the public eye, my family and I are under constant scrutiny. So I ask that you keep anything to do with me and Hazel under wraps. You will *not* speak about the details of your job to anyone. You will not post about it on social media. You will not take any photos or videos while you're under this roof or out with Hazel. While I'm accustomed to being under the media's spotlight, I will not let my daughter be subjected to it."

"Of course. I understand."

"Then we're on the same page. You'll sign an NDA before you start, but that's nothing more than a piece of paper." Valerie rested an arm on the counter next to her and leaned forward, her eyes fixed on Abby. "What I want, what I value more than any legal document, is your word."

Abby nodded. "You have it."

"Good."

Silence fell between them. But Valerie didn't take her eyes off Abby. Instead, she studied her even more intently.

"There's one last question I have for you," Valerie said. "One thing I'm curious about. What made you change your mind about taking this job?"

"Well, my old job was the only thing stopping me from taking you up on your offer," Abby said. "So after I quit, I didn't want to miss this opportunity. This job sounds great. And Hazel seems like a good kid."

"So that's why you called me up in the middle of the night?"

"Right." Abby glanced down sheepishly. "Sorry about that."

"I didn't mind. I was glad to hear from you. So tell me, why did you quit your old job?"

Abby shrugged. "Honestly? The kids' parents treated me like crap, and I decided I wouldn't stand for it any longer."

Was it a mistake to be so honest with her new boss? It wasn't exactly professional.

But Valerie only nodded. "Good for you. Rest assured, you won't be mistreated while working for me. As I told you the other day, a good nanny is worth her weight in gold, and I will treat her as such."

Valerie's words echoed in Abby's mind again. *I'll make sure you're treated right.*

Just like you deserve.

Abby's pulse fluttered. Why did those words send all kinds of indecent thoughts racing through her mind?

Valerie straightened up. "If you don't have any more questions for me, I'll see you out."

As Valerie led her to the door, Abby pulled herself together. And when she left the house and made her way to her car, she could feel Valerie's eyes following her.

CHAPTER 7

Valerie took another bite of her lunch as she scanned the script on the desk before her. It was Friday, but her week was far from winding down. She had less than an hour before she was due to meet with some investors to secure extra financing for a film project, and she needed to prepare.

So she'd holed herself up in her office, giving her assistant instructions that she wasn't to be disturbed unless there was an emergency, and silenced her phone, with an exception for Abby's number in case any problems arose with Hazel. It had been five days since Abby started working for her, and so far, she hadn't needed to call Valerie once. She and Hazel got along flawlessly, and Abby was competent enough to handle her without any help.

She was proving to be the perfect nanny. But there was one problem. Despite her best efforts, Valerie couldn't stop thinking about her. About her pink lips, plump and enticing. Her curves bursting from her flirty sundresses.

Her silken red hair, which Valerie longed to caress, to twine through her fingers, to grasp by the handful while she did all kinds of wicked things to her...

Focus. Valerie returned her attention to the script, ignoring the paperwork stacked on her desk and the unanswered emails in her inbox. The script wasn't for just any film. It was for a passion project of hers that was years in the making. Not only was she producing it, but she was directing it personally, for the first time in years.

Because the film had the potential to be bigger than any she'd helmed before. It was an international ensemble cast rom-com, the cast packed with some of the biggest stars in Hollywood along with up-and-coming actors who would soon be household names. But what made this film different from any other was that the entire cast was queer and diverse. It told the story of people like her finding the kind of fairy tale love that only existed on the screen.

That was a hard sell in Hollywood, but she'd sold it. She only needed a few more investors to truly bring her vision to life.

She scribbled a note in the margin of the script. *Location: Greece? Italy? Spain?* She'd titled the film *The Resort* because of the luxury vacation setting. The location needed to be somewhere glamorous, romantic, grand. For the film to succeed, she needed to go big.

There was a knock on her office door. She looked up from her desk to see Elle striding into the office.

Valerie's assistant was at her heels, an apologetic look on his face. "I told her you were busy, but—"

"It's fine, Alex," Valerie said. "You can leave us."

The young man nodded and left the room, closing the door behind him.

"That assistant of yours…" Elle took a seat in front of Valerie's desk. "Is he new? I don't think I've seen him before."

Valerie flipped to the next page of her script. "Don't get any ideas, Elle. He's gayer than me."

Elle feigned offense. "I don't know what you mean."

Valerie set the script aside. "So, what brings you by?"

"Nothing much. I was in the neighborhood, so I thought I'd drop in and see you." Elle settled into her seat. "I'm sure you've heard the news by now?"

"The news?" *Of course. That's why she's here.* "Your ex. The engagement. So you've heard?"

"Everyone's heard. Her face is all over the news, along with her new fiancée's. It's impossible to ignore it. Never date someone famous."

"You're telling me," Valerie murmured. "Do you want to talk about it?"

"There's nothing I'd rather talk about less."

It was the answer Valerie expected. Elle didn't need a shoulder to cry on, just someone to briefly commiserate with. "If you change your mind, I'm here."

"Thanks, but that's enough about me." Elle leaned in. "Did you hear? Marissa Ashton is interested in investing in Club Velvet."

"Yes, Simone mentioned it." Marissa Ashton was the head of the most influential family in Los Angeles. And one of the wealthiest.

"I can't deny how surprised I was to hear it. The Ashtons have always been a traditional bunch. But we all know the most conventional people are rarely so conventional behind closed doors." Elle crossed one leg over the other. "Speculation aside, she could be a valuable investor. She's from an old money family, and she has all the connections that come with that. She can pull strings the rest of us can't, deal with all the petty local politics."

Valerie murmured in agreement. The Ashton name would add a certain legitimacy to their club. Not everyone was thrilled about the existence of a ladies-only BDSM club, including several local councilors and politicians. It made getting permits and building approvals difficult. Ashton held enough political influence to overcome that.

"So?" Elle said. "What do you think?"

"I agree. Ashton could be a valuable business partner. But I haven't given it any thought until now. I've been far too busy."

"I can see that." Elle peered at the piles of paperwork on Valerie's desk. "You're busier than Simone lately. The difference is, she likes it that way."

"Things are a little hectic at the moment. We're doing reshoots for that historical drama series, and everything that could go wrong has. I'm also in the process of getting my rom-com project off the ground, which is taking up most of my time. And there's Francesca, who won't stop calling me." But Valerie's ex was the last thing she wanted to talk about. "Did I mention that Hazel is going through a phase where she bolts at every opportunity? I have my hands full."

"So you still haven't found a new nanny?"

"I may have found someone. I'm trialing her for the week."

The week was almost over. All Valerie had to do was say the word and the job would be Abby's.

And Abby would be hers.

Valerie cleared her throat. "However, I'm having second thoughts about taking her on permanently."

"Oh? Does Hazel not like this one either?"

"No, she likes her. Loves her, even. She's the only nanny I've found who Hazel likes."

"Then what's the issue?" Elle asked.

"I simply have some reservations about her. She's a bit younger than I'd like. I'd prefer someone more mature, more experienced."

"If she's good at her job, why does it matter how old she is? Sounds to me like you're afraid to have a hot young nanny working for you."

Valerie scoffed. "Don't be ridiculous."

"Oh? Don't tell me I hit a nerve." Elle raised an eyebrow. "Really, Val? The babysitter? How scandalous! You're supposed to be the responsible one."

Valerie held up her hands. "It isn't like that."

"I'm sure it isn't."

"I mean it, Elle. Nothing has happened between us, and nothing will. But I'll admit, there's some chemistry there. Just having her in the house for a week…" Valerie shook her head. "I underestimated just how challenging it would be. How *tempting* it would be."

"All the more reason to hire her."

"That's exactly why I *shouldn't* hire her. I can't risk anything happening between us. I'd be her boss. It wouldn't be right."

A smile crossed Elle's lips. "Only if she doesn't want it to happen."

Valerie said nothing. Since day one, she'd been steadfastly ignoring the matter of Abby's attraction to her. Even that day in the park, there had been signs. And there had only been more since. Coy smiles, flirtatious looks, the way she'd blush and stammer whenever Valerie issued her a command.

The way Abby obeyed her without question.

"It doesn't matter what she wants. I can't be the person who has a torrid affair with their nanny. That would make me no better than *them*." Valerie folded her arms across her chest. "You know who I mean. The men of Hollywood's old guard who abuse their power to exploit young women."

Valerie was all too familiar with those types. When she was a young, up-and-coming screenwriter, she'd had more than her share of encounters with those men. It didn't matter that she wasn't interested in them, or in men at all. They expected her to cave to their advances out of desperation and fear like so many women eager to break into the industry did.

But she'd rejected their advances every time. And she was lucky it hadn't cost her her burgeoning career.

"That's the kind of behavior I've spent my entire career battling," Valerie said. "I'd be a hypocrite if I did the same."

"I hear you," Elle said. "And I understand. Abby is off-limits. But that doesn't mean you can't hire her. You obviously need the help. And you said yourself that Hazel loves her. If you won't hire her for you, hire her for Hazel. Doesn't she deserve the best?"

Valerie gritted her teeth. The two of them had been friends for long enough that Elle knew exactly which buttons to push. But this time, she had a good point.

"You're right," Valerie said.

"When have I ever been wrong?" Elle got up from her chair. "You can thank me later. You're clearly busy, so I'll get out of your hair. But keep an open mind about this nanny of yours. I know you're Little Miss Plays-by-the-Rules, but some rules are meant to be broken. And life is much more fun that way."

With a mischievous smile, Elle swept out of the room.

Barely a second later, Valerie's assistant appeared in the doorway. "I know you don't want to be disturbed, but, uh—"

"Yes, Alex?"

"There's some trouble on set. It's Jackie."

"Of course it is. What is it this time?" Jackie Jameson was the star of Valerie's historical drama series. Her name alone was enough to get viewers to tune in. And since going public about her relationship with her popstar girlfriend, Jackie was more popular than ever, especially with the younger demographic.

But working with Jackie came at a heavy price. And not just in terms of money.

"She's refusing to wear her dress for the ball scene. Says it makes her look like—" Alex glanced at his notes, "*a freaking wedding cake*. She's trying to bully wardrobe into letting her wear something else."

"The rest of the scene was shot months ago, with her in that dress. Does she expect us to reshoot *the entire scene*?"

Alex shrugged.

Valerie let out a heavy sigh, making a mental note to speak to the head of wardrobe again and give them a generous bonus. This wasn't the first time they'd been the target of one of Jackie's costume-related tantrums.

"Give me five minutes," she said. "I'll go down and sort out this mess. And call the investors and tell them to meet me on set instead of in the office. I'll frame it as a way to give them a behind-the-scenes look at one of my productions."

Alex nodded and left the room, shutting the door behind him. Valerie checked the time. She wouldn't have long to speak with Jackie before the meeting, but she didn't need more than a couple of minutes. She had no patience for Jackie's diva act. It would only take a few firm words to set her straight.

Valerie rubbed her temples. Dealing with Jackie was just another part of her job. But lately, it seemed like all she did was put out fires—at work, at home. There was only one part of her life where she was free of all her responsibilities, and she hardly had the time for it.

All the more reason to hire Abby permanently.

Valerie closed her eyes. She needed to do what had to be done. She could handle the biggest diva in Hollywood. She could handle running her production company and Club Velvet at the same time. She could handle raising a toddler all by herself.

She could handle having Abby work for her, living in her home day after day, intimately close.

She wouldn't be tempted. She wouldn't let herself be.

Valerie grabbed her leather tote bag that doubled as a briefcase, slipping the script inside and slinging it over her shoulder. As she left her office, she took out her phone and dialed Abby's number.

"Hello, Abby," she said. "About the job."

CHAPTER 8

Abby unbuckled Hazel from her car seat. They'd spent the afternoon at the beach, and Hazel had fallen asleep before they'd made it back to the car.

She picked up the sleeping toddler, balancing her on one hip as she made her way into the house and up to Hazel's bedroom. Once inside, Abby set her down on her bed carefully. She stirred, but didn't wake up.

Abby crept out of the room and shut the door. She had an hour before Valerie came home, which would give her a chance to relax once she cleaned the place up a little. Valerie had a housekeeper who came in every day, but Abby had enough spare time to tidy up here and there. Hazel was an easy kid. Abby had never had an easier nannying job.

Not to mention, a cushier one. Working for Valerie Kane had its perks. On top of the spacious bedroom Abby now called her own, she had free use of the entire house, along with all the other luxuries it had to offer.

The job was perfect, except for one thing. She couldn't stop fantasizing about her boss. Every time Abby was around her, it took all her willpower not to turn into a flustered mess that betrayed all the naughty thoughts in her mind. And living in Valerie's house meant that there was nothing she could do to escape her, to escape those thoughts, those *feelings*. When she lay awake in bed at night, she longed to quench her thirst herself, all while imagining her own hands were Valerie's.

But every night, she resisted the urge. She didn't need to add more fuel to the fire.

She made her way downstairs and began tidying the living room, putting away the art supplies scattered across the coffee table and making sure to set Hazel's latest drawing aside for Valerie. She'd instructed Abby to save all of Hazel's artwork for her. Was she actually keeping it? She didn't seem like the sentimental type. And most of the parents Abby had worked for didn't care about those kinds of things. Any crafts their children made for them ended up in the trash.

She headed into the kitchen and stacked Hazel's bowls in the dishwasher, then started it up and returned to the living room. Stretching herself out on the couch, she took out her phone and began flicking idly through her social media feed. A girl she'd gone to high school with had gotten engaged. A distant cousin had posted photos of her wedding. Erin had shared a selfie she'd taken with her boyfriend, the caption underneath it consisting of nothing but heart emojis.

Romance was in the air. At least for everyone else.

As she scrolled on, another photo caught her eye. It had been shared by her mom, who posted obsessively on social media. So did her stepdad. They were the stereotypical image-obsessed Los Angeles couple, flaunting their extravagant lifestyle for all to see. But Abby knew the truth. They were nowhere near as well-off as they pretended to be. Their lifestyle was a thin facade funded entirely by credit card debt.

Abby studied the photo. In it, her mom stood on a beach in a bikini and sarong, her face filtered to look far younger than her 40 years. She had an arm around her husband's waist, the other hand on the shoulder of one of her two teenage sons, who stood at either side of their parents. All four of them had gleaming white smiles and beach blond hair. Beneath the photo was the caption, *Family vacation!*, followed by a long spiel about how lucky she was to have such a beautiful family.

A family that didn't include Abby.

Suddenly, she heard the tap of footsteps down the glass stairs. She put away her phone quickly. While Valerie didn't mind if she relaxed when she was done with all her tasks, she didn't want to push her luck, especially while she was still new to the job.

A moment later, Valerie appeared at the bottom of the stairs in a stylish pantsuit, her hair gathered into a tight bun at the top of her head. Even dressed in workwear, she sent all kinds of sinful thoughts rushing through Abby's mind.

"Valerie," she said. "I didn't know you were home."

"I left the office early. Too many people wanting things from me. I needed some peace and quiet so I could actually get some work done." She joined Abby by the couch. "Is Hazel down for her nap?"

Abby nodded. "Out like a light."

"You must have done a good job tiring her out today. I don't know how you manage."

"It's easy. Hazel is a smart kid. Give her something to do that challenges her mind, and it's as good as having her run around for hours."

"I'll keep that in mind." Valerie reached up and freed her curls from her bun, then drew her fingers through her hair. "I have something for you. Come."

Abby got up and followed her through the house. When they reached the door to the garage, Valerie stopped.

"I've been meaning to talk to you about your car."

Abby winced. "Right." She'd been driving the same car since she got her learner's permit in high school. It was older than she was, and it looked like it too. "I know it's a little old—"

"That's an understatement. I can't have my daughter being driven around in a death trap."

Abby couldn't argue with that. It was falling apart. It was just one breakdown away from being written off entirely.

"Fortunately, I have a solution." Valerie opened the door to the garage and turned on the light. "Go on in."

Abby stepped into the garage. It was big enough to fit half a dozen cars, but there were only three inside. A sporty Porsche, which she'd never seen Valerie drive. An SUV with a child seat strapped into the back. And a third car, one Abby hadn't seen before. It was a sleek, matte black Mercedes with an oversized red ribbon on the hood.

"The bow is a bit excessive, but the dealership insisted," Valerie said. "What do you think?"

"About what?"

"About the car. It's yours."

Abby stared at her. "You're giving this to me?"

"For as long as you're working for me, yes. Come, take a closer look." Valerie led her to the car and opened the driver's side door. "Have a seat, get comfortable."

Abby slid into the driver's seat, the scent of new leather filling her head. Inside, the car was as luxurious as outside, with plush leather seats and gold accents.

Valerie got into the passenger seat and shut the door behind her. "It has all the latest safety features, including an advanced collision avoidance system. Not to mention heated seats, a state-of-the-art sound system, a mini-fridge. Everything you could possibly need."

"No kidding," Abby said. "This is great."

"I'm glad you like it. As I said, it's yours to use whenever you want. You can even use it on your days off. It doesn't make sense to have you juggling two cars."

"Really?"

"Yes, really."

Abby shook her head. "I don't know what to say. This is awfully generous."

"Like I told you when I offered you the job, I always make sure that every one of my nanny's needs is taken care of."

"Well, I appreciate it. Thank you."

"You can thank me by continuing to do a good job."

Abby nodded. "I will."

Valerie rested her arm on the center console between them. "I have to admit, I was skeptical about hiring such a young nanny, but you've proven to be more competent than many of the others I've tried."

"I have plenty of experience. I've been nannying full-time since I was eighteen, but I did a lot of babysitting as a teenager. And I spent lots of time looking after my brothers growing up. I was much older than them, so I ended up being a kind of third parent. Actually, I was more like the only parent."

"Oh?"

"Yeah, my mom and stepdad were around, but they didn't exactly do much parenting. They wanted kids the same way some people want pets—for the cute family photo ops, but not the sleepless nights and tantrums. All the benefits with none of the hard work."

Abby trailed off. She was rambling again. Maybe seeing the photo her mom posted had thrown her off balance.

But Valerie only gave her a sympathetic nod. "I'm familiar with the type. And I'm sorry you had to look after your brothers when you were still a child yourself."

"It wasn't so bad," Abby said quickly. "And it taught me a lot about kids, about what they need. That's part of why I became a nanny. I want to make sure the kids I look after have someone they can count on. And I genuinely enjoy the job too."

"It shows. You really have a way with Hazel."

"She's a great kid. Makes it easy."

That was the truth. Hazel was the complete opposite of most of the rich kids Abby had cared for, like Connor and Owen. Their parents barely paid any attention to them, so they'd never learned boundaries. And they got so little love from their parents that misbehaving was the only way they knew how to get attention.

Abby understood that from experience. Her mom had never paid much attention to her either. She'd gotten pregnant at 16, but she hadn't wanted to be a mom so young. She'd tried to hide it, but Abby had sensed it.

"I'm glad the two of you get along so well," Valerie said. "Truth be told, you're the only nanny she's ever felt comfortable with. Perhaps even the only *person* other than me. She's really opened up to you. I could hardly believe that she told you her name at the park. It was a long process just to get her to say a few words to *me*. She's never said a single word to anyone else. Not until you."

"Wow. I never would have guessed it. I guess some kids start talking late, but they catch up."

"That's what the doctors said. And her speech therapist. They think it's because she was premature. She was born with some serious health issues, so she spent the first eighteen months of her life in and out of the hospital."

"That must have been hard for you," Abby said.

"It was harder on her than me. While it's in the past now, it took its toll on her. All those doctors prodding and poking at her made her anxious and wary of strangers. That's why it's been so difficult to find a nanny for her. And that's why, when I met you in the park, I offered you the job on the spot. I've learned over the years to trust my instincts. And my instincts told me I needed to hire you for Hazel's sake."

Abby studied Valerie's face. The woman was so reserved in her emotions, except for when it came to Hazel. Whenever she left her daughter with Abby, she could see the struggle in Valerie's eyes as she wrenched herself away from her child. Whenever she and Hazel reunited at the end of a long day, Abby could feel the relief radiating from her. Whenever she spoke about her daughter, Abby could hear the love in her voice.

Seeing this commanding powerhouse of a woman melting in her daughter's presence? It made Abby's heart flutter.

"I understand," she said. "And I'll make sure you don't regret giving me this job. You can count on me. So can Hazel."

Valerie nodded. "That's all I want. It's all any parent wants. Someone I can be confident will keep Hazel safe. Someone who has her best interests at heart. Someone who genuinely cares."

"I do. It hasn't been long, but I've already come to care about her."

"I can tell." Valerie gave her a gentle smile. "Now, let me give you the keys. They should be in here."

She opened the glove box and took out a set of car keys. As she handed them to Abby, their fingers touched. At once, Abby was sent hurtling back to that moment in the park. On her knees. At Valerie's feet. The woman's hand grasping hers, her fingertips caressing her skin, her gaze locked on Abby's.

Deep within her, desire sparked to life. All of a sudden, the spacious car was tiny, and Valerie was so close, close enough to feel the warmth of her body, to hear the whisper of each breath that emerged from her luscious red lips. Valerie's fingers lingered on hers, her skin soft and smooth, her other hand stretched toward her on the center console, just inches from Abby's bare leg. Her dark curls cascaded down her shoulders, framing her breasts, which peeked out from her half-unbuttoned blouse in the most tantalizing way…

Heat rose through Abby's body. She looked up at Valerie's face. And suddenly, she couldn't look away. She was pinned in place by Valerie's gaze.

"Abby," she said softly. "There's something I need from you."

Abby's breath hitched. "Yes?"

Valerie leaned toward her, lips parting slightly. But no words emerged from them. Was she, like Abby, mesmerized? Was she desperately fighting the urges inside her too?

No, she was Valerie Kane, Abby's *boss*. The thought was outrageous.

Was it?

A shrill buzzing filled the air. Valerie's phone, vibrating in her jacket. She tensed and pulled her hand from Abby's, reaching into her pocket to grab her phone.

As she glanced at the screen, her face warped into a grimace.

"Is everything okay?" Abby asked.

It took a moment for Valerie to answer her. "Yes." She silenced her phone and slipped it back into her pocket, leaning back in her seat. "Now, where was I? Ah, I need you to start early tomorrow. I have to be at work by six for a shoot."

Abby blinked. "Okay. Sure."

But before she could say another word, Valerie opened the door and stepped out of the car.

She straightened up her jacket and smoothed down her hair. "Take the car for a test drive. You need to get a feel for it before you start driving Hazel around. Make sure you're back in time for dinner."

With that, she shut the door and left the garage.

Abby let out a long, slow breath, her pulse racing. One moment, Valerie had been warm toward her. The next, she couldn't get away fast enough.

What the hell had happened?

CHAPTER 9

Hazel surveyed the collection of crayons strewn across the table, her brows drawn together with concentration. "I want… orange trees!"

"You're the boss," Abby said.

Hazel picked up the orange crayon and began scribbling on the sheet of construction paper blanketing the coffee table, humming tunelessly to herself. Abby doodled absently on the opposite end of the paper. It had been a week since Valerie had given her the car. A week since Valerie had turned from hot to cold.

And it had only gotten worse since.

Abby returned her attention to Hazel, who had put down her crayon and was scrutinizing her drawing again. "All done?"

Hazel shook her head. "I want green. Green sky."

But before she could grab another crayon, the sound of a key in the front door reached them.

"Mommy!" She climbed to her feet and sprinted toward the front door, her drawing forgotten.

"Hazel," Abby warned. "We walk inside, remember?"

But she was already halfway to the front door.

Abby sighed and went after her, meeting her by the door just as Valerie stepped through it.

"Hi, sweetie." She swept her daughter into her arms and planted a kiss on her cheek. "Did you have a nice day today?"

Hazel beamed. "We went to the park. I pet a dog."

Valerie glanced at Abby. "Did you, now?"

Was that disapproval in her voice? "It was the neighbor's dog," Abby said quickly. "It was friendly."

"I'm sure it was."

"So, how was work?" It was the only thing she could think to say.

"It was fine." Valerie didn't look at her as she set Hazel down on her feet. "It's almost time for dinner. I'll get Hazel cleaned up. Has she had a bath yet?"

"Not yet. I know you like to do bathtime with her, so I waited until you got home. But I can do it if you—"

Valerie held up a hand. "I'll take care of it."

Abby's stomach sank. No matter what she did or said, Valerie responded with businesslike firmness. And she seemed to be avoiding speaking to Abby any more than she needed to.

"And dinner?" Valerie asked.

"It's in the oven. Should be done in half an hour or so."

Valerie gave her a curt nod. "Come," she said to Hazel. "Let's get you into the bath. I'll fix your hair afterward."

As Valerie led her daughter to the stairs, Abby's stomach churned. It was as if Valerie couldn't stand to be in her presence. Had she done something wrong? She must have. But what was it?

She clenched her hands into fists. She couldn't hold it in anymore.

"Valerie, wait."

Valerie turned back to her. "Yes?"

"I was wondering…"

But Abby couldn't just accuse her boss of being cold to her. What if it was all in her head?

Abby took a deep breath. *Stop being weird. Be professional.* "So, now that I've been working here for a few weeks, do you have any feedback for me? Anything I can do better?"

Valerie shook her head. "Nothing comes to mind. Hazel is happy and well looked after, and that's what matters."

"Oh. Okay. Well, let me know if anything comes up."

Valerie nodded. And without another word, she took Hazel's hand and led her carefully up the stairs.

Abby headed into the kitchen, pushing down the anxiety simmering in her stomach. While Valerie's private chef prepared meals for them every other day, Abby occasionally had to stick something in the oven or put the finishing touches on a dish. And it was her job to make breakfast and snacks for Hazel.

She grabbed a knife and chopping board, along with some fruit and vegetables which would serve as Hazel's snacks for the next day. As she set about cutting them up, the conversation with Valerie replayed in her mind.

Valerie claimed she was perfectly happy with her work. So why was she behaving the way she was? If it wasn't anything Abby had done, was it something she'd said? It wouldn't be the first time she'd put her foot in it.

Or maybe it's because you keep acting like a schoolgirl with a crush whenever she's around. Abby couldn't help it. That afternoon in the car had only made things worse. For a moment, she'd felt this chemistry between them, this electricity...

Abby shook her head. She was imagining things. With how cold Valerie was being toward her, it was obvious that her feelings were one-sided. It was silly to even fantasize about it.

Abby portioned out the carrot sticks and apple slices into snack-sized containers and put them in the fridge, then checked on the lasagna in the oven. The cheese was bubbling, and it smelled more heavenly than anything she'd ever eaten. The chef-prepared meals were yet another perk of working for Valerie. But with the tension between the two of them hanging heavy in the house, it was hard to enjoy any of the luxuries that came with the job.

As she shut the oven door, her phone began to buzz. She pulled it from her jeans pocket. Erin was calling her.

She glanced in the direction of the stairs. Hazel's bath would take at least another fifteen minutes, and Abby had nothing left to do but wait for dinner to cook.

She answered the call. "Hey, Erin."

"God, you won't believe the day I had." She didn't give Abby a chance to get another word in. "You know that guy from work? The one who kept flirting with me? Turns out he thought I was single this whole time. He thought Dan was my *brother*, if you can believe that."

Abby murmured along as her friend continued. Erin had always been a magnet for male attention. But she'd been in a relationship with her boyfriend since middle school, and she only had eyes for him.

Abby didn't understand what she saw in Dan. He still acted like he was in high school. But he made Erin happy, and that was all that mattered.

And a part of Abby envied her. Would she ever find that one person she wanted to spend the rest of her life with? It didn't matter to her whether they were a woman, a man, or anything else. What mattered was that they understood her—what she wanted, what she desired. More than that, they embraced those desires, taking command of her in the way she'd always craved.

"So yeah, he made this dramatic apology in front of everyone," Erin said. "But five minutes later, he was flirting with Amanda. Let me tell you, she is *not* going to be as nice as I was when she turns him down. But enough about my job. How's your job going?"

"It's going great," Abby said. "It's the best job I've ever had."

"Glad it's working out for you. Aren't you happy you quit your old job?"

"Yeah, but I still feel bad about abandoning the Hendersons. The kids, not their parents. I didn't even get to say goodbye to them."

"Like you said, they're old enough now that they barely need looking after. They'll be fine without you. You had to do what was right for you."

"I guess."

"Well, *I'm* happy for you. I miss living with you, though."

"I miss you too. But I don't miss that tiny room." Abby was still renting it to store some of her things, and her job was new enough that she wanted to keep her old room just in case, at least for a few more weeks. Valerie was paying her generously enough that she could easily afford it.

"You should come by sometime," Erin said. "Then you can tell me all about what it's like working for Valerie Kane."

"You know I can't tell you anything. It's a privacy thing."

"Okay, but you can at least tell me what she's like, can't you? Do you still think she's intimidating?"

"A little. But intimidating in a kind of… sexy way? It's like, every time I'm around her, my whole body screams *I want you*." Abby groaned. "I don't know what's wrong with me."

"Nothing's wrong with you. So you're into her. If I liked women, I'd be into her too. She's hot as hell. And she's a lesbian, right? Used to be married to Francesca Moreno? You know, that actress who was in half her movies."

"Yeah, and?"

"So it means you have a chance with her."

Abby scoffed. "I don't think so. She's my boss. And she's *Valerie Kane*. There's no way she'd ever be into me. If anything, it's the opposite."

"What do you mean?"

Abby leaned back against the countertop. "I don't know. Things between us are kind of… tense."

"Isn't that normal for a new nannying job? You always say things with the parents are awkward at first, especially if you're living with them."

"This is different, though. It isn't just the usual adjustment period. The way Valerie is acting, it's like she's mad at me. And it feels like she's avoiding me. I thought maybe I messed up somehow, but I asked her about it, and she said I was doing a good job. So maybe it isn't about my job. Maybe it's personal." Abby's stomach flipped. "I don't know. All I know is that she's upset with me."

"I can't imagine you doing anything to upset her. You're, well, *you*. There's a reason you're a nanny. You're basically a real-life Mary Poppins, but way hotter."

"Uh, thanks?"

"What I'm saying is, you're a total sweetheart who would literally throw herself in front of a bus to save whatever kid you're looking after. If Valerie has an issue, it's on her, not you. Don't beat yourself up about it. I know your shitty parents did a number on your self-esteem, but you need to stop being so hard on yourself."

Abby opened her mouth to argue. But her friend was right. They'd known each other since they were kids. She knew what Abby's family was like. In her parents' eyes, her brothers were angels who could do no wrong. Abby? She could never do anything right.

Abby sighed. "You're probably right. Maybe it's not me. Things are just tense. It's starting to eat at me, you know?"

"You can't let her get to you," Erin said. "You've gotten through worse on jobs before. Just hang in there. I'm sure it'll work itself out."

"I hope so." Abby glanced at the oven. Dinner was almost ready. She turned to grab the oven gloves from the counter. "I just wish she'd tell me why—"

She froze in place. Standing in the doorway to the kitchen, only a few feet away, was Valerie.

And her eyes were fixed on Abby.

Her stomach sank. How long had Valerie been standing there?

How much had she heard?

"Hello?" Erin's voice echoed through the phone. "Are you there?"

Abby swallowed. "I have to go."

She hung up the phone, heart thumping. And as Valerie stepped toward her, her heart stopped altogether.

"We need to talk," Valerie said.

CHAPTER 10

Valerie crossed her arms. She'd only heard part of the phone call, but she'd heard enough.

"Valerie." Abby's cheeks turned crimson. "I, um... I thought you were upstairs?"

"Hazel wanted out of the bath early," Valerie said. "But it's not her I want to talk about."

"Right. I-I'm sorry. I didn't know you were listening. I shouldn't have—"

"I don't want apologies. I want to hear the truth from you. What you said just now, about me. Is that how you really feel?"

The blush on Abby's cheeks deepened. "I..."

"You think I'm upset with you."

"Oh. Yeah." Abby shook her head. "I shouldn't have said that. I was just venting. It's probably nothing, I've just been getting the feeling you're avoiding me. Like you don't want to talk to me or be around me. That's why I asked you if you had any feedback for me. I wanted to know *why.*" Her gaze dropped. "I wanted to know what I'd done wrong."

Valerie felt a pang of guilt. She'd been too harsh. She'd only intended to keep Abby at a professional distance. Instead, she'd made her think she was upset with her.

"Abby," she said. "Look at me."

Abby obeyed.

"I'm not upset with you, okay?"

Abby nodded unconvincingly.

"I mean it. I'm *not* mad at you. But you're right about one thing. I *have* been avoiding you. But it's not because of anything you did or said."

"It's… not?"

"Of course not. You've been amazing since day one. With Hazel, with everything else. You're everything I've been looking for and so much more. And that's why I've been keeping my distance."

Confusion and doubt swam behind Abby's eyes. And for a moment, all Valerie wanted was to seize her by the waist and press her lips to hers in a kiss that said more than words ever could.

Instead, she placed her hand on the countertop next to her, grounding herself. "You said that there's no way I'd ever be into you. Nothing could be further from the truth." Her fingers curled around the edge of the counter, gripping it tightly. "The truth is, if circumstances were different, then yes, I'd be interested. Perhaps I'd even want to pursue something with you."

Abby gazed back at her expectantly. But she'd already said far more than she should have.

"But you're Hazel's nanny. And I'm your boss. I *won't* be that person. Nothing can ever happen between us."

Abby lowered her head for a fraction of a second. And when she glanced up at Valerie again, her eyes glimmered.

"Not even if I want it to?" she said softly.

Valerie tensed. "Abby…"

Abby stepped toward her, gliding her hand along the countertop beside them. Her eyes, still locked on Valerie's, simmered with lust, her lush pink lips teasing her, inviting her.

Desire stirred deep within Valerie. *This is wrong.*

But as Abby slid her hand closer, grazing her fingers over Valerie's hand tentatively, her body acted of its own accord.

She placed her hand on Abby's, stopping it in its tracks. But she didn't push it away. Instead, she wrapped her fingers around Abby's wrist, pulling her into her as she drew her other hand up the back of Abby's neck, fingers twining through her hair.

Abby gasped, a visible tremor rolling through her. She pressed her body back against Valerie's, her eyes fluttering shut as she leaned close—

"Mommy?" Hazel's voice echoed through the house. "Mommy, where are you?"

Valerie pulled away. Not a second later, Hazel appeared at the entrance to the kitchen, clutching a wooden toy train.

"I'm hungry," she declared.

Valerie took a few steps back. "Okay, sweetie. Dinner is almost ready, right, Abby?"

She glanced at Abby, who nodded. "Uh, yes. Just a couple more minutes."

Valerie strode over to where Hazel stood and picked

her up. "Let's go put away your toys, then we'll wash your hands."

"I can do that for you," Abby said.

Valerie shook her head. "I'll handle it."

"It's no trouble—"

"Just stay here and finish with dinner."

Abby nodded and looked away. But Valerie could feel the disappointment radiating from her.

She stifled a curse as she left the kitchen. She'd slipped up, let herself get carried away.

It wouldn't happen again. She'd make sure of it.

Dinner came and went, Hazel chattering animatedly through the entire meal. Valerie attempted to make conversation with Abby, but she wouldn't say more than a few words. She could barely look Valerie in the eye.

And as soon as Hazel finished her last bite, Abby jumped up from the table to clear away the dishes before telling Valerie that she was going to her room.

Valerie didn't stop her. Instead, she set about getting Hazel ready for bed, a process that took an entire hour. She insisted on taking care of Hazel's bedtime routine herself whenever she was home. The older Hazel got, the more Valerie realized how precious her time with her was.

Once Hazel was finally asleep, Valerie went into the kitchen and poured herself a glass of wine. She leaned back against the counter and took a long, slow sip, then picked up her phone, which she'd left silenced in the kitchen while putting Hazel to bed.

She flicked through her notifications. She'd missed a message from her assistant. That could wait until morning. She'd also missed a message from Francesca, along with two phone calls.

Valerie, we need to talk. Call me.

She put down the phone. She had more important things to deal with right now.

She raised her glass to her lips again, drinking deeply. No amount of wine could prepare her for what she had to do, but she needed to do it.

She needed to talk to Abby.

Abby was hurt. She was confused. And Valerie couldn't blame her. She'd let things go too far. While they'd been interrupted before they could go any further, the damage had already been done.

She needed to clear the air between them. And she needed to make sure Abby understood that nothing like that could ever happen again, no matter how much they both wanted it.

And oh, how Valerie *wanted* it.

But even if Abby wasn't off-limits, Valerie didn't have room in her life for romance. And after Francesca, she didn't want to get involved with anyone now, or perhaps ever.

She finished off her wine. It was getting late. She needed to speak with Abby before she went to sleep. And she needed to do it without crushing her in the process.

She set her glass down and made her way upstairs, walking quietly as she passed Hazel's room. When she reached Abby's bedroom, she knocked on the door.

"Abby? Can I come in?"

"Yes." Abby's voice was quiet and muffled through the door.

Valerie opened it carefully. Inside, the room was dark, the only sources of light a lamp on Abby's nightstand and the moon outside the half-open window. The crisp white curtains swayed in the wind, the evening breeze cooling the warm air.

As Valerie's eyes adjusted to the dim light, the bedroom coalesced. On the bed, in the center of the room, lay Abby, her head thrown back and her eyes closed, her mouth open slightly, heavy breaths rising from her chest. The covers were thrown back in the heat of the night, the thin bedsheets tangled around her outspread legs, her nightie bunched up around her hips. One hand was sprawled on the sheet beside her, fingertips digging into the mattress. Her other hand moved between her thighs, faster and faster and faster.

"Yes..." A moan flowed from Abby's chest. "God, *yes*..."

Valerie's breath hitched. In the still silence of the room, it was enough to stir Abby from her trance.

Her eyes flew open, her gaze falling upon the doorway, a whispered word spilling from her lips.

"Valerie?"

CHAPTER 11

Abby pulled her headphones from her ears, her stomach sinking. When had Valerie come in? How long had she been standing there?

How much had she *seen*?

Abby's body began to burn. She cinched her thighs together and yanked her nightie down, her fingers gripping tightly at the hem. She needed to shield herself, to pull up the sheets, to hide under the covers until Valerie went away.

But she didn't move.

And neither did Valerie.

"Valerie," she said again.

But the woman didn't say a word. Her gaze was fixed on Abby on the bed. And even in the dim light, Abby could see—Valerie's eyes, her expression, her stance.

They were filled with *lust*.

Abby's heart pounded, her whole body throbbing with it. The moment Valerie touched her in the kitchen that evening, it had ignited something inside her. She'd wanted nothing more than for Valerie to take her on the kitchen counter right there and then.

And even after she walked away, leaving Abby alone in the kitchen, that feeling didn't dissipate. No, it grew and grew, until Abby couldn't take it anymore. She shut herself in her room. She got into her bed. She closed her eyes and tried to drown out her feelings.

And she finally broke.

It had only been minutes. Just a few minutes spent imagining all the things she longed for Valerie to do to her while she touched herself the way she wanted Valerie to. And now, the woman from her imagination was standing right there in her doorway.

It was humiliating. At least, it should have been. But it only made Abby hotter.

So did the way Valerie was looking at her.

You said that there's no way I'd ever be into you. Nothing could be further from the truth. Those had been Valerie's words. A part of Abby had doubted them, but it was undeniable now.

"Do you…" Her lower lip quivered. "Do you want me to stop?"

Again, Valerie said nothing. But there was the faintest deepening of her breath, the slightest tremor in her body. Abby's skin sizzled under Valerie's gaze, but she resisted the urge to look away, meeting Valerie's eyes as she slid a hand up her thigh.

"May I—" She bit her lip. "May I keep going, please?"

Still, Valerie was silent.

Slowly, Abby slid her hand higher up her thigh, dragging her nightgown up with it, hoping, *praying* that Valerie would command her to keep going—

Valerie's voice cut through the still air.

"Stop."

Abby froze. Had she read Valerie wrong? Was she making a fool of herself? Any minute now, Valerie would turn around and leave her there, pretending she hadn't seen anything at all.

She reached for the door handle. But she didn't leave the room. Instead, she closed the door and stepped toward the bed, stopping at the end of it.

Then, she issued a command.

"Keep going."

A shiver rippled through Abby's body. She closed her eyes, her hand trembling as she slipped it underneath her nightgown—

"Open your eyes," Valerie said. "Look at me."

Abby obeyed.

"Pull your nightgown up. All the way up."

Abby pulled the hem of her nightie up around her waist tentatively, her exposed skin prickling.

"Good. Now spread your legs wide for me."

Abby parted her legs, a thrill rising through her. Valerie's eyes skimmed along her body, devouring her with her gaze.

"Go on," she said.

Taking a deep breath, Abby slid her hand down her stomach, all the way to where her thighs met. Parting her lower lips with a finger, she glided it up and down between them. Her fingertip grazed her clit, sending sparks through her.

"Slowly now, Abby."

Desire swelled inside her at the sound of her name.

Valerie's velvet-smooth voice was so enthralling. She was powerless to do anything but obey.

"That's it," Valerie whispered. "Touch yourself for me, just the way you like it."

Abby let out a breath, drawing a finger down to circle her entrance. A tremor rolled through her. She'd been wet and ready before Valerie had walked through the door. And now, she was right back there again.

She dipped a finger inside, then another, electricity darting deep into her body.

"Yes, just like that," Valerie whispered. "Keep going."

Abby drew her fingers in and out, curling them against that sweet spot inside. She bit down on the inside of her cheek, holding back a moan. Aside from Valerie, there was no one around to hear her. But what they were doing felt so forbidden. She couldn't acknowledge the illicit moment they were sharing. She couldn't make a sound. She couldn't break the spell.

She peered up at Valerie, pleading with her wordlessly. Abby yearned for her to kiss her, touch her, ravish her with her fingers and tongue and lips, with her whole body.

But all Valerie did was command her once again.

"Keep going," she said. "But don't come. Not until I give you permission."

A shudder rolled through Abby. Her fingers still inside her, she drew her other hand down between her legs, stroking her swollen clit, sending pleasure flowing through her. She squirmed atop the silken sheets, her head tipping back against the pillows.

"Faster," Valerie said. "But don't come yet."

Abby exhaled softly, her fingers moving frantically

between her legs. How was she supposed to hold back with Valerie gazing down at her with ravenous eyes? How was she supposed to contain herself when just the sound of Valerie's voice set every inch of her ablaze?

How was she supposed to keep herself together when Valerie's presence made her want to fall to pieces?

Her hips arched, pleasure rising within her. She couldn't hold back any longer.

"You're close, aren't you?" Valerie said.

Abby nodded feverishly. "Can I come?"

"Only if you ask nicely."

"Please…" A quiver shook her. "Please, can I come for you?"

"Yes," Valerie whispered. "You can come."

Her words were all it took to release the avalanche of ecstasy inside Abby. Her eyes fell shut, a gasp erupting from her chest as she arched up from the bed. She held back a cry as wave after wave of pleasure flooded her, until finally, she couldn't take any more.

She collapsed back down to the bed, breathing hard, her skin flushed and damp with sweat. But she barely had a moment to come to her senses before Valerie spoke again.

"Taste yourself."

Heat crept up Abby's cheeks. What could she do but obey?

What did she want but to obey?

Gazing up at Valerie, she drew her hand up to her mouth and licked her slick, wet fingers clean.

Valerie let out a slow, trembling breath. And just like that, Abby was as wet and ready as she had been moments ago.

Please. Abby didn't dare to plead out loud. Instead, she kept her eyes locked with Valerie's as she silently begged her to give her what she so desperately wanted, what *Valerie* so desperately wanted.

But the woman only stood up from the bed, the mattress swaying beneath her. "Good night, Abby. I'll see you in the morning."

Without another word, she turned and left the room, closing the door behind her. And just like that, she was gone, leaving no trace behind.

Abby's pulse raced. Her thirst had been quenched. Her desire had been sated.

But now, she ached for Valerie's touch even more.

CHAPTER 12

"Valerie, you're needed on set," Alex said.

"I'll be there soon. I just need to find this damn script." Valerie searched the papers on her desk, but it was nowhere to be found. "I must have left it in my other bag at home."

"Do you want me to go get it?" her assistant asked.

"No, you have too much to do already. I'll sort it out."

Alex nodded and disappeared from her office. Valerie picked up her phone. At this time of day, Abby would be at home with Hazel. She could bring the script to her.

Valerie had never intended to give her tasks that were outside her job description. However, Abby had noticed how busy Valerie was and had offered to help her out when she could. Valerie had taken her up on the offer and had given her a generous bonus in return, ignoring Abby's attempts to turn it down. She was so eager to please. So ready to serve.

That night in her bedroom had proved that a thousand times over.

Valerie let out a long, slow breath. She'd been steadfastly trying not to think about that night. The morning after had been like any other. And ever since, neither of them had spoken a single word about what happened. That was exactly what Valerie wanted, no, needed. She *needed* to pretend it hadn't happened at all.

She dialed Abby's number. It took a dozen rings for her to pick up.

"Hello Abby," she said. "Did I catch you at a bad time?"

"No, it's fine—Hazel, sweetie, let me get that for you." There was a loud clatter at the other end of the line. "Sorry, Hazel's a little restless today. We're about to go for a walk. Did you need something?"

"Yes, actually. I left some important documents at home. They're in my bag by the door. Can you bring it to me?"

"Sure, whatever you need. I bet Hazel will be excited to see you."

"Good. I'll be on set, but I'll make sure security knows you're coming. Thank you, Abby. I appreciate it."

Valerie hung up the phone, leaned back in her chair, and closed her eyes. Just hearing Abby's voice sent her back to that night in her bedroom, that night when she truly saw Abby for the first time.

From the moment they met, Valerie had been inexorably drawn to her. Now she knew why. Abby tempted an innate part of herself that was embedded deep in her soul. And catching Abby in the throes of self-pleasure had made that part of her roar.

That part of herself? It was pure, unbridled *need*. A need for control. A need for obedience.

A need to see Abby on her knees.

Can I come for you?

Five words. Five simple words.

Had Abby known then that those words would make Valerie come undone?

~

"Cut!" the director yelled. "Okay everyone, let's take ten."

Chatter broke out as the crew scrambled to adjust the set and the actors and extras wandered off, pulling out phones that were incongruous with their period-accurate Regency clothing and hair. The director, a stout, middle-aged woman, marched over to Valerie.

"Thank god you're here," she said. "This morning was a disaster. If Jackie ruins one more take…"

She rattled off a list of complaints, most of which were about Jackie. Valerie assured her that she'd take care of it, but that did nothing to stop the director's tirade.

Mercifully, Alex appeared nearby, glancing at her as if trying to catch her eye.

She cut the director off as politely as she could. "I hear you, and I'll handle it. Now, if you'll excuse me."

As the director made herself scarce, Alex hurried over to Valerie. "Abby and Hazel are here."

She nodded. "Bring them in."

A moment later, Abby appeared at the entrance to the set, pushing Hazel in her stroller. As the toddler fidgeted with the visitor's lanyard around her neck, Abby looked around in awe. Film and TV sets were nowhere near as glamorous behind the scenes, but there was a certain beauty in their chaos.

Abby wheeled Hazel over to her. "Valerie, hi." She glanced over her shoulder. "Was that Jackie Jameson?"

"Yes, and she better be worth all the trouble she's causing," Valerie murmured. She leaned down, unbuckling Hazel from her stroller and picking her up. "Hi, sweetie. How has your morning been?"

But Hazel just nestled her head shyly in Valerie's shoulder. There were too many people around.

She turned to Abby. "Do you have it?"

Abby nodded and unslung the tote bag from her shoulder. "Everything should be in there."

"You're a lifesaver." Valerie handed Hazel to her and took the bag, pulling a folder from it and flipping through it.

But her relief soon disappeared.

"It isn't here." She cursed and began searching the bag. "Where the hell did I put it?"

"What's the matter?" Abby asked.

"The script. I could have sworn it was in here." Valerie pinched the bridge of her nose. "I must have left it on my desk in my study."

"Do you want me to go back and have a look for it for you?"

"I can't ask that of you. You've done enough already."

"It's no trouble. I don't mind."

Valerie kept her study locked for a reason. But she needed that script today. She had no choice but to trust that Abby wouldn't snoop.

"All right," she said. "I'll write down the title for you so you know what you're looking for. I need some paper."

She looked around until she found her assistant, who jumped to attention and came rushing over. At Valerie's request, he took a notepad and pen from his pocket and handed them to her before scurrying off again.

"Here." She scribbled the script's title on a blank page, then ripped it out and handed it to Abby. "I wrote down the code for the door too. If the script isn't on my desk, you'll have to look around for it."

"Got it. Want me to—"

"Valerie?" A woman's voice cut through the air, loud and crisp. "Valerie, darling, is that you?"

She tensed and turned around. A woman strode toward them, tall and slender, with olive skin, raven black hair, and an air of elegance. She paid no mind to the people scattered around. The people, on the other hand? They were entranced.

It was exactly that charisma that had propelled her to fame. To everyone else, she was actor and Hollywood darling Francesca Moreno.

To Valerie? She was her ex-wife.

Francesca stopped before her. "Hello, Val. It's so good to see you."

Valerie crossed her arms. "What are you doing here?"

"Why, I'm working, of course. I'm shooting my next film nearby. Did you hear? I'm starring in Martin's new picture. Rather, it was written for me. Marty thinks it's a real Oscar contender."

"How wonderful for you," Valerie said flatly. "What are you doing on *my* set?"

"What do you think? I came to see you." Francesca flashed her a smile. "It's been so long since we've spoken. I just wanted to talk to my wife in person."

"*Ex*-wife," Valerie corrected.

Beside her, Abby shifted Hazel from one hip to the

other. Valerie had been so focused on Francesca that she'd almost forgotten they were there. She couldn't let her ex set her sights on either of them.

"Abby, take Hazel back to the house and look for that script, will you?"

Abby nodded. "Sure, I'll just—"

"Leave Hazel here," Francesca interrupted. "I want to see her."

"No," Valerie said. "Absolutely *not*."

"But Valerie." Francesca brought her hand to her chest, projecting her voice to carry across the set. "You wouldn't deny a mother a chance to see her daughter, would you?"

Valerie spoke through gritted teeth. "Hazel—" She looked around. Everyone in the room was pointedly avoiding looking in their direction, but Valerie didn't miss the murmurs and whispers that rose from the crowd.

She held back a curse. This was exactly what Francesca wanted. And Valerie had no choice but to play along.

For now.

"*Fine*," Valerie said. "Abby, leave Hazel with me. You can pick her up when you come back with the script."

Abby glanced from Valerie to Francesca and back again. "Uh, sure." She handed Hazel over. "I'll be right back."

As she turned and walked away, Francesca flashed Valerie another smile.

"Now, where were we? Ah, yes, Hazel." She leaned down, her face level with the toddler's. "Hello there, Hazel. You've gotten so big."

Hazel clung harder to Valerie, burying her head in her mother's chest.

Francesca scowled. "What's her problem?"

"She can tell when a stranger can't be trusted," Valerie said.

"Still as sharp-tongued as ever, I see."

Valerie ignored the barb. "You want to talk? Let's talk. But not here."

She buckled Hazel into her stroller and marched off the set, Francesca following close behind her, until they were out of earshot of anyone else. Depriving her of an audience meant she had no one to manipulate.

But that didn't stop her from trying.

She twirled a lock of her hair around a finger. "Eager to get me alone, are you?"

"What do you want?" Valerie said.

"Straight to the point, I see. You always did like to play the ice-cold bitch, didn't you?"

"I'm not doing this with you, so cut the bullshit. You're not here to see Hazel. So just tell me what you want."

"I don't know what you mean. I can't come by for no reason other than to see you both?"

Anyone else would have believed her. Francesca was a star for a reason. She knew how to put on a show. She knew how to tug at her audience's heartstrings. She knew exactly what to say, to do, to charm whoever she wanted.

But Valerie knew her better than anyone.

"*Enough*," she said. "These games of yours? They don't work on me. So drop the act and tell me why you're really here."

"All right." Francesca crossed her arms. "You want the truth? I've already given it to you. I came here because I want to talk to you. You refuse to pick up my calls. You refuse to respond to my messages. What choice do I have but to come see you face to face? And I wasn't lying about wanting to see my daughter."

"She's *not* your daughter. She never has been. We divorced before she was even in the picture. You have no claim over her." Valerie had made sure of that before Hazel was conceived. She'd cleared it with her lawyers and had started over at a new IVF clinic to eliminate any doubt.

"But she was meant to be *ours*. We were meant to have her together. I wanted to stay. I wanted to work things out. I wanted a family with you."

"We both know that's not true. Or have you actually started to believe your own lies? You never wanted a child. You wanted an accessory to show off to the cameras." That realization had been the straw that broke their relationship.

No, it had been broken long before then.

"You've only ever thought of other people as pawns for you to use to your advantage. Even now, you're using Hazel as a pawn to get to me." Valerie gestured toward the set. "All those people? They don't know that she isn't yours. You knew I couldn't say no to letting you spend time with her in front of everyone without looking like a monster." It took all of Valerie's willpower to keep her voice calm so she wouldn't upset Hazel. "You have some nerve."

"I'd never—"

"I'm done entertaining you. You need to leave."

Francesca scoffed. "*You're* making demands of *me*? After everything you did to me?"

"*Leave,*" Valerie repeated. "Or I'll call security and have you thrown out."

"Honestly, Val. Do you really think that's going to work? I'm a star, darling. The goons in security wouldn't dare lay a hand on me."

Valerie put her hands on her hips. "Let's find out if that's true, shall we?"

Silence fell over them. Francesca held Valerie's gaze.

But only for a moment.

"All right," Francesca said. "I'll leave. But you're going to wish you'd listened to what I have to say. You're going to—"

"*Leave, now.*" Valerie leaned in close, dropping her voice to a firm whisper. "And if you *ever* use Hazel to manipulate me again, I'll make sure you regret it."

"All right, all right. I'm leaving."

Valerie didn't take her eyes off Francesca until she was out of view. As she took a deep breath to settle her anger, she noticed Alex nearby, trying his best to look as if he hadn't been listening.

"Yes, Alex?" she said.

He scurried over to her. "It's just, well… it's Jackie. Her girlfriend called, and they started fighting, so she locked herself in her trailer and won't come out."

"I swear to—" Valerie let out an exasperated sigh. It had been a long day. It was only mid-afternoon, but they'd started filming early in the morning. The crew was exhausted. The director was losing her patience. Everyone needed a break.

She needed a break.

"Let's call it a day," she said. "Tell everyone to go home. We'll start again tomorrow. And tell Jackie if she's not on set first thing in the morning, I'll kill off her character and replace her with someone who knows how to behave like an adult!"

Alex nodded. "Understood."

As he headed back to the set, Valerie peered into Hazel's stroller. She was due for her afternoon nap, and she was struggling to keep her eyes open.

"Looks like it's time to go home." She drew her fingers through Hazel's baby-soft curls. "I'll let Abby know we're on our way."

Abby. Sweet Abby. She'd be waiting for them at home, eager and ready to serve as always. And as always, Valerie would suppress her attraction to her, ignore the chemistry between them.

But it was becoming harder and harder to resist.

All it would take was a word, and Abby would be so much more than just her nanny. Abby wanted to be hers. She yearned for it. It only made Valerie want her more.

And her resistance was starting to crumble.

CHAPTER 13

Abby punched the code into the keypad outside Valerie's study. A second passed. Then, the door unlocked with a click.

She pushed it open and stepped inside. In the center of the room was a large mahogany wood desk, a plush leather chair behind it. The wall to one side of the desk was made up of the same floor-to-ceiling windows as the rest of the house. The other three walls? They were entirely covered in bookshelves, bursting with books.

She stared at the shelves. She'd never seen so many books outside of a library. She could spend hours in this room just flicking through them. But she had a job to do.

She walked over to Valerie's desk and slipped into the leather chair, resting her arms on the armrests as she spun around in it. It was even more comfortable than it looked, and it was big enough to curl up in with a good book and a cup of cocoa. Or a glass of wine. That was more Valerie's speed. Lounging in her chair in nothing but one of her long, silk dressing gowns, a glass of wine in her hand, her copper-brown legs crossed one over the other, dark hair cascading down bare shoulders to her breasts, which peeked out from the top of her robe…

Focus, Abby. You're not here to fantasize.

But she couldn't stop herself. Since that night in her bedroom, she'd been consumed with thoughts of Valerie. Her voice, sultry but firm as she whispered each command. Her presence, so regal, so overpowering that Abby could feel it without Valerie even touching her.

Her body, and the way Abby's own body obeyed Valerie's words before her mind did.

She leaned back in the chair and closed her eyes. She should have felt humiliated by what had passed between them, by the way Valerie had left her alone right after. A part of her *did* feel hurt. But an even bigger part of her wanted *more*.

She needed to tell Valerie that. She needed to talk to her about what had happened. But every time she tried, her tongue tied itself into knots and her body grew weak.

And she just couldn't do it.

But it was obvious that Valerie didn't want to talk about that night either. While she'd stopped avoiding Abby and seemed to have warmed up to her again, she hadn't said a word about what had happened. Abby didn't understand it. How could Valerie ignore what had happened between them when it was all Abby could think about?

She swiveled around in the chair, facing Valerie's desk. That night? It had probably meant nothing to her. Sure, she'd admitted she was attracted to Abby. But could Valerie ever be seriously interested in someone like her when she had a Hollywood superstar like Francesca Moreno beating down her door?

Abby could never compete with that. Especially since Francesca and Valerie had years of history. They'd been married. They had a kid together.

Her stomach churned. Never in her life had she felt smaller than she had in Francesca's presence. The woman was so glamorous, so magnetic. She dominated the room in a way that Abby had only ever seen in, well, Valerie.

But Valerie hadn't even bothered to introduce Abby to her. It was like she'd forgotten that Abby existed. But why would either of them pay any attention to her? She was just the nanny.

Abby sighed and began looking through the papers blanketing Valerie's desk. There were a few official-looking documents, but most of them were scripts, all annotated in Valerie's graceful handwriting. None of them matched the title she'd written down. Neither did any of the scripts in the drawers of the desk.

Abby got up from the chair and wandered over to the small table by the window. The script wasn't there either. And it probably wasn't in the filing cabinet. Most of those drawers were locked.

There was nowhere else it could be.

Abby cursed. She'd have to call Valerie to tell her. But she'd left her phone in her purse, and she'd left her purse on the hall table.

She glanced at the bookshelves. Valerie's collection of books seemed endless, and more than half of them were vintage. Would she ever get the chance to see inside Valerie's study again?

It couldn't hurt to take a closer look.

She turned to the nearest bookshelf. It was filled with contemporary novels of all genres, from literary fiction to thrillers. Had Valerie read all of them? She was a writer *and* a producer, so it made sense for her to be well-read and up to date with the latest fiction. Some of her films had been based on novels.

Abby pulled a book out at random and read the title. Her face flushed. It was a romance novel, one she'd read before, and it wasn't for the faint of heart. Erin had caught her reading it years ago and had teased her mercilessly about it for an entire week before sheepishly asking to borrow it. That had been the last time she made fun of anything Abby was reading.

She returned the book to its place and wandered over to the shelf on the opposite wall. The books here were older, mostly classics. Most of them looked older than Abby herself.

She ran her hand along the shelf, taking care not to let her fingers touch the books. But as she scanned their spines, her eyes fell on a copy of *Wuthering Heights*. It was one of her favorite books. And Valerie's copy was ancient, but it was in pristine condition.

Is this... is this a first edition? There was only one way to find out. But she needed to be careful not to damage it.

Abby glanced back at the door, then reached up and pulled the book out from the shelf gingerly. But it only came out halfway before getting stuck.

She tugged on it again, harder this time. It didn't budge. But something behind the book clicked.

And the entire bookcase *moved*.

Abby backpedaled, looking around frantically. *What did I do? How do I stop this?*

But it was too late. The bookcase slid to the side, revealing an *entire room* behind it.

Abby's pulse pounded. She stepped toward the newly formed doorway, peering inside. But the lights were off and the curtains were drawn. All she could make out in the darkness were vague shapes.

I shouldn't go in there. I shouldn't even be looking at this. I need to leave and tell Valerie what happened. It was an accident. She won't be mad.

But something made her hesitate. And before she knew it, she'd stepped past the bookcase and into the room.

The moment she crossed the threshold, the lights flickered on, illuminating the vast room. Abby blinked. *A bedroom?* It looked like one. A large four-poster bed made up with silken sheets and arrayed with pillows sat on a platform at the far end of the room. There were a dozen chests of drawers and cabinets and trunks scattered about, which seemed excessive. But otherwise, it looked just like any other bedroom in the house.

Abby frowned. Why would Valerie have a secret bedroom locked away behind her study?

She scanned the room again. Her eyes fell on a large, framed canvas above the head of the bed. It was a black and white painting of a woman, completely naked and bound with ropes that were artfully tied around her body, immobilizing her completely...

Wait. Wait. Abby stepped toward the four-poster bed, examining it closer. The wrought-iron bed had little rings attached to the frame every foot or so in a way that almost looked like a part of the elaborate design.

Almost.

She swiveled around. Nearby was a bench that was shaped like a sawhorse, but padded and upholstered with leather. It clearly wasn't designed to sit on. And the wall beside her? It had thick, black leather cuffs bolted to it three-quarters of the way up the wall.

She took a step back, her thighs hitting an ornate dresser made of dark wood behind her. She turned and opened a drawer at random. It was filled with toys. *Adult* toys. Whips and floggers, riding crops and canes, blindfolds and handcuffs and ropes.

Abby's body began to burn. This was why Valerie's study was off-limits. It wasn't the study itself that she wanted to keep hidden. It was this room.

And there was only one purpose for a room like this. One reason Valerie would have one in her house. From the moment they'd met, Abby had felt it. The way Valerie was always in control. The way she could make Abby's knees weak with just a look. The way she commanded every room she was in.

The way she commanded Abby in her bedroom that night.

Her heart thumped. This was why she'd been so drawn to Valerie from the very beginning. She'd never understood it when others talked about what they were attracted to in a person. Their looks, their job, their gender. None of that mattered to her.

What mattered was that they made her want to fall to her knees and vow to be *theirs*.

She closed her eyes, running her fingertips over a soft velvet blindfold. As she did, she imagined Valerie slipping it over her head, fingers caressing her face as she whispered all the dirty things she was going to do to her—

A voice broke through her trance, clear and sharp. "What do you think you're doing?"

Abby yanked her hand back and whirled around.

Standing in the doorway, her arms crossed and her eyes fixed on Abby, was Valerie.

CHAPTER 14

Abby slammed the drawer shut behind her. "I, um..." But what could she say? She'd been caught red-handed. And Valerie's icy expression made one thing clear —she was furious.

Abby swallowed. Was she about to get fired? She opened her mouth to speak, but nothing came out. As Valerie stepped into the room, heels clicking on the marble floors, Abby's pulse surged.

"Well?" Valerie stopped before her, her penetrating gaze freezing her in place. "I asked you a question. What are you doing in here?"

Abby lowered her eyes, every inch of her skin alight. Even now, her body betrayed how much she wanted Valerie. "I'm sorry! I was looking for the script in your study, but I couldn't find it. Then I saw the books on your shelf, and I..."

Abby glanced up at Valerie. Her expression was still hard as stone, the fire in her eyes blazing even hotter. But as Abby met her gaze, her stomach fluttered. It wasn't anger in Valerie's eyes. No, it was something else entirely.

It was *desire*.

"Where's…" Abby's voice quavered. "Where's Hazel?"

"Asleep. She won't be disturbing us. It's just you and me." Valerie ran her hand along the top of the chest of drawers next to Abby. "So now you see why I keep my study locked. It's to keep this room hidden from prying eyes. Yet here we are."

Valerie took another step toward her, leaving barely a foot between them. Abby trembled, transfixed by her plump red lips, the scent of her hair, the heat of her body.

"Valerie…" But she could barely breathe, let alone speak. It was taking all of her willpower to keep herself from falling to pieces.

Until Valerie whispered a single word.

"Kneel."

And Abby lost herself completely.

Her mind went blank as she fell to her knees, her hands on her thighs and her eyes downcast. Heat rose through her body. She'd obeyed without hesitation, as if it were a reflex. No, it was something even deeper. It was instinct.

Above her, Valerie let out a satisfied murmur. "So eager to obey. I'm not surprised. I could tell from the moment we met that you're in dire need of a Mistress. And I see it now, the way your body begs to serve me." She reached down and drew her fingers up the center of Abby's neck, tilting her head up to face her. "Am I wrong?"

Abby's whole body flushed. She shook her head.

"Again, I asked you a question. Am. I. Wrong?"

"No," Abby said softly. "You're not."

Valerie traced the backs of her fingers up Abby's cheek. "How does it feel to be on your knees before me? Does it feel good? Does it feel *right*?"

"Yes," Abby whispered. "So right."

The corners of Valerie's lips curled up slightly. "You look delectable on your knees."

Abby let out a long, slow breath. In all her wildest fantasies, she'd never imagined anything like this. But this? It was hotter than anything she could ever dream up.

"What's your safeword?" Valerie asked.

Again, Abby spoke without thinking. "Topaz."

"Good." Straightening up, Valerie reached behind her head and released her hair from its bun, shaking it out until it tumbled over her shoulders in perfect curls. "Do you want to please me, Abby?"

Abby nodded. "Yes."

Valerie's eyes didn't leave Abby's as she reached down and took the hem of her skirt in her fingers. With a shimmy of her hips, Valerie drew her skirt up around her waist, baring her smooth, bronze thighs and a pair of black panties made of silk and lace.

"Then you know what to do," she said.

Abby's breath trembled, desire rising inside her. Valerie was right. She knew what to do. Casting her eyes down again, she slid her hand up the inside of Valerie's calf, up past her knee, up her thigh, all the way to her hip.

She peered up at Valerie's face as she tugged at the waistband of the woman's panties. "May I?"

Valerie nodded. "You may."

Slowly, Abby drew Valerie's panties down her thighs, all the way to the floor. Valerie stepped out of them, one high-heel after the other, then leaned back against the wall and spread her legs wide, parting her thighs.

Abby's pulse throbbed. Valerie was so wet she was almost dripping. And Abby was even wetter.

"Go on," Valerie said. "I know how much you want to taste me."

Abby leaned in close, Valerie's scent flooding her head. She ran her tongue up the inside of Valerie's thigh until she reached her warm, slick folds, and glided it up and down, licking and stroking gently.

"Oh yes," Valerie murmured. "Just like that."

She arched her back, pushing her hips out toward Abby. Abby drew her hands up the sides of Valerie's thighs, grasping onto her full, round hips to anchor herself as she buried her head between Valerie's legs. She flicked and teased, circled and swirled, dipped her tongue into her entrance. And as she skated it up to her clit, Valerie's legs trembled, a muted moan rising from her.

"Don't stop," she said. "Don't stop."

A thrill rippled through Abby's body. Seeing, hearing, *feeling* Valerie in the throes of pleasure felt so illicit. Her grip on Valerie's hips tightened, fingers digging into the soft flesh of her ass cheeks as her mouth moved faster between her legs. Valerie's breaths grew heavy, tremors shaking her body with every sweep of Abby's tongue, every brush of her lips. Her hands fell to Abby's head, fingers twining through her hair as she pulled Abby into her, hips bucking back against her mouth.

"Yes!" Valerie cried. "Oh, yes—"

She stiffened, then shuddered, her thighs clenching around Abby's ears as an orgasm rocked her body. A gasp echoed from her, her grip on Abby's hair tightening.

But Abby didn't let up. Not until Valerie's hands fell from her head and she slumped back against the wall, breathing hard.

Abby sat back on her heels, peering up at Valerie. Her eyes were closed, the lightest sheen of sweat on her chest.

"Did I—" Remembering herself, Abby lowered her gaze. "Did I please you?"

"Oh, yes," Valerie said between breaths. "Let me show you just how much."

She pulled Abby to her feet. Her head spun. She was dizzy with desire, drunk on Valerie's scent, on the taste of her.

But Valerie didn't give her a moment to catch her breath. Grabbing her by the waist, she spun Abby around and pushed her up against the wall behind her, taking hold of Abby's wrists and pinning them at either side of her head.

Abby gasped, her whole body trembling. Valerie was barely an inch from her, her lips close enough that she could almost feel them on her. Out of the corner of her eye, she could just make out the leather cuffs hanging from rings in the wall several feet away.

Valerie leaned closer, whispering softly. "You have no idea how many times I've imagined this. Pushing you up against the wall. Feeling you quiver in my grasp. Making you beg me to come, just like you did the other night."

Abby's lips parted with a silent breath. But Valerie didn't kiss her. Instead, she released one of Abby's wrists and snaked a hand down the front of her dress, between her breasts, down her stomach, down to the skirt of her sundress. It was the same long, floaty sundress she'd worn at the park the day they met.

She dragged it up to Abby's waist and slipped a hand between her thighs. "You're already dripping underneath these panties, aren't you?"

Abby shivered, a surge of pleasure rolling through her at Valerie's touch. "*Yes...*"

"I can tell." She drew her lips down Abby's neck. "I can tell how hot just being in this room makes you. I can see how much it turned you on to be on your knees before me." She ran her hand up to Abby's stomach again, then slid it inside her panties. "I can feel how wet it made you to serve me."

She slipped a finger between Abby's lower lips, skating it over her clit and down her folds. Abby's legs trembled as she sucked in a sharp breath, Valerie's touch almost bringing her to her knees again.

She ran her finger down, teasing Abby's entrance before easing it inside. "This is how you like it, isn't it?" She slid another finger into her and began drawing them in and out, her fingertips curling with every thrust. "This is how you touched yourself for me the other night?"

"Yes..." Abby shuddered, bolts of pleasure shooting through her. "God, yes."

Fingers still moving inside her, Valerie swept her thumb up to circle her clit. "Every single night since I walked in on you, I've touched myself to the vision of you on the bed, your legs spread at my command. Every single night, I imagined myself touching you instead."

A moan rose from Abby's chest. She closed her eyes, her head tipping back as Valerie moved her fingers faster, harder. Abby's free hand scrabbled against the wall behind her, her other arm still trapped firmly in Valerie's grasp.

"Valerie..." she whimpered. "God, *please—*"

Her words were cut off by a climax that shattered her body, her hips arching against Valerie as pleasure flowed through her, unrelenting. But Valerie didn't stop. She held Abby in place, thrusting and stroking between her legs, until every last drop of pleasure had been milked from her.

Abby let out a hard breath. And before she could take another, Valerie's hands were at her cheeks, and her lips were on hers in a blistering, blazing kiss.

Abby sighed into her lips, dissolving against her. Her head swam, intoxicated by Valerie's heat, by the scent of her skin, the taste of her lips, the press of her body. And for one exhilarating moment, she lost herself in bliss, and in Valerie.

A shrill chiming pierced the air, coming from the study. Valerie pulled back slightly, hands still cupping Abby's face.

"The baby monitor," she said. "I need to check on Hazel."

Instead, she drew Abby into a kiss again, hot, hard, *hungry*. Abby murmured into her lips. She didn't want Valerie to stop. But they couldn't ignore the chiming.

They couldn't ignore reality.

Valerie pulled away, freeing Abby from her hold. "I'll go check on Hazel." She smoothed down her skirt and straightened up her blouse. "Take a moment to collect yourself, then lock up my study."

Abby nodded. But her heart was racing, along with her mind. What just happened between them? It wasn't something they could simply walk away from.

No. Not again.

As Valerie turned to leave, Abby grabbed her hand. "Valerie, I…"

But she didn't need to say anything more. Because Valerie pulled her into a final, urgent kiss before releasing her hand again.

"We'll talk tonight," she said.

And with that, she disappeared through the doorway, leaving Abby alone in the hidden room.

CHAPTER 15

Valerie shut Hazel's bedroom door. It was late in the evening, and she'd spent the better part of an hour getting her daughter to sleep. Just one more book had turned into three, an indulgence Valerie rarely allowed.

But she'd broken all the rules today already.

She went into her bedroom and picked up her phone from her nightstand. She had a dozen missed calls and messages, all from the last hour. Was there an emergency at work?

She unlocked her phone and scrolled through her notifications. The calls and messages? All were from Francesca.

I'm sorry about today. I just wanted to see you.

I've been thinking about you lately. About the way things ended between us.

Why won't you answer me? I just want to talk to you.

Answer the phone, Valerie.

Stop ignoring me.

She dismissed the messages. Francesca was becoming a problem. Valerie needed to deal with her.

But right now, she had something more important to do.

She made her way to Abby's bedroom and knocked on the door. "It's Valerie. Can we talk?"

This time, she waited for Abby to give her a clear answer. "Come in."

Valerie opened the door and entered the room. Inside, Abby sat on her bed, her legs crossed and a book face-down beside her. Her hair was loose, and she was dressed in a thin cotton tank top and a pair of pajama shorts that left little to the imagination. But that didn't stop Valerie's imagination running to wicked places.

Just one word and I could have her on her knees again. But they had already gone too far today, much further than Valerie should have allowed without prior discussion and negotiation. That was a rule she enforced even with the most experienced of submissives.

It couldn't happen again. No, if they were going to do this, they needed to do it right.

She shut the door behind her. "Am I interrupting?"

"Not at all." Abby grabbed a bookmark and slipped it into her book, then set it on top of the stack of books on her nightstand.

"That's quite the collection," Valerie said. "You like to read?"

Abby nodded. "Always have. Books were a big escape for me growing up. Actually, that's why I ended up in your... room." She averted her gaze. "I got a little excited when I saw all those books. I wanted a closer look. But I'm sorry, I shouldn't have snooped."

"Yes, well, clearly we both need to stop marching into rooms uninvited."

A blush spread across Abby's chest and up her cheeks. Was she, too, remembering the last time Valerie had come into her room?

"So, um, I didn't find that script in the end," Abby said.

"Oh, that? It was in the car wedged beside the seat. It must have fallen out of my bag. But that's not why I'm here." Valerie sat down at the end of the bed. "It's time we talked about what happened today."

"Right. Look, I know you're going to say that you're my boss, so we can't get involved, but I want this. I—"

Valerie held up her hand. "That's not what I was going to say. But you're right. Yes, I'm your boss. Yes, this goes against everything I stand for. Yes, my life is complicated enough already." Saying it out loud was almost enough to change her mind.

Almost.

"But there's no denying what's between us. And we both have something to offer each other. Something we both want." She locked eyes with Abby. "I want a sub. And you clearly *need* a Domme."

Abby's lips parted silently. Those lips? They begged to be kissed. And her body begged for so much more.

"Well? What do you have to say to that?" Valerie drew a hand along Abby's thigh. "Don't keep Madame V waiting."

"You're…" Abby glanced away before looking up at her again. "You're not wrong. I've been a submissive for as long as I remember, even before I knew what that meant. But I've never had a Domme of my own. I've had casual play partners and one-off things, but that's it."

"I suspected as much. I could tell that you know who and what you are, but you've never had someone truly tame you the way you want to be tamed."

Abby bit her lip. Was she imagining just that? Because Valerie was.

Abby tucked her legs to one side. "I guess that's true. That's what I've always wanted. But not with just anyone. I want it to be someone I have a real connection with. Someone who I can just be myself with. Someone I can feel safe with."

"It's only natural to want that. Submission puts you in a vulnerable place. Trust between a Domme and her sub is paramount. And it's my job to make you feel safe, all right?"

Abby nodded.

"So what I need to know is what you like, and what you don't like. What are your limits? What are you comfortable with?"

"Well, hard limits are anything that falls under edge-play. Degradation too. I'm okay with discipline, dirty talk, things like that. But I don't like being humiliated. I don't like being made to feel worthless."

"I hear you. And you should know, that's not my style. While discipline has its place, I treat any submissive of mine like the precious treasure she is." Valerie traced her fingers up the front of Abby's thigh. "In exchange for her devotion, of course."

Abby quivered. Valerie felt a pang of satisfaction.

"What else?" she asked.

"That's pretty much it. Other than that, I'm up for most things. Bondage, impact play, toys." Abby paused. "Except for maybe anal? I guess you could say it's a soft limit. It's a little intimidating. I've never felt comfortable enough with anyone to try it, you know?"

Valerie squeezed Abby's thigh gently. "I understand. Is there anything else?"

Abby shook her head. "That's it."

"All right. So those are your limits. But you haven't told me much about what you like. I want to know what really excites you. What *thrills* you."

Abby hesitated. "There's nothing in particular. Besides, that's part of the thrill of it for me. You know, experimenting, trying new things. Letting someone else take control and make those decisions for me."

Valerie studied Abby's face. *What aren't you telling me? What secret desires do you harbor?*

But now wasn't the time to push her. "That's what I enjoy the most too. Delving deep into my submissive's desires, exploring the parts of her she's never explored before. Pushing her to challenge her boundaries, her beliefs about herself and what she's capable of. It requires a certain amount of intimacy and trust."

"That sounds… intense," Abby said.

"It is. But the rewards are greater than you can imagine." Valerie took her hand. "Just know that I will never push you further than you can handle. And ultimately, it must be you who chooses to step across that line. Your power is yours to give. I can only take it if you offer it to me willingly."

"I understand. And I don't mind you pushing me a little."

Valerie took Abby's chin in her fingers. "You don't need to worry. I'll keep you safe."

Valerie kissed her gently. But as Abby deepened the kiss, Valerie drew back.

"We can't," she said. "I have an early start tomorrow."

"Oh." Abby peered up at her from under her eyelashes. "Is there anything I can do to change your mind?"

"Not unless you want to stand before the investors I'm meeting with tomorrow and explain to them why I'm late in *intimate* detail."

Abby sighed. "Okay."

Valerie caressed her cheek. "Don't you worry. We'll get to have our fun soon enough. After all, I need to punish you for going into that hidden room of mine without permission."

Abby's face flushed crimson. *That will give her something to think about while she lies in bed tonight.*

"But until then, I'm your boss, and you're my nanny," Valerie said. "And *nothing* else. Especially around Hazel, understand?"

Abby nodded. "I understand."

Valerie squeezed Abby's hand, then got up from the bed. But when she reached the door, she stopped and turned back to Abby.

"One last thing. I expect you to keep what's between us under wraps. It goes without saying that I can't have this getting out. It would cause a scandal that could end my career."

"Of course," Abby said. "I can't imagine how stressful it is to have the media digging through your personal life."

"Then we're on the same page."

But that was only half the truth. It wasn't just the media that Valerie couldn't risk finding out about them.

But the less Abby knew about Francesca, the better.

CHAPTER 16

The moment Abby stepped out of her car, Erin squealed at her from the sidewalk.

"Oh. My. God." She made a beeline for the matte black Mercedes, nearly bowling over a couple standing nearby. "This is really yours?"

"Kind of." Abby shut the car door behind her. "It belongs to Valerie, but it's mine to use whenever I want." She still hadn't gotten used to driving around in such an expensive car, especially when she didn't have Hazel with her. But she'd already gotten rid of her old car. It hadn't made sense to keep it.

"I still can't believe Valerie Kane bought you a Mercedes," Erin said. "You're so lucky."

"Just keep it down, okay?" Abby glanced around. The car was parked in front of a busy coffee shop, and they were getting more than a few stares. Luxury cars were a dime a dozen in LA, but that didn't stop people gawking at them.

"Sorry." Erin lowered her voice. "I know I'm supposed

to keep everything about your job hush-hush, but it's just so exciting. I've been dying to ask about it. Let's go inside so we can talk."

They headed into the coffee shop and ordered two iced coffees before taking a seat at a table on the sidewalk. It was late in the afternoon, and the weather had finally cooled down, so there were plenty of people outside.

Erin sat back in her seat, sipping her drink. "So? What's been going on with you? How's working for Valerie Kane? I have so many questions. It's been too long since we caught up properly."

"Where do I even begin?" Abby hadn't talked to Erin in person since the day she'd moved into Valerie's house. So much had happened since then.

"Let's start with your job. How's everything going with Valerie? Last time you mentioned her, you said things were kind of weird between you."

"Right." Abby stirred her iced coffee with her straw. How could she even explain what had happened between them? Plus, Valerie had told her not to tell anyone about their secret affair.

But Abby couldn't keep it to herself any longer. She had to tell *someone*. Not because of her excitement. Because of her doubts. She hadn't been able to shake them, and they were threatening to overwhelm her.

And Erin was her best friend. They'd known each other since grade school. Abby had shared all her deepest, darkest secrets with her, and she'd never told a soul. She could trust Erin with this secret too.

"Look," Abby said. "It's a long story. But I can't tell you anything unless you promise you won't say a word to anyone about this. Not even Dan."

Erin nodded. "Of course. I swear on our friendship, I won't tell anyone. You can trust me."

"Okay." Abby took a deep breath. "So, it turns out Valerie wasn't mad at me at all. Things were tense between us because she was into me too."

"Seriously? Wow. Not that I'm surprised. Like I always say, you're a catch. Of course she's into you. So that's why she was acting weird?"

Abby nodded. "She was trying to keep her distance because she didn't want anything to happen between us. You know, because she's my boss and all. She was worried she'd be taking advantage of me. But then one thing led to another, and, well..."

"*And?* Don't leave me hanging. You kissed? You had hot sex on the kitchen table? What?"

"Not exactly."

Abby told Erin everything, minus a few details. Her friend didn't need to know that Valerie had caught her red-handed playing with herself one night. And she *definitely* didn't need to know about Valerie Kane's hidden sex room.

Erin's eyes widened. "Wow. That's... wow. But hey, what did I tell you? I knew you had a chance with her. So are the two of you like, a thing now?"

Abby shrugged. "I don't know. I know she wants a sub, but we haven't exactly talked about anything beyond that."

"Well, you should. You're banging this hot rich lady who's the Domme of your dreams, and she's into you too. You need to lock that down."

"I don't know. It's just hard to believe that she's interested in me that way. She was married to *Francesca*

Moreno. Who I've met, by the way. She's a total smoke show. I can't compete with that."

"You don't need to. They're not together anymore."

"I guess. But they have a kid together. And, it sort of feels like they have some kind of unfinished business."

"Oh?" Erin leaned forward. "Got some insider gossip I don't know about?"

"No, it's just a feeling."

Abby didn't know much about what had happened between Valerie and Francesca, but she knew a little. She didn't follow celebrity gossip, but when their relationship ended, it had been all over the news. They'd claimed the breakup was mutual and amicable, but they'd been tight-lipped about the details. And the entire time Abby had been working for her, Valerie had never mentioned Francesca once.

But that day on set, the tension between them had been thick enough to cut with a knife. And Francesca had made it clear that she was still Hazel's mom, and she still thought of Valerie as her wife.

Did Valerie feel the same?

"Anyway, I don't think she wants anything serious with me," Abby said. "She never wanted anything to happen between us in the first place. Plus, she wants to keep us a secret, and for good reason. She has a reputation to maintain. She's not going to risk her career over me."

"Maybe. Maybe not. You'll never know if you never talk about it."

Abby shook her head. "I don't even know what I'd say. And I don't even know if I want something serious with her."

Erin let out an exasperated sigh. "I swear to god, you do this every single time."

"Do what?"

"*This.* You find someone you like, fall head over heels for them, then you freak out and sabotage things by finding an excuse to push them away."

"I do not. And I'm *not* head over heels for Valerie."

"Uh-huh. Then why do you blush every time you say her name?"

"I—" Abby crossed her arms. "Okay, maybe I like her. A lot. But I don't want to rush into anything. I'm just going with the flow. Whatever happens, happens."

"Right. Keep your expectations low so you don't get hurt. Typical Abby. This is exactly why you're always single."

Abby said nothing. There was no point arguing with her, even when she was wrong. Which she *definitely* was.

Erin seemed to sense that she'd gone too far. "Anyway, speaking of relationships, I have some news. Dan and I have decided to move in together."

"That's great," Abby said. "That's a really big step for you two."

"Yeah, well, we've been talking about it for a while now. And you mentioned that once you're settled into your job, you're going to move out properly. So I was thinking, instead of finding a new roommate, Dan could move in. He can use your room as an office, and you could even keep storing your stuff in the closet if you'd like. What do you think?"

"That's a great idea. I'm on board."

Erin grinned. "I can't wait to tell Dan. I'm just so excited that we're finally taking the next step. We've been together for so long, but we were never really ready. Well, *he* was never ready. You know what he's like."

Abby just took a sip of her drink. She knew exactly what he was like. Erin had been coming to her with her relationship drama since they were teenagers. But for reasons that were beyond Abby's understanding, he made Erin happy.

She let out a wistful sigh. "I think he's finally started to grow up. He's even been talking about us getting married, if you can believe that."

Abby smiled. "Sounds like things are going well for you."

"Yep. Everything's just perfect." Erin reached across the table and put her hand on Abby's. "Thanks again for letting him move in. You're such a good friend. And that's exactly why I'm always on your back about your love life. It's why I'm rooting for you and Valerie too. I just want you to find the kind of happiness I have with Dan. You deserve it."

"That's sweet of you," Abby said. "I'm sure I'll find it, just in my own time."

Her phone buzzed inside her purse. She pulled it out.

"It's from Valerie. Give me a second, I should read this. It could be important." It was Abby's day off, and Valerie was strict about giving her space when she wasn't on the clock. Was there an emergency?

But Valerie's message wasn't about her job.

I've arranged for the babysitter to look after Hazel for a few more hours. How do you feel about ending your day off a little early and serving me this evening instead?

Abby couldn't reply fast enough. *I would love that.*

Good. It'll be just the two of us, and I'm going to take full advantage of that.

Her heart skipped. Ever since Valerie had come into her bedroom for the second time, Abby had longed for just a moment alone with her.

She typed out another message. *What do you have planned?*

You'll have to wait and see. Let me know when you're on your way home.

Whatever you say. I'm yours to command.

Abby set her phone down on the table. "Sorry, I'm all done." She picked up her drink and swirled it around in her cup. "So, when do you think you'll have Dan move in?"

Erin raised an eyebrow. But a second later, she launched into her plans with her boyfriend. She could never resist a chance to talk about Dan.

As Abby sipped her drink and nodded along, her mind was filled with thoughts of Valerie.

No, not Valerie. *Madame V.* That was what she'd called herself the other night.

Was Madame V as irresistible as the Valerie she knew?

CHAPTER 17

That evening, Abby returned to Valerie's Hollywood Hills mansion. As she unlocked the front door and headed upstairs, her stomach flitted with butterflies. The house felt unnaturally quiet and still. But Valerie was in her room at the end of the hall, waiting for her.

Come to my bedroom and knock on the door. That was what Valerie's message had said. She'd felt a pang of disappointment when she read it. Since discovering the hidden room inside the study, she'd been yearning for Valerie to take her back inside.

But that wasn't happening tonight. Valerie wanted her in her bedroom. And she was the boss, in more ways than one. But Abby had a quick stop to make first.

She went up the stairs and into her bedroom, slipping into the ensuite bathroom. She'd been out all day and needed to freshen up. She splashed some water on her face and tied back her hair, but didn't change out of the clothes she'd worn to meet up with Erin. While the outfit was casual, the short skirt and low-cut neckline of her top showed off her body in an undeniably flattering way.

She inspected herself in the mirror. *That'll have to do.* She didn't want to keep Madame V waiting.

She left her bathroom and made her way to Valerie's bedroom at the end of the hall.

Then, taking a deep breath, she knocked.

"Abby," Valerie said from inside. "Kneel in front of the door and wait for me."

Abby got down on her knees, her hands flat on her thighs, her head down, and waited. Seconds passed, then minutes, then what felt like hours. All the while, her mind and body simmered with anticipation.

Finally, Valerie spoke again. "You may come in."

Abby got to her feet, opened the door, and stepped into Valerie's bedroom. She'd caught little more than a glimpse of it when Valerie had shown her the house for the first time. In the middle of the room was a king-sized bed made of dark wood, surrounded by a thick white rug that was soft under Abby's feet. Above the bed was an enormous abstract painting that looked like it cost more than the car Valerie had bought her, and the glass doors leading out to the balcony had the best view of all the rooms in the house, overlooking the Los Angeles cityscape and the ocean beyond as the sun set over it.

But there was one thing in the room that was even more breathtaking than the view.

Valerie.

She sat in the corner in a leather armchair, half shrouded in darkness. Her hair was loose, flowing down her shoulders in dark curls and coils, and her lips were an alluring shade of crimson. She was dressed in babydoll lingerie made of intricate ivory lace, and her feet were adorned in raven black heels.

Mistress. Siren. Goddess. Valerie was all those things and more.

And Abby was *enthralled.*

With a wave of her hand, she beckoned Abby to her. Up close, Valerie was even more captivating. The ivory lace of her lingerie contrasted her deep bronze skin, and it was sheer enough that Abby could see the faint outlines of her nipples underneath.

"Like what you see?" Valerie skimmed her eyes up Abby's body appraisingly. "Because I certainly do."

Abby's skin grew hot. She lowered her gaze.

Valerie murmured with satisfaction. "Oh, I'm going to have fun with you tonight. But business must come before pleasure." She crossed one long, lean leg over the other, her hands on the armrests of her chair. "You might be wondering why we're in here and not my little hidden playroom."

Abby nodded.

"You should understand that I don't take just anyone in there. That privilege is earned. And you haven't earned it… yet. Which brings me to another matter—your punishment for going inside that room in the first place."

Abby's mouth fell open. Hadn't Valerie only been teasing her when she said that? Was she really going to punish her?

Abby peered up at her face. Valerie was dead serious.

And that only made Abby hotter.

"I couldn't possibly let such a thing slide," Valerie said. "I wouldn't be a very good Mistress if I did, don't you agree?"

Abby lowered her eyes again. "Y-yes."

"You will address me as Madame V."

"Yes," Abby said again, more clearly this time. "Yes, Madame V."

"Good, we understand each other." Valerie rose from her seat. "Get onto the bed and lie down on your stomach."

Abby did as she was told, positioning herself on Valerie's bed. It wasn't until she was lying down that she noticed a pair of black leather cuffs sitting on the bed next to the pillows. They were attached to each other with a short gold chain that was barely a couple of inches long.

Valerie picked them up. "Hands behind your back."

Abby obeyed. Valerie took her hands, rearranging them so that they sat folded in the small of her back, one on top of the other, then fastened the cuffs to her wrists.

"There." She drew a hand along Abby's shoulder. "How does that feel?"

"Um, good, Madame V." The cuffs were snug around Abby's wrists, but not so tight that they were uncomfortable. She pulled at the cuffs, testing them. They didn't budge. And the short chain between them meant she could barely move her arms at all.

She glanced at Valerie. The woman's expression hadn't changed, but there was a glimmer in her eye that made Abby's heart skip.

"Now that I have you exactly where I want you, let's begin."

She swept her fingers down the back of Abby's neck, between her shoulder blades, along the length of her spine. As she disappeared from view, Abby felt fingers at the zipper at the back of her skirt.

And in one swift motion, Valerie pulled the zipper down and tore the skirt from Abby's legs.

Her breath hitched. It wasn't hard to figure out what kind of punishment Valerie had in mind. Just thinking about it made her burn all over.

"I can see that you're eager to get started," Valerie said. "But keep squirming like that and I'll make you wait even longer."

Abby stilled. She hadn't realized she was moving.

"Now, where was I?" Valerie traced her hands up to the waistband of Abby's panties, hooking her fingers underneath it and tugging gently. Abby lifted her hips, allowing Valerie to pull her panties down her legs. But Valerie made no effort to remove them, leaving them tangled around her ankles.

Her pulse began to race. Her hands were bound. Her ass was bare, exposed. She was at Valerie's mercy.

At *Madame V's* mercy.

She peered over her shoulder. Valerie was standing beside the bed in line with Abby's hips.

"Eyes forward," she said firmly, waiting for Abby to obey before continuing. "It's a pity the rest of my toys are downstairs in that little room of mine. But I don't need them to have my fun with you tonight. You see, I'm not only going to punish you. I'm going to find out exactly where your limits lie."

Abby's breath quickened. Valerie skimmed her fingertips over Abby's ass cheek, her touch feather-light.

"Yes, I'm going to find out just how much you can take," she said. "When you've had enough, ask me for mercy, understand?"

"Yes, Madame V."

Abby drew in a breath. Seconds passed, the silence stretching out.

It wasn't until she let out her breath and relaxed into the mattress that Valerie brought her hand down on her ass cheek.

Abby inhaled sharply through her teeth. The impact had shocked her more than it hurt. But Valerie was only getting started.

She brought her hand down again, a sharp smack on Abby's ass cheek. Abby winced, reflexively pulling her hands even higher up her back. That one stung. So did the one that followed.

She whimpered into the pillow beneath her head, the heat between her legs growing with every strike.

"Oh?" Valerie drew her hand over Abby's ass cheek, soothing her inflamed skin. "Sounds like you're enjoying this far too much. You really are a naughty girl, aren't you?"

"Yes, Madame V," Abby panted.

Valerie chuckled softly. "Then I must be going too easy on you."

She struck Abby again, hard enough to make her jolt against the bed. Abby hissed. That one had *hurt*.

But that was what she wanted, no, *craved*. To be pushed to her limit. To drown in sensation. To lose herself completely and fall into that space where the rest of the world slipped away.

Because in that space, she could truly let go.

In that space, she could truly surrender.

She shut her eyes as Valerie rained her hand down on her ass cheeks and the backs of her thighs, once, twice, three times, on and on and on. Each sliver of pain only amplified her desire, each impact sending aftershocks through her. The skin of her ass and thighs burned tender and raw, her whole body blazing.

Every part of her was sensitized. Every part of her throbbed.

Every part of her ached for Valerie.

She brought her hand down, harder than before, the loud crack filling the air. Abby cried out. The pain, the pleasure—she couldn't tell the difference anymore. The onslaught of sensation, the *need* inside her, was too much to handle.

"Mercy," she said, breathless. "Mercy."

Valerie's hand stilled, silence falling over the room. Valerie's name spilled from Abby's lips, then Madame V's, then Valerie's again, until both melded into one.

And in the space of a heartbeat, she was right there beside Abby on the bed. "I'm here," she said. "I'm here."

Valerie cradled her face in her hands, turning it toward her before parting Abby's lips with her own. Abby returned the kiss, tenderly at first, then desperately, urgently. With her hands cuffed behind her back, she could do little more than kiss her, strain toward her, urge her on with pleading moans.

Valerie murmured into Abby's lips. "Do you want me inside you?"

Abby looked down. There was something hard pressing against her hip. A strap-on? She'd been so drunk with desire that she hadn't noticed Valerie put it on.

She tipped Abby's chin back up with a finger. "Do you want me?"

"God, yes." Abby's words were barely a whisper. She needed Valerie so badly that she could hardly breathe.

"Lie back down for me."

Abby lay down on her stomach again, sinking into the bed beneath her. Valerie drew her lips down the side of Abby's neck and the back of her shoulder blade, moving down to straddle Abby's thighs. Abby lifted her hips from the mattress impatiently. She wanted to feel Valerie inside her and all around her all at once.

But Valerie didn't make her wait. Grabbing hold of Abby's hip with her hand, she guided the strap-on between Abby's thighs, skating it over her clit then back up to her entrance before burying herself inside.

Abby exhaled sharply, the ache in her core rising. She needed Valerie deeper inside her, harder inside her. She pushed back against her, urging Valerie on. But she only shoved Abby's hips down to the mattress, pinning her to the bed with the weight of her whole body as she plunged deeper into her, filling her completely.

She gasped. And as Valerie began moving inside her, she sent wave after wave of pleasure through her body.

"Valerie," she pleaded. "*Valerie...*"

She turned her head until her lips found Valerie's, kissing her feverishly. Abby was consumed by her. By Valerie inside her. By the press of her breasts against her back. By her lips, her scent, the whisper of her breath on her neck and the embrace of her body.

"Madame V," she murmured. "Oh—"

Abby cried out as pleasure erupted deep within her. Her back arched and her hips rose from the bed, her feet and toes curling. Every part of her was alight, every fiber of her being overcome with ecstasy. And Valerie was right there with her, inside her, all around her, drawing out her climax until there was nothing left but bliss.

And Valerie.

~

"Here." Valerie set the glass of water down on the nightstand. "Let me know if you need anything else."

"I'm okay," Abby murmured.

Valerie slipped into the bed beside her once again. After freeing her from the cuffs, Valerie had wrapped her up in her arms and kissed her until neither of them could breathe. Only then had she allowed Abby a moment to come back to herself.

Abby stretched her body out, settling into the bed on her stomach. Her ass and the backs of her thighs still burned, but it was a pleasant, calming burn.

Valerie traced a gentle hand over Abby's tender skin. Abby purred. Nothing had ever felt so heavenly.

"Tell me," Valerie said. "What are you thinking about right now?"

"Nothing at all," Abby replied. "I'm still on cloud nine."

"You enjoyed that, did you?" Valerie propped herself up on her side, drawing a line along the back of Abby's thigh with her fingertip. "So, are you going to tell me what else you enjoy? I want to know what really gets you going. And don't tell me 'nothing' like you did the other night. I know you're holding something back."

Heat crept up Abby's cheeks. How did Valerie know? "It's… it's just, well, I've never admitted it out loud before."

"Whatever it is, it's nothing to be ashamed of." Valerie's gaze softened as she draped a hand across the back of Abby's waist. "Our desires are a gift. They're an expression of all the innate, complex, wonderful parts of us that we keep hidden, sometimes even from ourselves. There's beauty in that. In embracing those parts of ourselves. Especially in a world that likes to tell us otherwise."

"That's…" Abby chewed her lip. "I've never thought about it that way."

"Tell me, then. What are your deepest, darkest desires?"

Abby hesitated. *Am I really telling Valerie this?* "I like… being watched."

"Oh?" Valerie's voice dropped low. "Like how I watched you in your bedroom that night?"

"Well, yeah. But not just that. I like the idea of *people* watching me. Of all of their eyes on me…" Abby shook her head. "But I haven't been game enough to try it before. So much can go wrong when you're vulnerable like that, you know?"

"I understand. It requires a great deal of trust, both in those around you and in any partners involved. You need to know you're safe. And you need someone you feel confident will look out for you."

Abby nodded. "Yeah. Something like that."

"Is this something you'd like us to explore together?" Valerie asked.

Abby hesitated. If there was one person to try something like that with, it was Valerie. She was an experienced Domme. She knew what she was doing.

But more than that, there was something about her that made Abby feel at ease. Was it the way she was just as warm and kind and patient as she was firm and commanding? Was it the way she seemed to understand exactly what Abby wanted, *needed*, without her having to say a word?

Was it the way that when Valerie looked at her, it made her feel like she was the only person in the world?

"Yes," she said. "I'd like that."

Valerie gave her a soft smile. "How about this? One night soon, I'll take you somewhere we can explore exactly what you want more deeply."

"Like where?" Abby asked.

"Have you heard of Club Velvet?"

"Are you kidding?" She sat up on the bed. "Of course I have. Ever since it opened, I've been dying to go, but it's impossible to get in. The place is always packed. And the events are always booked out."

"That's something we're working on. We don't want Club Velvet to become another exclusive LA venue for the elite and no one else. From the very beginning, it was important to us that the club be open to everyone, but interest has been greater than we anticipated."

"Wait, what do you mean *we*?"

"The club's owners. I'm one of them."

Abby blinked. "*You own Club Velvet?*"

"Yes, alongside a few close friends. So getting in won't be a problem. And at Club Velvet, we won't have to worry about privacy. There are rules, both unwritten and written, that whatever happens in the club stays in the club. Which means we can be as open as we want."

Abby smiled. "That sounds amazing."

Valerie squeezed Abby's arm. "Just give me some time to get a babysitter sorted, and I'll take you there, okay?"

Abby nodded. "I can't wait."

"Now, come here."

As she lay back down, Valerie drew her into an embrace. Abby melted into her body, a sigh swelling in her chest. Never in her life had she felt so content. But Valerie made her feel safe in a way no one else ever had.

Was Erin right? Was she falling for Valerie? It didn't make sense. She was Abby's boss. Their relationship was forbidden. They could never be together without risking everything.

But at the back of her mind, Abby wondered.

Would it be so bad if she simply let herself fall?

CHAPTER 18

I 'm on my bed in my panties. What do you want me to do next, Madame V?

Abby's message greeted Valerie as she got out of her car. It was late in the evening, and she'd been messaging Abby all day long, teasing her with increasingly salacious instructions. By now, she was in a state of desperation.

What next? There were so many possibilities, each more delicious than the last. Valerie had already instructed her to strip off her clothes, piece by piece. She could make Abby go into her bedroom at the end of the hall and lie down on her own bed instead. She could make Abby touch every inch of her body, all while imagining Valerie's hands on her. She could make Abby play with herself without allowing her release.

But Valerie wanted to keep her waiting a little longer.

Send me a photo, she sent before slipping her phone back into her purse. She'd have given anything to go home right that instant and finish what she started. That night in her bedroom? It had made her need for Abby even more insatiable. Whenever they were alone, they were barely able to keep their hands off each other.

But with a two-year-old in the house, they rarely had the chance to be alone. So they'd had to make do with subtle flirtations and not-so-subtle messages. Each and every one made Valerie ache with desire. Was there any sweeter torture?

She made her way down the sidewalk in the direction of Club Velvet. Every part of her life had fallen into place. She'd finished reshoots for her historical drama series. She'd secured the funding she needed for *The Resort*, her most ambitious project yet. Her location scouts had found an island off the coast of Italy that would make the perfect location for the film, and Valerie planned to see it for herself as soon as she had the time.

And Club Velvet? It was thriving. From the day it opened, there had been lines out the door every night, and tickets for every event had sold out, including their masquerade-themed party this weekend. It was the hottest venue in the city's queer and kink scenes. And Valerie and the other owners were determined to keep it that way.

Which was why, instead of going home to Abby after a long workday, she was on her way to Club Velvet to put out another fire.

She reached the club and pushed the door open. As she stepped inside, she was greeted by the sound of power tools and raised voices. The club had been closed for the last few days for some minor renovations, but they'd hit a snag.

She walked past the bar and into the large space they'd dubbed The Playroom. At the far end of the room, a stage was being erected. And in front of the stage, a dark-haired woman with olive-brown skin dressed in a stylish pantsuit was squaring off with a man twice her size.

"No, *you* listen to *me*," Olivia said. "The plans were clear. This is *not* what we asked for. If you think—"

"What seems to be the problem?" Valerie interrupted.

Olivia turned to her. "Thank god you're here. Would you look at this?" She gestured toward the stage. "It's all *wrong*."

Valerie examined the stage. Olivia was right. It was smaller than it was supposed to be.

"This is a complete disaster." Olivia turned back to the foreman. "You need to fix this, *now*."

"Look, lady," the man said. "This is what you asked for."

Olivia crossed her arms. "We most certainly did not."

"All right, let's take a step back," Valerie said. "Let me see the plans."

The man handed the plans to Valerie. It didn't take long for her to find the problem.

"Here." She nodded to Olivia. "There's a drafting error on page 2. We should have caught that. It was our mistake."

Olivia huffed.

Valerie turned to the foreman. "But the rest of the plans have the correct dimensions. You should have noted the discrepancy and clarified it before starting construction."

The man mumbled an excuse. Valerie held up her hand. "Pointing fingers isn't going to help. We need to work out how we can fix this. How about you extend the stage so it reaches the sides of the room? You'll need to adjust the catwalk in the middle to compensate." It wasn't a perfect solution, but it was close enough. "Can you get that done before the weekend?"

"Yeah, yeah," the man grumbled. "We'll get it done."

"Good. Now, I'm sure you and your team have plenty to do, so we'll leave you to it."

The man grunted and walked away.

Olivia let out a heavy sigh. "You're a lifesaver, Val. Honestly, after the day I had, I could *not* deal with this."

"Work again?" Valerie asked.

Olivia nodded. "Things are tense. The rumors of a merger are becoming hard to ignore. Just when I had that promotion in the bag." She threw her hands up. "I've been gunning for the top spot for years, and now this?"

"They're just rumors. They're not worth your time." Valerie wasn't being dismissive. Olivia was a straight talker, and she preferred the same in others. "And if the rumors prove to be true, you'll find a way to take advantage of the situation like you always do."

Olivia murmured wordlessly. That was as close as she'd come to admitting Valerie was right.

Her phone dinged. "One moment." She pulled it from her purse. It was a message from Abby. She opened it up.

And was greeted by a photo of Abby lying on her bed in nothing but a pair of tiny pink panties, her bare, flushed breasts on display.

Olivia cleared her throat.

"Right. Yes." Valerie put her phone away. "You were saying?"

Olivia raised an eyebrow. "Forget about me. Who was *that*? I know what that look means."

"It was just the nanny. She had a question."

"Did she now?" Olivia looked Valerie up and down. "So, are the two of you fucking yet?"

"Why would you…" Valerie pinched the bridge of her nose. "What did Elle tell you?"

"Not much. Just that you and your nanny have this intense chemistry and it's only a matter of time before you crack. She bet me a bottle of Macallan 1938 that you wouldn't last a month."

"Of course she did. So, who else knows? Simone?"

Olivia shrugged. "No idea. I've barely seen her at all lately. She's been spending every spare moment with her girlfriend now that they're finally official."

Simone was one of Valerie's dearest friends. Olivia and Elle were a few years younger than both of them, so Valerie and Simone had a closer relationship. She'd be hurt if she found out about Abby secondhand.

"So?" Olivia asked. "How long did it take?"

Valerie held up her hands. "I'm not saying a word. I want nothing to do with this bet of yours."

"Sounds like I owe Elle that bottle. She's going to be so smug about this." Olivia brushed some construction dust off her designer jacket. "But it's good to see you moving on from Francesca. She was a nasty piece of work. You deserve to be with someone who's worthy of you."

"I wouldn't say things between us are that serious. It's simply been a long time since I've had a submissive. And Abby? She's perfect."

"So it's entirely unromantic?" Olivia scoffed. "I find that hard to believe."

Valerie couldn't deny she had feelings for Abby that went beyond physical attraction. With Abby living in her home, being around her every morning and every night, it was hard not to develop a closeness.

And seeing her with Hazel only intensified that feeling. Abby had a way with her that was unlike anyone else before. It was almost like she was a part of the family.

And that was what gave Valerie pause. After Francesca, she couldn't risk letting someone into her life—her heart—again. And there was the risk to her professional life on top of that.

"I can't get serious with her," Valerie said. "It's bad enough that we're involved in the first place. She's my nanny. If anyone finds out about us, it could tank my entire career."

"You're talking to the future CEO of LA's top publicity firm. I know more than anyone how easy it is to spin a scandal into something palatable. Advantageous, even. It's a non-issue."

"So now you're confident you'll get that promotion?"

"And *you're* trying to change the subject." Olivia folded her arms across her chest. "Look, you know how I feel about relationships. I'm far more flexible than most, and settling down with one person for the rest of my life sounds like my own personal nightmare. But we're polar opposites in that regard. You need one person, one woman, to serve all your needs. It's why you stayed with Francesca for so long, despite her being the conniving monster she is."

Olivia had never been one to mince words. But Valerie didn't disagree.

"You need to move on, Val. It's time."

"I moved on long ago," she said.

"Moving on from Francesca was one thing. Moving on

from the pain she left you with? That's something else. You can't let it stop you from living your life. Who knows, you might end up finding someone who, god forbid, actually makes you *happy*." Olivia glanced at her Cartier watch. "I need to go. I'm having drinks with a client later. Will I see you on Saturday night? The masquerade ball was your idea, after all. And Ashton is coming, so we'll need to impress if we want her to invest in the club."

Valerie nodded. "I'll be there."

The two of them left the club, parting ways at the door. It was a warm night, but a slight breeze cooled the air. As Valerie made her way down the sidewalk, images of Abby filled her mind.

But it wasn't the sensual moments they'd shared that played in her mind's eye. It was the mundane. Abby smiling as she greeted Valerie at the door. Abby cradling a sleepy Hazel in her arms. Abby giving Valerie a chaste kiss before she went to bed.

Each kiss? It was even sweeter than the last.

As Valerie approached her car, she noticed a woman standing a few feet away, dressed in a long black coat, a wide-brimmed hat, and dark glasses. It was as if she was trying to look inconspicuous. But in the evening heat, with the sun already gone, the outfit only made her stand out more.

And as Valerie got closer, she realized why the woman was in disguise. It was Francesca. And she was hiding from the paparazzi.

A second later, she spotted Valerie and strode over to her. "Val, it *is* you. I thought I recognized your—"

"What the hell are you doing here?" Valerie hissed, glancing around to check for paparazzi. The last thing she needed was for photos of her screaming at her ex-wife to appear on every gossip site tomorrow. "Are you following me now?"

"Of course not. I was having dinner across the street. I saw your car, so I thought I'd come say hello."

Valerie scoffed. While there was a trendy new Spanish restaurant across the road that was a hotspot for the rich and famous, the timing was too much of a coincidence.

"I just want to talk to you," Francesca said. "There are things I need to tell you. Important things. Please, let's go somewhere and talk, just the two of us."

"I don't have time for this," Valerie snapped. "Just say whatever it is you want to say to me, or leave me alone."

"All right, all right. What I've been trying to tell you is…" Francesca took off her sunglasses. "I miss you. There, I said it. Are you happy?"

Valerie shook her head. "What?"

"I said, *I miss you.* I can't stop thinking about you. About *us.*"

"Francesca, why are you telling me this?"

"Because I want you back! You, and Hazel too. When we ended things, I thought what I wanted was to be free and unfettered, to live as I please, to experience life as a single woman in her prime."

Valerie said nothing. Francesca had certainly achieved her goal. Her exploits had been the talk of the tabloids. In the three years since they'd divorced, she'd been with half of the out women in Hollywood. And not all of them had been single.

Hearing that news had only confirmed what Valerie already knew—she had no feelings left for Francesca whatsoever. She hadn't felt sadness, or jealousy, or anything else. She'd felt nothing at all.

"But I've come to realize something," Francesca said. "That life, it isn't all it's cut out to be. And now that I know that, I'm ready to come back to you. I'm ready for us to be a family again."

"You can't be serious."

"Of course I am."

Valerie studied Francesca's face. This wasn't an act. She was being sincere.

"Fran, you can't honestly think I'd agree to that."

Francesca threw her hands up. "What do you want from me? To admit that I was wrong? That I made a mistake? Well, here I am, admitting just that. I messed up. I should never have let you go. And now, I'm paying the price. Since we split, everything in my life has gone wrong. No one wants to work with me. No one will cast me in anything!"

"What about that film with Martin? The one you were working on when you showed up on my set?"

"There is no film. I just didn't want to admit the truth. My life is falling apart. It's been years since I starred in anything. The only auditions I can get are for side parts, never starring roles. The last part my agent sent me was for the mother of the leading man! And I didn't even get it. They cast someone five years younger than me!" Francesca's voice faltered. "It wasn't meant to be like this. I'm a star. I always have been. And you understood that."

"So that's what this is about? You realized you were riding on my coattails all along, and you want me to make you a star again?"

"No, that's not—" Francesca shook her head. "I just

want my old life back, *our* old life back. I want *you* back. So let's put all this behind us and be a family again."

Valerie crossed her arms. "We're *done*. We were done years ago, even before we ended things. Even before the hell you put me through when I broke it off. There's nothing you can say or do that can change that."

Francesca lowered her head. "Please, just give me another chance."

"No, Fran. I can't."

Silence fell over them. And as it stretched on, Francesca's shoulders began to shake. Was she crying?

But when she lifted her head, there were no tears in her eyes. No, there was something more sinister.

Cold, hard rage.

"You're making a mistake, Val," she said. "You're never going to find anyone who understands you like I do. The *real* you. Not the person the rest of the world sees. Not even the illustrious Madame V. The person you are behind closed doors."

Anger boiled in Valerie's chest. "I'm not going to stand here and listen to this."

"Why not? Guilty conscience?" Francesca's lips twisted into a smile. "What would everyone think if they knew the truth about you? What would everyone think if they knew what you did to me?"

Valerie's blood ran cold. That was a threat. A veiled threat, but a threat nonetheless. And it wasn't the first time Francesca had made it.

"I'm done," Valerie repeated. "You need to leave me alone. And if I *ever* see you again, I'm calling the police."

Without another word, she walked to her car, got into the back seat, and told her driver to take her home.

As the car took off, Valerie raised the privacy screen and sat back in her seat, taking a deep breath to calm herself. She wasn't going to let Francesca's accusations get to her.

And she wasn't going to let Francesca stop her from living her life.

She took her phone from her purse. She hadn't replied to Abby yet. And she had something to tell her.

Valerie typed out a message.

You look delectable. I'm going to enjoy devouring you on Saturday night.

Abby's reply was instant. *What's happening on Saturday night?*

I'm taking you to Club Velvet.

Valerie could almost feel Abby's excitement through the screen. *Really? I can't wait!*

That's not all, my pet. You're going to need something to wear. Go shopping tomorrow and buy yourself a new outfit. Something to wear to the club, and something for underneath. Put it on my card. Consider it a reward for being a good pet.

Thank you, Madame V. Did you have anything in mind?

I'll leave the details to you. Just make it something scorching hot. Something that will drive me wild and have me dying to tear it off. Something that will have the whole club staring at you.

Something that will make them jealous that you're mine.

Abby held up the dress in front of the mirror in her bedroom. Saturday was finally here. It had taken a whole day of shopping before she'd found the perfect outfit in a small boutique on Melrose Avenue. When the sales assistant told her the price, she'd almost put it back. But Valerie was paying for it. And she'd told Abby to buy something that would have every eye in the club on her.

This dress? It would turn heads.

She slipped it on and zipped it up at the side. The short, lacy black dress was woven with subtle threads of gold that shimmered in the light, and it had a low, plunging neckline and thick straps that crisscrossed over her breasts. Luckily, it had built-in support, because it was far too revealing to wear a bra underneath. But where they were going, no one would bat an eyelid at such a risqué outfit. And harnesses and straps were trendy, so it could easily pass as a high fashion piece.

Valerie's voice echoed from down the hall. "Are you ready, Abby?"

"Almost!" she said. "One minute."

She turned back to the full-length mirror, inspecting herself from head to toe. The dress looked even better on her tonight than it had when she tried it on in the store. She'd left her hair loose, framing her breasts, and had added a pair of sparkling gold earrings. Her legs were lengthened by her glossy black high heels, and the straps over her chest emphasized her breasts in a subtly provocative way. One strap sat high on her neck, almost like a collar.

She traced her fingertips over it. What would it feel like to have a real collar around her neck, to mark her as the treasured possession of her Domme?

What would it feel like to belong to Valerie, body, mind, and soul?

Something fluttered inside her chest. Ever since Valerie told her they were going to Club Velvet, she'd been filled with butterflies.

Was it a date? No small part of Abby hoped it was. But that did little to quiet the voice at the back of her head. Valerie wasn't interested in a real relationship with her. Why would she be, when it risked everything she had? When she never wanted anything to happen between them in the first place?

When she insisted on keeping Abby a secret?

"Abby?" Valerie's voice again, this time from right outside her door. "Is everything okay?"

"Yes, I'm fine!" Abby silenced the doubts in her mind. "I'm coming."

She stole one last glance at the mirror. Even she had to admit that she looked good.

Would Valerie think so too?

She grabbed her purse and a light jacket, then opened the door to find Valerie standing in the hallway. She was dressed in black stilettos and a long, dark coat, her hair loose and her lips a deep, rich crimson.

Abby's heart skittered. No matter what Valerie was wearing, she always left her enthralled.

So it took her a moment to notice Valerie staring back at her with ravenous eyes.

"You are *exquisite*." She drew her fingertips up Abby's cheek. "Every woman in the club is going to be looking at you tonight. Every single one is going to wish they were you. Every single one of them will know that you're *mine*."

Abby's breath caught in her chest. And for a moment, all she wanted was for Valerie to drag her back into her bedroom, toss her onto the bed, and take her there and then.

Instead, Valerie drew her hand back. "Shall we get going?"

"Here we are," Valerie said. "Club Velvet."

The car pulled to a stop at the side of the busy West Hollywood street. Abby glanced out the window. On the sidewalk, a long line of people stood queued on a red carpet. All were women. And all wore masks or carried them in their hands.

"Tonight is our very first masquerade ball," Valerie said. "An entire night dedicated to indulging in your every wicked desire, all from behind the anonymity of a mask." She reached into her purse and produced an ornate domino mask, holding it out to Abby. "I had some made for us, just for tonight. This one's for you."

Abby took it from her carefully. It was made of delicate threads of gold filigree woven like lace, with tiny diamonds scattered across it.

She traced her fingers over the intricate design. "Are these *real diamonds?*"

"Of course," Valerie said. "Fake diamonds wouldn't look right next to 24-karat gold."

"This is… It's beautiful."

"It will look even more beautiful on your lovely face." Valerie took the mask from her. "Allow me."

Abby turned around. With an expert touch, Valerie swept Abby's hair aside and drew the mask over her eyes, tying it securely at the back of her head before rearranging her hair to cover the ribbons.

"Now, let me see you."

Abby turned back around. Valerie examined her face carefully before taking the sides of the mask and adjusting it slightly.

"There," she said. "Perfect."

She reached into her purse again, producing a second mask, which she slipped over her head. It was the pair to Abby's, with the same gold filigree and diamonds. But it was less delicate, more elaborate, with flourishes that flowed down Valerie's cheekbones and fanned out at either side of her head.

It was a mask fit for a queen.

The driver opened the back passenger door and stood aside. Valerie slid out of the car and held her hand out for Abby. Abby took it, stepping carefully out onto the sidewalk. And together they made their way to the club, breezing past the line.

When they reached the front door, the bouncer, a butch woman almost twice Abby's size, gave Valerie a nod. "Madame V."

She unhooked the velvet rope across the doorway and gestured them inside. Valerie guided Abby into the lobby, where a woman sat behind a desk with a tablet. She greeted them warmly, then handed the tablet to Abby.

"Just the standard paperwork," Valerie explained. "Club rules, NDAs, the standard waivers. Being a guest of mine comes with certain privileges, but everyone needs to sign these the first time they come here, no exceptions."

Abby nodded. It wasn't her first time at a BDSM club. She flicked through the paperwork on the tablet, then scribbled her signature at the end and handed the tablet back to the woman, who offered to check their jackets.

As Valerie slipped hers off, it was all Abby could do to keep herself together. Because underneath her coat? Valerie wore a fitted black corset dress made of soft, supple leather overlaid with lace that cinched in her waist and emphasized her chest. It was short enough that Abby could see the garter belt she wore underneath, which held up a pair of lace-topped thigh-high stockings. The outfit was even more risqué than Abby's. But on Valerie, it looked sophisticated, elegant, oh so *sensual*.

A blush rose up Abby's cheeks. She was staring. And Valerie had noticed.

"I… You look…" Abby shook her head. "*Wow.*"

Valerie laughed softly. "Is this all it takes to render you speechless? Oh, tonight is going to be so much fun." She took both their coats and handed them to the woman. "Shall we go inside?"

Placing a hand on the small of Abby's back, she led her into the club.

And for the second time that night, Abby was speechless.

It was as if she'd stepped into a different world, a world of luxury, sex, *sin*. Lush velvet chairs and crystal chandeliers contrasted with neon purple lights and vintage wallpaper. Myriad women filled the room, dressed in everything from cocktail dresses and suits to corsets, nipple tassels, thongs. All wore masks in every style imaginable, and many accessorized with harnesses and nipple clamps, floggers and riding crops.

And they didn't hesitate to use them. In one corner of the room, a tall brunette lounged on a chaise, a smaller woman stretched across her lap on her stomach, her skirt pulled around her waist. The tall woman held a leather paddle in her hand, which she slapped against the short woman's bare ass as she conversed with a couple who sat across from them. A handful of other women watched, sipping their drinks casually. All the while, black-clad servers with white domino masks wove through the scene, delivering cocktails and refilling glasses with complimentary champagne.

"It's extraordinary, isn't it?" Valerie said.

Abby nodded. "This is incredible. I've never seen anything like it."

"I felt the same way on opening night. This place is everything we wanted it to be and more. It's a place for women to explore their every desire, without judgment, without guilt. Tonight, more than ever. These masks? They give us the freedom to truly let go."

Abby's eyes fell on a pair of women nearby. One was completely naked, save for the thick ropes bound artfully around her breasts, stomach, and hips like a spider's web. Her wrists were tied behind her back with the same ropes, and a bright red ball gag was fitted to her mouth. She was entirely at the mercy of the other woman, who teased her nipples and between her thighs with unrelenting fingers. All the while, those around them looked on, mesmerized.

Abby's whole body throbbed. What would it feel like to be the woman bound in rope? To be teased and tormented and pleasured by her Mistress while everyone watched, knowing who she belonged to?

"Of course, the effect is all in the mind. A flimsy eye mask can't truly hide one's identity. It's about what it represents." Valerie drew a hand up Abby's cheek, fingertips grazing her mask. "These masks give us permission to surrender to our true desires. And that's exactly what we're going to do here tonight, together."

Abby's breath trembled. Valerie hadn't even glanced at the bound, naked woman, or any of the other salacious things going on around them. Her eyes were fixed on Abby's with an intensity that set the fire inside her raging.

"All this? It's just the tip of the iceberg." Valerie nodded toward a wide doorway at the far end of the room. "Through there is The Playroom. That's where the real fun happens. It's set up with all kinds of naughty tools and toys for anyone to play with while others watch. Of course, there are private rooms, equipped with every sensual delight imaginable." She leaned in close. "But I know how much you prefer an audience. Which reminds me, we just had a stage built."

Abby's pulse quickened. "A stage?"

"That's right. It's booked tonight for a professional performance. But perhaps one day I can take you up there and we can put on a show of our own. Would you like that?"

"I—" Abby's skin flushed. The thought alone made her throb between her thighs. "Yes, Madame V. I would love that."

"I thought you might, my pet. Some other night, then. For now, let's sit down and have a drink."

She led Abby over to a loveseat at the side of the room. As soon as they sat down, one of the black-clad servers appeared, a white domino mask over her eyes and a tray of champagne in her hand.

"Madame V." She held the tray out to Valerie. "Champagne?"

Valerie plucked two glasses from it, handing one to Abby and giving the server a nod. "Thank you."

"Let me know if you need anything else." With that, the server disappeared.

Abby took a sip of her champagne, sinking into the plush chair. They were getting the royal treatment tonight.

"So, does everyone know you as Madame V here?" she asked.

Valerie nodded. "The name commands a certain respect. And it carries with it a reputation."

"I can tell." Abby glanced around the room. "Everyone is staring at you."

"That's where you're wrong, my pet." Valerie drew a

finger up the side of Abby's throat. "They're staring at *you*."

Her breath hitched. And once again, she was pinned in place by Valerie's gaze.

She took Abby's chin between her fingers, her breath whispering against Abby's cheek. "They're staring at you, wishing that they were you, just like I said they would. Every single one of them would give anything to be in your place. But none of them hold a candle to *you*."

She drew Abby's lips to hers and kissed, soft and slow and demanding. Abby quivered, desire rising within her. Even with her eyes closed, she could feel the stares of those around her. But Valerie only drew her closer, kissed her deeper, claiming her for all to see.

Abby murmured into her lips, urging her on. Her hands traveled down Abby's shoulders, pushing her against the armrest of the loveseat and sliding down to her chest, her fingers tracing over pebbled nipples through her dress.

Abby arched against her, a soft moan rising from her lips. *Brand me. Take me. Show everyone I'm yours.*

Valerie snaked a hand up Abby's thigh, slipping it under her dress. Abby parted her legs, just enough for Valerie to brush a finger between them.

"You really do like being watched," Valerie purred. "You're already so wet."

She pushed aside Abby's thong, teasing her folds with her fingertips. Abby shivered, pleasure darting through her.

"As much as I'd love to make you come right here, right now, we have so much to explore tonight. And I want you wet and aching for me the entire time." Valerie drew her fingers up and down between Abby's thighs. "The performance in The Playroom is due to begin soon. We're going to watch it as a little appetizer. And afterward, we're going to have some fun with all the equipment scattered around, where anyone passing by can watch and see what a good little pet you are." She skated her fingertip up to Abby's clit. "And if you serve your Mistress well? At the end of the night, I'll grant you what you so desperately want."

Abby's breath shuddered. Valerie's feather-light touch only inflamed her more.

"So, will you serve me well tonight, my pet?"

"Yes," Abby whispered. "Yes, Madame V."

"Good. Because I want to—"

"Val, thank god!"

Valerie pulled back. Abby opened her eyes to see a statuesque blond woman in a pearlescent eye mask marching toward them.

"We have a problem…" The woman stopped in her tracks, noticing Abby on the couch next to Valerie. "You're with someone. I apologize, I didn't realize."

Valerie cleared her throat. "Simone, this is Abby. Abby, Simone. She's one of the other owners of the club."

"Uh, hi." Abby glanced between the two women. Wasn't Simone the person Valerie had told her to contact in case of an emergency back when she hired her? The two of them had to be close. But it was obvious that Simone had no idea Abby existed.

Her stomach churned. Was she Valerie's dirty little secret?

Valerie nodded to Simone. "What's the problem?"

But before Simone could say a word, a dark-haired,

curvy woman wearing a matching eye mask appeared beside her. "Oh good, you found her. Hey, Valerie." She looked at Abby. "And, uh…"

"Jade, this is Abby," Valerie said. "Abby, Jade. Simone's girlfriend. Now, can we *please* get to the problem?"

"It's the performer for tonight," Simone said. "She got into a minor car accident on the way here. She's all right, but she's not going to make it."

Valerie cursed. "Can we find someone else?"

"We're trying. Elle and Olivia are making calls, but they haven't had any luck. It looks like we need to call the performance off."

"We can't. Not tonight. Ashton is here. She's expecting a show, and so is everyone else. She isn't going to invest in the club if we can't deliver on our promises."

"I don't see what else we can do," Simone said. "We're not going to find anyone else at such short notice."

Valerie glanced at Abby. "I may have a solution."

Abby blinked. *Wait, what?*

"But first, I'll need to talk to Abby here," Valerie said. "Will you give us a moment?"

Simone nodded and led Jade out of earshot. Valerie turned back to Abby, her eyes smoldering.

"So," she said. "How would you like to be tonight's entertainment?"

CHAPTER 20

I *can't believe I agreed to this. Why did I agree to this?*

Abby drew in a deep breath. She and Valerie were due on stage any minute now. After a long discussion about what Abby was comfortable with, Valerie had left her sitting in the empty VIP room that overlooked the club while she prepared the stage for their performance.

What that performance would involve? Only Valerie knew.

She took another deep breath. Valerie had made it clear that she could back out at any time. But she *wanted* this.

So why was she nervous?

A hand touched her shoulder. She jumped. It was Valerie.

"It's time." She held out her hand. "Let's go."

Abby took her hand and got to her feet. As Valerie led her downstairs and into The Playroom, her pulse thrummed in her ears, drowning out the music booming through the club. The Playroom was packed, the crowd buzzing with electricity.

And soon, that crowd would be looking at her.

When they reached the stage, Valerie led her into the wings and out of view of the audience. "There are still a few last-minute preparations to be made, but it won't be much longer. The stage was set up for a professional rope artist. While I'm partial to bondage, I'm no shibari expert. I had to tweak things, have some supplies brought over."

Abby peered out at the stage, where a woman dressed in black was looking over the equipment set up behind the drawn curtains. A metal suspension frame, slightly taller than a person and shaped like a tripod, took center stage. Next to it was a small table arrayed with equipment. From the wings, Abby couldn't make out what any of the equipment was. The possibilities sent her mind racing.

But her excitement couldn't dissolve the lump in her throat.

The stagehand gave Valerie a nod before disappearing into the wings at the other side of the stage. That could only mean one thing.

It was go-time.

Abby's heart thundered inside her chest. *Am I really doing this? What if something goes wrong? What if I humiliate myself? What if—*

Valerie's voice interrupted her thoughts. "Are you ready?"

Abby nodded.

Valerie took both of her hands. "Are you sure? It's not too late to back out. Just say the word."

She shook her head. "I don't want to back out. I want to do this."

"All right. What's your safeword?"

"Topaz."

"Good. You can handle this, okay?"

She nodded again.

"Abby, look at me," Valerie said.

Abby obeyed.

"I know you're feeling anxious. Tell me, what's going on in your head right now?"

"I…" Abby bit her lip. "I don't know. I want to do this, but I can't stop thinking that it's all going to go *wrong*. I'm going to make a fool of myself, and it'll be humiliating, and…"

She swallowed. Saying it out loud only made her more nervous.

"Let me ask you a question," Valerie said. "Do you trust me?"

"I do. I wouldn't have agreed to this if I didn't."

"And do you think that I would ever, for a second, let anything bad happen to you?"

"Well… no."

"That's right. So trust me when I say that I will be in complete control of everything that happens on that stage. Trust me when I say that I won't let anything go wrong. I'll take care of you. I'll keep you safe. And I *won't* push you harder than you can handle."

Abby nodded. "Yes, Madame V."

"And I'll do more than take care of you," Valerie said. "I'll make you feel so good that nothing else will matter. Not your nerves. Not the crowd. *Nothing.* I'll make you so intoxicated with pleasure that everyone watching will feel what you feel, will wish they were in your place. I'll make you feel so divine that the only word on your lips will be my name as you beg me for release." She cupped Abby's cheek in her hand, her lips brushing Abby's ear as she whispered. "I'll make sure *every single person* in this club knows how deeply and utterly you're *mine*."

Valerie pressed her lips to Abby's, kissing her softly. Abby trembled, desire rippling through her. She closed her eyes, dissolving into the kiss, her doubts, her anxieties crumbling to dust.

And in their place was an unquenchable *need*.

Valerie broke away. "Now, do you still want to do this?"

"God, yes," Abby said.

"Then there's one thing left to do before we begin."

Valerie reached over to a shelf next to them. On it was a thick leather collar and leash, accented with gold.

Valerie picked up the collar. "Turn around. I'll put it on for you."

Abby turned. Valerie slipped the collar around her neck, the heady scent of new leather filling the air.

"This isn't exactly my style, but at such short notice, I had to take what I could get." Valerie leaned in, the heat of her breath tickling the back of Abby's neck. "When you get a real collar from me, it will be a collar worthy of my submissive. A collar you can wear proudly that will show the world how precious you are to me."

Abby let out a quivering breath. A collar of her own, a Domme of her own, someone she could truly belong to?

Nothing excited her more.

Valerie fastened the collar and turned Abby around to face her. "How does that feel?"

"It feels…" Abby brought her hands to her neck, tracing her fingertips over the collar. It fit snuggly, but it didn't feel tight or constricting, and it had a reassuring weight to it. "It feels perfect."

Valerie drew her fingers down Abby's cheek, then picked up the leash from the shelf and clipped it to the collar. "Let's go put on a show."

As if on cue, the music in The Playroom faded, and the lights above the stage flickered on. The chatter of the crowd dropped to a murmur, silence settling over the room.

Then, the music began again, softly to start. And as the curtains rose, the music rose with it.

"Follow my lead," Valerie said. "You'll know what to do."

Abby nodded. And, leash in hand, Valerie drew her onto the stage.

A cheer rose from the crowd. Abby stole a glance at the audience. It was as if all the women in the entire club had packed into the room. Every eye was on them.

Abby lowered her gaze, staying a few steps behind Valerie as she led her to the metal frame at the center of the stage. With a tug of the leash, she reeled Abby in to her until barely an inch separated them, then used the leash to tip Abby's chin up. There was a command in Valerie's eyes, the same command she'd given Abby that day in the hidden room behind her study.

And just like that day, Abby obeyed.

She dropped to her knees. Hands on thighs. Head lowered. Facing Valerie, her back to the audience. Valerie was right. Abby didn't need to be told what to do. She simply did what was natural in the presence of her Mistress.

Valerie leaned down and cradled the side of Abby's face, drawing her thumb along her bottom lip. Abby nuzzled against her hand, relishing her touch.

"That's it." Valerie spoke softly so that only Abby could hear. "Give in to your Mistress. Just let go."

She drew her hand down to the collar and unclipped the leash from it, coiling it up and setting it aside on the table. From her knees, Abby could barely see the top of the table. But she could just make out some rope and a riding crop.

Anticipation throbbed inside her. It was no accident that Valerie had her with her back facing the audience. They'd have the perfect view of what was to come.

She watched from under her eyelashes as Valerie picked up a coil of rope from the table, unfurling it carefully. Was the audience transfixed by her, just like she was? Were they hypnotized by this siren in stilettos and lace, by the way her hands danced as she tamed the rope with sensual fingers?

Her performance? It wasn't a performance at all. It was Madame V in her element. It was Valerie set free.

And in that moment, Abby wanted nothing more than to be *hers*.

Rope in hand, Valerie turned back to her. But she didn't tie her up, not at first. Instead, she slipped a heeled foot between Abby's knees in another wordless command.

Abby parted her legs obediently, shifting her weight to sit back on her heels. But Valerie slipped a finger into the ring at the front of her collar and drew her up onto her knees, exposing the backs of her thighs to the audience.

She circled Abby slowly, inspecting the pose from every angle. Satisfied, she took the rope and began binding each of Abby's limbs. First, her wrists, which she tied to the metal frame above her a few feet apart, leaving her arms stretched up and out in a Y shape. Then, Abby's legs, which she bound by tying a piece of rope just above each of her outspread knees and tying the free ends to the frame at either side of her body.

And when she was done, Abby was left spreadeagled on her knees, her legs held open by the ropes, her arms and body stretched almost to their limits. She couldn't move. She couldn't close her legs or shield herself in any way.

All she could do was kneel helplessly before the watching audience.

All she could do was give in to Madame V's command.

Valerie reached down, tilting Abby's face up to look at her. "Everyone out there is watching. Everyone out there is expecting a show. I need you to be a good girl and give them just that."

Abby's lips parted silently, a soft breath escaping them. The intensity, the desire in Valerie's eyes, in her voice, sent tremors through her.

"Show them," Valerie whispered. "Show them how devoted you are to me. Show them that you belong to me."

"Yes, Madame V. I'm yours."

Valerie grabbed the back of Abby's neck and pressed her lips to Abby's in a deep, possessive kiss. But only for a moment. Only long enough to make her ache.

She broke away and drew Abby's hair over one shoulder, exposing her back, which was almost bare in her low-cut dress. Then, Valerie took the hem of Abby's dress and pulled it up around her waist.

Heat rose to her skin. All she was wearing underneath was a tiny thong made of crimson lace. Like the dress, she'd bought it just for tonight. But she hadn't expected that the whole club would see it, along with her bare ass cheeks.

Valerie ran her hands up the front of Abby's chest and pulled the top of her dress down. Her breasts flushed, her nipples tightening.

"Oh? Nothing at all underneath?" Valerie skimmed a hand down the side of Abby's breast. "If only I could turn you around to show these pretty pink nipples off to the audience."

She brushed her fingertip over a pebbled nipple. Abby quivered, desire stirring in her core.

"But they'll have to make do with the view from behind. Because now, we must show our adoring crowd exactly why you're mine."

Valerie straightened up and retrieved not one, but two floggers from the table. Dangling them from a finger, she returned to stand before Abby.

"Are you ready?" she asked.

"Yes, Madame V." Every part of Abby's being burned for her. For her touch, her kiss, the sweet sting of pain that would come at her hand. And for the thrill of all the eyes that would watch them.

"Then let's show them," her Mistress purred. "Let's show them why I chose *you*."

Valerie disappeared from view, heels clicking on the stage floor behind her. Abby tensed, the tails of a flogger trickling down her back, her bare ass, her thighs. But the strike she was waiting for never came. Only the brush of the flogger's falls over every inch of her skin.

Her pulse sped up. Valerie was drawing things out, stringing her along. Was it for the audience's benefit? For Abby's? Or for Valerie's own pleasure?

But it wasn't her place to question her Mistress. Her sole purpose, her duty, was to submit to Madame V's control.

She closed her eyes, breathing slow, steady breaths. She let the sweep of the flogger's tails, the vibrations of music, the rapt silence of the audience all wash over her. She fell deeper into her trance, deeper under Madame V's spell.

And when Valerie raised one of the floggers high in the air and brought it down on her ass cheek, it was with the lightest touch, light enough to do little more than tease her. But it was only the warm-up.

Valerie struck her again, on the other cheek this time, then the other, then the other, in a practiced rhythm that grew faster, harder with every impact. And soon, the gentle kisses of the floggers became sharp bites that made Abby's skin sizzle.

She exhaled slowly, but didn't make a sound. She didn't moan, or whimper, or beg for more. She was Madame V's devoted pet. Valerie had taken her, tamed her, and now, she *owned* her. Abby needed to prove that to each and every person watching.

So she knelt silently in place as Valerie drew stripes across her ass cheeks and the backs of her thighs. She bit down on the inside of her cheek, desire pulsing between her outspread legs. And when the floggers stopped falling, there was nothing left to distract her burning, aching need.

Valerie circled around her, caressing her cheek with her fingertips. "Are you still with me?"

"Yes," she said softly. "Yes, Madame V."

"Good. Because the whole audience is watching, reveling in the way I make you tremble and shiver, admiring the beautiful pink streaks I'm painting all over that pretty ass of yours. And I think they want to see more. Why don't you take a look for yourself?"

For the first time since she'd walked on stage, Abby turned and peered out into the crowd. And she found the crowd staring back at her, an endless sea of women. Some stood by with drinks in their hands. Some were kissing and touching and groping. Some were doing far more.

But all of them were watching. All were *entranced*. They wanted her. They wanted to *be* her.

They wanted more.

"So," Valerie said. "Do we give them what they want?"

"Yes," Abby whispered. "*More.*"

Valerie's lips curled up in a smile. She released Abby's face. "Eyes forward for me."

She looked straight ahead as Valerie set the floggers on the table, exchanging them for a long, thin riding crop. And with a twirl of the crop, Valerie disappeared behind her.

Abby braced herself. This time, Valerie didn't start slow, bringing the riding crop down on her ass and the backs of her thighs, again and again and again. While the floggers were a dull smack that sent shockwaves across her skin, the crop was a sharp sting that rippled deep into her.

She bit back a moan. Her whole body crackled with electricity, every inch of her primed and sensitized. And nowhere more than between her thighs.

And when the riding crop fell upon her again, she couldn't stop herself from crying out. At once, Valerie's hand was on her ass cheek, soothing her tender skin.

"Had enough, my pet?" she asked.

Abby shook her head. "Please, keep going."

"Just a little more." Valerie kissed the back of her neck. "You're doing so well."

She reached for the table again, this time picking up a long, thin whip. She had saved the most intense for last.

Abby shut her eyes, bracing herself. As the whip hit her skin, she couldn't hold back the moan building in her chest. The whip seemed to pierce right through her, penetrating down to her core. It was even more delicious than the riding crop.

Valerie struck her again, over and over and over. Abby shuddered and moaned. She couldn't hold back any longer. As the storm of sensation consumed her, she let go, let herself fall into it.

She surrendered.

And then Valerie was before her, and her lips were on her in a searing, aching kiss.

Abby sank into her lips, straining against her bonds. Her knees were numb, and the ropes rubbed at the skin of her wrists. But the throbbing inside her, the unrelenting desire drowned out everything else.

Valerie murmured into the kiss. "I can tell how much you want me. I can tell how much you *need* me."

She slipped her hand inside the waistband of Abby's

thong. Abby trembled, a desperate whimper spilling from her.

"You're going to come for me, right here in front of everyone," Valerie whispered. "And it'll only take seconds. Because your body is mine. I command it. And if I want you to come, you'll come."

"Yes," Abby said, breathless. "Yes, Madame V."

As the crowd looked on, Valerie parted Abby's lower lips with her finger, drawing it up and down her folds. Her fingertip skated over Abby's clit, sending sparks through her body. Her head fell back, pleasure swirling and swelling inside her.

Until at last, she shattered, her cry echoing through the room as pleasure overtook her. The audience, the club, the world faded away. And as the waves of her orgasm propelled her deeper into nirvana, it was with Valerie's name on her lips.

Valerie. Her goddess. Her Mistress.

Her everything.

And when she came down from her climax, her body slackening in her bonds, Valerie was there, holding her face with her hands.

"I've got you. I've got you." Her warm breath caressed Abby's cheek. "Let's get you out of here. I want you all to myself for the rest of the night."

CHAPTER 21

Abby was barely aware of Valerie untying her. She was barely aware of Valerie taking her home, and laying her down in the bed in the main bedroom. Her mind was a haze of sensation and bliss.

And *need*. A deep, unquenchable need.

Valerie slipped into the bed beside her, drawing her hand through Abby's hair. "How are you feeling?"

Abby's lip quivered. She could barely think, let alone speak. It was like everything she'd ever felt for Valerie—all the desire, all the doubt—was swelling up inside her at once. And the maelstrom of emotions was threatening to overwhelm her.

Valerie drew her in close. "I'm here. Whatever you need from me, I'm here."

Abby rested her head against Valerie's chest and closed her eyes, the gentle thump of the other woman's heartbeat reverberating through her body like it was her own. This was what she needed. This closeness, this vulnerability, not from Madame V, but from Valerie.

Abby opened her eyes and gazed into Valerie's. She cupped Valerie's face in her hand.

And she kissed her.

Valerie wrapped her arms around her, her lips dancing against hers. A sigh rumbled inside Abby's chest. She deepened the kiss, pressing her body against Valerie's, caressing bare skin and delicate lace. But she wanted so much more.

She drew her hands up the front of Valerie's chest, her fingers searching out the clasps that kept the corset dress in place. Valerie's breath hitched. She drew back, her hands falling to Abby's to pull them away.

Abby's heart sank. Had she crossed an unspoken line?

But as she opened her mouth to speak, Valerie pressed a finger to her lips. Then, she reached up and unhooked the clasps of her dress one by one, pulling it over her head and laying it carefully at the end of the bed. Her panties followed, leaving her in nothing but her garter belt and lace-topped thigh-high stockings.

She stretched out beside Abby again. Abby's breath caught in her chest. She hadn't seen Valerie naked before. Her bronze breasts framed perfect brown nipples, her luscious hips giving way to full thighs and long legs. And between those thighs was a patch of neatly trimmed hair that hid the treasures Abby first tasted on her knees that day inside the forbidden room behind the bookcase.

Abby longed to taste her again. She longed to feel Valerie's body against hers, flesh against flesh, skin against her skin. And as Valerie stripped off Abby's dress and drew her panties down her legs, the gentle pulsing between her thighs turned to throbbing.

Valerie lowered her gently back down to the bed.

Abby's heart raced. There was something in Valerie's eyes that ran deeper than lust. It was a profound yearning that mirrored the need Abby felt deep in her soul.

Valerie's lips met hers again, her hands roaming Abby's body. Abby explored her body in return, tracing her fingertips over each curve, each dip, each swell. She painted her lips across every inch of Valerie's skin. She took her nipples in her mouth, relishing the way they tightened at her touch and sent tremors through her body. She slipped her hand between Valerie's thighs, stroking slick folds, grazing her swollen clit.

And as Abby slid a finger down to Valerie's entrance and slipped it inside, the sigh of pleasure that heaved through Valerie's body was enough to make her ache. She savored every murmur and moan, every shiver and shudder, as she brought Valerie's pleasure to a crescendo.

And when she finally cried out in climax, no sound had ever been sweeter. It was that sound, that sight, that echoed in Abby's mind, even as Valerie pushed her back down to the bed and straddled her body, bringing Abby to release, again and again, until finally, they fell into that sweet oblivion together, unable to tell where one began and the other ended.

The door to the bedroom opened and shut, Valerie's footsteps growing louder. Abby kept her eyes closed, nestling deeper into the nest of cushions and pillows on the bed. She wasn't ready to come back to reality yet.

"Here." Valerie set something down on the nightstand. "Something for you to eat and drink."

Abby opened her eyes reluctantly. On the nightstand was a tray holding a jug of water and some glasses, along with juice, a selection of fruit, chocolate, nuts, and other snacks.

"I can get you something warm to drink," Valerie said. "Or anything else you'd like. Just let me know, and I'll make it happen."

"I'm okay," Abby said. "I don't need anything."

"Yes, you do. We put your body through the wringer tonight. You're going to crash hard if you don't replenish it."

Abby murmured wordlessly. Her mind was still foggy with endorphins.

Valerie sat down at the edge of the bed. "How about this? You drink a glass of water and eat something. And I'll give you the most exquisite massage you've ever experienced."

Abby chewed her lip. "That does sound pretty good. Okay."

She sat up, clutching the silk sheet to her chest. She was still naked, and there was a slight chill in the room. Valerie was naked too, but the cold didn't seem to bother her at all.

She poured a glass of water and handed it to Abby. Abby gulped it down, then plucked some grapes from the platter of fruit and popped them into her mouth. Her stomach rumbled. She hadn't noticed how hungry she was.

"Mmph." She grabbed another handful of grapes and swallowed them down, followed by a chocolate-covered strawberry. "You're right. I did need this."

"Of course I'm right. Your Mistress knows best."

Valerie took a grape from the tray and slipped it into her mouth. "So, was being up on stage tonight everything you imagined it would be?"

Abby shook her head. "It was even better."

She grabbed a chocolate truffle from the tray, her fingers fumbling with the foil wrapper. Valerie took it from her and unwrapped it carefully before slipping it into Abby's mouth. Abby let out a sound between a giggle and a moan. She'd never tasted anything more delicious.

She fell back onto the pillow with a sigh. "This feels like the most heavenly dream. I don't want it to end."

"It isn't over yet. I promised you a massage, after all." Valerie drew the backs of her fingers along the curve of Abby's chin. "But I'm tempted to make you wait so I can enjoy this beautiful view."

Abby's cheeks grew warm. She'd dropped the sheet she'd been covering herself with while she was eating, and she was flushed and sticky with sweat. Her hair? It had to be a mess by now.

Did Valerie really find her beautiful this way?

"But a promise is a promise," Valerie said. "Lie down on your stomach."

Abby lay down and folded her arms under the pillow beneath her head. Valerie reached over to the tray on the nightstand and took a small bottle from it. She opened the lid, a sharp, sweet scent filling the air.

"Coconut oil. It has so many uses. And it's perfect for massages." Valerie climbed onto the bed next to her. "Close your eyes. Try to relax."

Abby shut her eyes. The bed swayed as Valerie straddled her body, her knees on either side of Abby's hips. A moment later, she felt the trickle of oil on her back, followed by Valerie's hands kneading the oil into her muscles, gently at first, then harder, then harder still, working her way up Abby's back.

A moan slid from her lips. "This feels incredible." Valerie was finding muscles Abby didn't even know she had. "Where did you learn to do this?"

"I had a professional teach me. A massage is an excellent form of aftercare, so I made sure to learn how to do it properly. Any submissive of mine deserves the best."

She reached Abby's shoulders and began kneading even more firmly, loosening every knot. Abby sank deeper into the bed, soft purrs rising from her.

"Besides, it's not every day that I find someone special enough to call my own," Valerie said. "So when I do, I like to be able to spoil her."

"I definitely feel spoiled right now," Abby murmured. "Thank you, Madame V."

"You're welcome, my pet."

She glided her hands down Abby's back again until she reached her ass. It was still sore, and from what she'd glimpsed of it, bright red. But Valerie's hands were gentle there, and on the backs of her thighs, her touch soothing Abby's aching skin.

Valerie moved down her calves and feet, working her muscles loose. Once she was done, she ordered Abby to turn over. As Abby rolled onto her back and stretched out her body, a question grew in her mind.

"I was wondering," she said. "How did you become Madame V in the first place?"

"I didn't become her. I've always been her." Valerie picked up the bottle of massage oil and squeezed it down the front of Abby's legs, spreading it over her shins and thighs. "But the name is something I adopted about ten years ago. It was around the time *LA Legal* was picked up. I'd worked as a screenwriter before, but *LA Legal* was the first show I created myself. I was young, so the studio was taking a big chance with me. But I knew I had something special, and they saw that too. Sure enough, the show became an international sensation. I went from being an unknown writer to a household name overnight."

She slid her hands up past Abby's knees, kneading her way up her thighs with firm thumbs. "I was thrust into the spotlight. And all of a sudden, every part of my life was under intense scrutiny, far more than my peers. I was an outsider to Hollywood in more ways than one—gay, Black, a woman, and I didn't come from the elite. I'd clawed my way up from a working-class background with zero connections. So I didn't have the luxury of mistakes, of scandals, of failure. I constantly needed to think about my image, about who and what I represented."

"That's a lot of pressure," Abby said. "I can't even imagine what that would be like."

"It wasn't easy. I started to feel like I needed a part of my life, a part of *myself*, that wasn't under constant scrutiny. Something that didn't belong to the public, that was mine and mine alone. I needed a way to simply *be*, without the weight of the responsibilities that came with the name Valerie Kane."

She moved on to Abby's other leg, working her thumbs deep into her muscles. "Finding that part of my life happened naturally. Kink was already a part of me, so I sought refuge in it, immersed myself in it, not as Valerie Kane, but as Madame V. It wasn't as if the moniker obscured my identity. And the BDSM community values privacy for obvious reasons, so there would be no harm in using my real name. But it wasn't about anonymity, or pretending to be someone else. Madame V isn't an alter ego or a false persona. She's a truer expression of myself than the person I am day to day."

Hadn't Abby thought just that on stage earlier that night? It was as if, for the very first time, she was seeing Valerie as she truly was, unburdened, uninhibited, free.

"Having that outlet to express myself became more important as time went on," Valerie said. "As I started my own production company, became a wife, then a single mother. The responsibilities piled on. The need to maintain a certain image grew, and it keeps growing every day. But as Madame V, none of that matters."

"I think I get it. Well, I'll never get what it's like to be you. To have all that pressure, to have to fight harder for acceptance than everyone else around you. But I understand the need for an escape. And I understand wanting the freedom to just be yourself."

She closed her eyes. Valerie was still massaging her legs, lulling her back into a trance with her soothing touch.

"Sometimes, I want the same thing," Abby said. "Sometimes, I just want to let go of it all and be who I truly am. But that's easier said than done. Because what's holding me back isn't other people's expectations, or my responsibilities, or anything else. It's just *me*. It's that voice inside my head telling me I don't deserve it. Telling me no one wants me and no one ever will. Telling me I'm useless, a burden, a nuisance, just like everyone always said I was."

"Abby..." Valerie's hands stilled. "Whoever told you that?"

Abby shrugged. "No one worth my time. I know that now that I'm older. And even though I've left all that behind, left *them* behind, it doesn't stop me feeling the way I do sometimes."

She didn't talk about her parents much. She'd moved on, built a life for herself without them. But their words still haunted her like specters from the past.

"My mom was a teen mom," she said. "Had me at sixteen because her family wouldn't let her get rid of me, but then they turned around and kicked her out for getting pregnant. My dad skipped town when he found out, so she was stuck raising me all by herself. She tried her best, but even as a little kid, I could tell she resented me for ruining her life. Then my stepdad came along when I was six years old. He'd made a little money selling a startup to some big company, and he wanted a hot young wife as a trophy. To him, I was just an inconvenience that came with her. My mom didn't care that he felt that way. All she cared about was that she had someone to provide for her and didn't have to struggle alone anymore."

Valerie stretched out beside her, her hand falling to Abby's arm. "I'm sorry. No child deserves that."

"It's hard to blame her. No teenager wants to be saddled with a baby. Because of my stepdad, she got to have a semblance of the life she would've had if she hadn't gotten pregnant at sixteen. And when my mom and stepdad had my brothers a few years later, she finally got a chance to start over with the perfect nuclear family. One I didn't fit into. It was like I became invisible to them overnight."

Abby stared up at the ceiling, just like she used to back

then, when she'd lain awake in bed at night, wondering what she'd done to make her parents shun her.

"I was just a kid," she said. "I didn't understand why they treated me the way they did. I thought it was my fault. I thought that if I tried hard enough, was perfect and well-behaved enough, I could win their affection. But nothing I did worked. And when I got older, I stopped trying and rebelled instead. It was just typical teenage stuff, but it made my mom and stepdad furious. They worried about what people would think of them, having a troublemaker like me as a daughter. But at least I had their attention. That was all I wanted. For them to see me. Because my stupid teenage subconscious thought that maybe if they saw me, they'd love me."

Her voice faltered. Valerie slipped her hand over Abby's, twining their fingers together.

"I guess one day, I went too far," Abby said. "It was my sixteenth birthday. We went out to dinner to celebrate, but in reality, it was just an excuse for my stepdad to go to this fancy restaurant he wanted to try. I wanted to go somewhere else, somewhere *I* liked, or at least invite some of my friends, but I didn't get a say. So I wasn't exactly enjoying myself, and I was acting like it too.

"I don't remember what I said or did that set my stepdad off. But I remember the moment he finally snapped and said out loud what I'd always known in my heart was true, but had wished wasn't. He said…" Abby swallowed. "He said that I wasn't his kid. That he didn't want me and never had, and neither did my mom. That they wished I'd never been born." Her voice quavered. "But the worst part is, my mom? She didn't defend me. She didn't say that it wasn't true. She didn't say anything."

"Oh, Abby." Valerie squeezed her hand, holding it tight. "I can't imagine how that must have felt."

"I'll never forget it. I'll never forget how much it *hurt*. After that, I checked out of the family entirely. I stopped trying to get my parents' attention. I stopped expecting anything from them. I started taking babysitting jobs and stashed away all the money I could. And the day I turned eighteen, I moved out.

"It wasn't easy. I had to abandon my brothers. My mom and stepdad weren't exactly parents of the year. They cared more about keeping up appearances than actually parenting. More often than not, it was on me to look after my brothers. They relied on me, and they were too young to understand why I was leaving. I'm sure they're okay, but I haven't seen them since, or anyone else in my family. My mom calls me now and then, says something about wanting to catch up, but she never follows through with it. She only called me once this year, on what she thought was my birthday, but she was a week late." Abby shook her head. "It doesn't bother me, not anymore. I moved on from them a long time ago. But sometimes, they get in my head and make me question myself."

Valerie reached out and stroked Abby's cheek. "I understand. It's hard to shake off the stories we're told when we're young, especially when they're about ourselves. And I'm sorry you went through all that. The way your parents treated you was cruel. You deserved better."

Abby glanced away. "Like I said, I'm over it. But I guess a part of me worries that if I get too close to someone, let my guard down, show them the real me? They'll reject me. But with you…" She met Valerie's eyes again. Her pulse quickened. "With you, tonight? You made me feel like I didn't have to worry about any of that. Like I could just *be*. I'm glad I trusted you tonight. And I'm glad you pushed me."

Valerie gave her a gentle smile, drawing her in close. "I'm glad you feel that way. Know this, Abby. I see you. The *real* you. And I'm not going to reject you for it. It's what drew me to you in the first place."

Valerie kissed her softly on the lips, sending warmth surging through her. She wrapped her arms around Valerie's neck, returning the kiss with greedy lips.

Valerie saw her. She understood her. She wouldn't reject her.

So why did a part of her still doubt those words?

CHAPTER 22

Valerie took a seat at a table at the corner of the small cocktail bar. It was late in the evening, and she had plans to meet with Simone. It had been far too long since they'd had the chance to speak one-on-one.

And after the masquerade ball, Simone would have questions for her.

As Valerie waited for her to arrive, she took out her phone and checked her messages. There were almost a dozen. And most were from Francesca.

I'm sorry about the other day. I just miss you.

Please, just talk to me, Val.

I want to go back to the way things were. I want us to be a family again.

Valerie held back a curse. She'd thought she'd gotten through to Francesca that evening outside Club Velvet. She should have known better.

As she set her phone on the table, more messages arrived, each barely a second apart.

Why can't you see that we're meant for each other?

I need you, Val. And you need me.

You'll never find someone like me again. Someone who understands you like I do. The real you.

Nobody knows who you really are. Nobody but me.

Valerie re-read the last message. There it was again, the threat hidden behind innocent words.

How long until Francesca made her threats a reality?

Valerie tapped Francesca's name on the screen and blocked her number. That would buy some temporary peace.

But soon, she'd have to deal with Francesca once and for all.

"Sorry I'm late." Simone slid into the chair across from her. "Traffic was a nightmare."

Valerie slipped her phone back into her purse. "Not a problem. I only arrived a few minutes ago."

A server came by to take their orders, a Manhattan for Simone and a whiskey for Valerie. She suddenly felt the need for a stiff drink.

Simone stuck to small talk until their drinks arrived. But as soon as the server was out of earshot, she crossed her arms and leaned back in her chair.

"So," she said. "When were you going to tell me about Abby?"

Valerie took a long swig of her drink. She knew the question had been coming, but that didn't make it any easier to answer. Simone was her closest friend. And while she wasn't letting it show, Valerie could tell she was hurt.

She set her glass down. "You're right. I should have told you. But the situation between me and Abby is... sensitive."

"Because she's your nanny?" Simone said. "Which, by the way, I only found out because Elle let it slip. Apparently, Olivia knew too."

"Simone, I'm truly sorry. And I didn't tell Elle and Olivia. They figured it out for themselves. To be honest, I didn't want to tell anyone, but especially not you. I warned you against dating your assistant. And now, I'm sleeping with my nanny? The hypocrisy is hard to ignore."

"You know I'd never judge you for that. Besides, you came around on me and Jade eventually. What did you tell me? 'Sometimes it's worth the risk'?" Simone swirled her drink around in her glass. "You were talking about Abby, weren't you?"

Valerie nodded. "Yes, and I meant it. Everything with Abby has been so, so worth it. But that doesn't make it any less complicated, or messy, or *wrong*. I'm her boss. This goes against everything I stand for. I'm putting my entire career at stake."

"You're right. It *is* complicated. It *is* messy. But it isn't wrong. Val, for years now, you've had women throwing themselves at you. At Club Velvet, at work, everywhere else. And you never gave them a second glance, not once. Then along comes this nanny of yours, and you're suddenly risking everything? Do you know what that tells me? It tells me that what you and Abby have is real. It tells me that you feel so deeply about her that you're willing to put everything you have, everything you *are*, on the line. How could that possibly be wrong?"

Valerie sipped her drink, letting the warm burn of the whiskey spread through her. Perhaps there was some truth in Simone's words.

"Here's what I want to know," Simone said. "What is it about her? What is it that makes her worth it?"

"I don't know how to put it into words. It's… a feeling. Whenever I'm with her, everything becomes brighter, warmer. And I feel this fierce need to protect that, to protect *her*. In a world that can be so harsh and cold, someone like Abby is precious. She deserves to be treasured."

An image of Saturday night flashed in her mind. Of the two of them lying together in Valerie's bed. Of Abby pouring her heart out, and the bittersweet kiss that followed. It was only that night that Valerie understood what was behind the quiet strength she'd always sensed in Abby, the maturity beyond her years. She'd been through so much, and she'd had no choice but to weather it alone. But she still carried her pain with her. And Valerie would give anything to take that pain away.

"She's obviously very special," Simone said. "And what the two of you share is obviously special too."

"It isn't only the two of us. You should see her with Hazel. Sometimes I wonder if Abby understands her better than I do." Valerie shook her head. "That should make me jealous. But with Abby? When I look at her and Hazel together, it feels…"

"Right?"

"Yes. It feels right." Valerie let out a heavy sigh. "There are so many ways this could go wrong. I don't want to hurt her."

"Why do you think you're going to—" Simone's brows drew together. "It's Francesca, isn't it? She's playing her games? Getting into your head?"

"She hasn't gotten into my head, but she's trying her

best. Her calls and messages have become increasingly persistent. And she just happened to run into me near Club Velvet the other day."

Simone's expression darkened. "She's stalking you? Valerie, you need to do something about this. Her behavior is escalating."

"And I'm handling it. I've blocked her, and I'm going to speak to my lawyers about the situation. But I have too many things on my plate right now, and I don't have the energy to deal with the inevitable fallout once she finds out I've gotten lawyers involved. I have that trip coming up. I need to focus on that."

Simone gave her a disapproving glare. "Just promise me you won't ignore this."

"I won't. I'll make an appointment with my lawyers first thing when I get back."

"All right." Simone sat back in her seat and took a sip of her drink. "So, about this trip. Where are you off to?"

"Italy. It's only for a few days. And it's business, not pleasure. I'm scouting a location for that rom-com project I told you about."

"And you're taking Abby with you?" Simone asked.

"Of course." Valerie hadn't told her yet. She'd only finalized the details of the trip earlier that day. "I don't want to be apart from Hazel for three days, and I'll need help looking after her while I work."

Simone raised an eyebrow. "Let me get this straight. You're taking Abby on a trip to a romantic island resort, and it's going to be all work and no play?"

"I wouldn't say that. While it *is* a business trip, I'm going to make sure the two of us get some alone time too. Abby works so hard. She deserves an escape."

Simone studied Valerie's face. "She makes you happy, doesn't she?"

"Yes. She does."

"I'm glad." Simone gave her a small smile. "You know, I never got to thank you for your advice with Jade."

"No need. I'm just happy it all worked out. So everything is going well with you two?"

Simone nodded. "It's going wonderfully. You were right. It was worth the risk. And I'm sure Abby will be too."

When Valerie returned home that night, she was met with a calm silence. But as she headed upstairs, the faint sound of Abby's voice reached her. It was coming from Hazel's bedroom.

She crept down the hall to Hazel's door. It had been left ajar. Taking care not to make a sound, she peered into the room.

Abby sat on the edge of the small bed, reading aloud from a picture book. Hazel lay tucked into the sheets, her eyelids drooping. She had a stuffed lion clutched to her chest, a green silk bonnet protecting her curls. Unlike other sitters and nannies, Abby had never forgotten it, not once.

Abby turned to the final page of the book and peered down at Hazel. The toddler had lost her battle to stay awake. Abby shut the book and set it aside, then stroked Hazel's forehead gently before getting up from the bed and slipping silently from the room.

She shut the door behind her, giving Valerie a warm

smile. "You're home. You should have said something. You could have come in and said good night to Hazel before she fell asleep."

"I didn't want to interrupt. She looked so peaceful." Valerie took Abby's hand and drew her to the stairs. They sat down on the top step. "I don't know how you do it. I always have my hands full getting her to sleep. You must tell me your secret."

Abby twirled a lock of hair around a finger. "But then you'd have no reason to keep me around."

"Oh, I can think of a few."

Abby's face flushed pink. Valerie felt a pang of desire. But she had an early start in the morning, and she still had a few things to do before bed. The first of which was telling Abby about the trip.

"I have some news," she said. "I need to go to Italy for a few days. Location scouting for a film. Do you have a passport?"

Abby nodded. "I got it for a trip I went on with a family I used to nanny for. But do you mean…"

"That's right. You're coming with me, along with Hazel. I'll need to work, of course, but I'll do my best to carve out some free time for us. The resort has sitters on staff, so we can take advantage of that to get a little alone time. That is if you're interested."

"Are you kidding? Of course I am."

"Good. Because this whole trip will be under the radar. We're flying in by private jet, and we'll be on a small, isolated Tuscan island where no one knows my face. Which means we won't have to worry so much about keeping things under wraps. We can be a little more free with each other."

Abby smiled. "That sounds perfect." She leaned over and kissed Valerie's cheek. "I can't wait."

Valerie stood up. "I'm going to take care of a few things before turning in for the night. I have a long day tomorrow."

Abby nodded. "I'm going downstairs to read for a bit. I'll see you in the morning."

Valerie headed to her room, a warm buzz in her chest. It was moments like these that made her want something more. For Abby to be not only her lover, her submissive, but her girlfriend, her partner.

And perhaps one day, her wife?

Valerie let the thought fade. She'd had one whiskey too many.

She stepped into her bedroom and shut the door. As she began to undress, her phone buzzed in her pants pocket. She pulled it out to find several messages from an unknown number.

But it didn't take her long to figure out who they were from.

Why did you block me? Just talk to me.

Is there someone else? Is that why you don't want me back?

Who is she? Whoever she is, she's all wrong for you.

You were meant to be with me.

Valerie's blood ran cold. How did Francesca know about Abby? Was she watching her? Had she hacked Valerie's phone?

But there was a simpler explanation. Francesca didn't know about Abby at all. She simply couldn't comprehend Valerie rejecting her unless there was someone else.

No, Francesca wasn't stalking her. Valerie was being paranoid. Clearly, her ex was starting to get to her.

And she wasn't done.

You're making a mistake, Val.

Does she know the truth about you? Does anyone?

Only I know who you really are, Valerie. Only I know what you did to me.

What would everyone think of you if they knew?

What would they do if they found out?

Valerie blocked the number, then set her phone on her nightstand. Until she came back from her trip, she wasn't going to give Francesca a single thought.

Valerie wasn't going to let her ruin what she had with Abby.

CHAPTER 23

Abby stepped off the gangway and onto the dock, Valerie beside her with Hazel in her arms. They'd landed in Pisa early in the morning before being whisked off to a yacht that had taken them to the small island off the Tuscan coast. Already, the trip had been luxurious beyond Abby's wildest dreams, and they hadn't even made it to the resort yet.

As porters streamed off the boat with their luggage, Valerie set Hazel down, holding tightly onto her hand to keep her from wandering off. Hazel was awestruck by all the new sights and sounds. And so was Abby.

They reached the end of the dock. Abby slipped out of her sandals and stepped onto the beach, burying her toes in the sand. It was fine and white, and it had been warmed by the morning sun. The turquoise waters beyond the beach were calm and crystal clear, and behind it, a blanket of trees stretched out into the horizon. In the distance, she could just make out the facade of a building that had to be the resort.

"It's beautiful," Valerie said. "Isn't it?"

Abby shook her head. "It looks too perfect to be real."

Valerie took off her sunglasses, gazing out over the island. "I can picture it now. Our cast of characters stepping off the boat with no idea that their lives are about to be changed forever. No, their *hearts* are about to be changed forever."

Abby studied Valerie's face. This wasn't the first time she'd heard Valerie talk about her work, but it was the first time she'd heard her speak about it so passionately.

"This movie means a lot to you, doesn't it?" Abby asked.

"It does. And my hope is that everyone who watches it will feel the same. I want every person in the world to be able to see something of themselves in it, no matter their gender, or race, or sexual orientation. That's always been important to me, but it became even more important when I had Hazel. I want her to grow up in a world where she gets to see herself on the screen, along with her mom, her aunties, everyone else around her. I want her and everyone else to know that they can find the kind of life-changing love that the characters in the film will find."

Butterflies flitted in Abby's chest. This side of Valerie —sentimental, romantic—was something she'd only ever caught glimpses of. And only when the two of them were alone. So what was different now?

What had changed?

Her thoughts were interrupted by a middle-aged man in a shining white polo shirt and khaki shorts, a sparkling gold Rolex around his wrist. He greeted them both by name in heavily accented English, introducing himself as the resort's owner and inviting them to follow him back to the resort.

As they made their way up the tree-flanked path running alongside the beach, the owner chattered away about all that the resort and the island had to offer. Abby took a cue from Valerie, responding only with polite nods. It wasn't long before Hazel began to tire, so Abby picked her up to carry her the rest of the way.

Finally, the trees thinned, and the resort came into view.

"Here we are," the owner said. "Palmieri Resort. It was named by my great-great-great-grandfather, who built it almost two hundred years ago. It's been here ever since."

Abby looked up at the building. The sprawling resort was even bigger than it seemed from a distance. The sandstone facade shone the same bright white as the sand on the beach, and it was surrounded by lush tropical gardens dotted with marble statues and fountains, all timeworn but pristine, just like the resort itself.

"No need to check in," he said. "I'll take you straight to your villa."

He guided them past the main resort building and down a path that led deeper into the trees. Other than a few staff milling about, they didn't pass any other people.

Finally, they reached their villa. It was more like a coastal mansion, spanning two stories with a private pool at the back. It was surrounded by trees, and the doors and windows were flung open to let in the cool sea breeze.

As the owner led them to the door, Valerie gave him a nod. "We can take it from here."

The man hesitated. It was obvious he wanted to keep

talking up the resort. But it was impossible to argue with Valerie.

He reached into his pocket and handed her a set of keys. "Let me know if you need anything. Anything at all. Just give me a call."

Valerie waited for him to leave before ushering Abby and Hazel through the door. "Thank god. I thought he'd never leave us alone. Now, why don't you put Hazel down for her nap so we can settle in?"

Abby nodded. "Sure thing."

"I asked the resort to set up a bed for her. It should be in the bedroom closest to ours."

"Ours?"

"Yes, the main bedroom. You'll be sleeping with me. Is that a problem?"

"No, of course not." It wasn't the first time they'd shared a bed, but most nights, they slept in their own rooms. And judging by the size of the villa, there were plenty of other bedrooms. But Valerie had said that they wouldn't have to hide while they were on the island.

Warmth bloomed in Abby's stomach. Maybe someday, they wouldn't have to hide at all.

She headed upstairs, Hazel in her arms. The toddler was already half asleep, having dozed off on the walk from the beach. Abby wandered the villa, peering into each room until she found the main bedroom. Their suitcases had been left inside, right at the end of the bed.

She went into the room next door. It was a smaller bedroom with a low bed that had safety railings around it. After placing Hazel on the bed, Abby returned downstairs to find Valerie on the couch in the living room, her laptop open on her lap and a stack of papers on the coffee table in front of her. How had she gotten unpacked so quickly?

Abby took a seat next to her. "Hazel is down. She's out like a light."

"I'm not surprised," Valerie said. "She falls asleep easier when we travel than she does at home. Handles jet lag better than most adults."

Abby glanced at the papers on the coffee table. "Getting to work already?"

"Unfortunately, I have to. There's plenty that I need to do while we're here, so I can't afford to waste time." Valerie set her laptop on the table. "But that doesn't mean we won't get to have any fun. I plan to explore every inch of this resort, along with the island itself. And I want you to come with me while I do it."

"You do?"

"Of course. My film is about lust, love, romance, and everything in between. How else will I know if this is the right location for it without seeing the resort the way the characters will? I need to experience everything the island has to offer. The sun and the sand. The sights and the sounds. The food, the wine, the beauty. I want to experience it all, with you by my side."

Abby's heart thumped. Valerie's eyes, her voice, were as impassioned as they had been on the beach when they arrived.

But this time, she was looking at Abby.

"We have three days," Valerie said. "Three days in paradise, hardly another soul around. Three days away from the hustle and bustle of Los Angeles, from the crowds and paparazzi. Three days to be as free as we please."

She drew a hand up Abby's thigh, sliding her dress up and leaning in close. Abby's breath caught in her chest, her eyes falling shut as Valerie's lips brushed hers—

The buzz of a phone on the glass coffee table pierced the air. Valerie sighed and pulled away, reaching for her phone. Abby bit back a groan. Just a brief kiss had been enough to get her all worked up.

But Valerie's attention was on her phone now. It was still ringing, but she didn't answer it. Her face was hard as ice.

Abby frowned. "What's the matter?" When she didn't answer, Abby put her hand on hers. "Is everything okay?"

Valerie silenced the call. "It's nothing. Now, where was I?" She set her phone down and picked up her laptop again. "I need to deal with these emails. Why don't you go unpack?"

"Oh. Yeah, sure."

"I won't be long. By the time I'm done, Hazel will be awake, and we can all go out and explore the island together, okay?"

Abby nodded and headed up to the bedroom, her stomach churning. She'd never seen Valerie so flustered before. And all over a phone call? Who was calling her? Why didn't she answer it?

Abby shook her head. It didn't matter. She had a whole weekend at an island paradise with Valerie.

And she was going to enjoy it.

CHAPTER 24

The rest of the day passed in a whirlwind, beginning with a helicopter tour of the island to give them a bird's-eye view of the scenic landscape. Lunch was a beachside picnic, complete with champagne and caviar for Abby and Valerie and finger food for Hazel, followed by a walk through the trees to a hidden waterfall.

They'd capped the afternoon off with a spa treatment and a relaxing massage, which was welcome after a day spent on their feet. There were no cars on the island, but Abby didn't mind walking. It was the best way to experience the island's natural beauty. And there hardly seemed to be anyone else on the island, which only added to the serenity. Even the staff seemed to be doing their best to remain unseen.

It was like they had a little island paradise all to themselves. The only reminder that it was a business trip and not a real vacation was that Valerie's attention was divided. But she had plenty of work to do. And she took notes everywhere they went.

By the time they returned to the villa in the evening, Hazel was fast asleep again. Abby dressed her in her pajamas and set her down on her bed before making her way back downstairs.

She collapsed onto the couch with a sigh. "Hazel is completely wiped out. So am I."

"Not too wiped out for dinner, I hope?" Valerie slipped out of the kitchen, a glass of wine in each hand. "I made a reservation for the three of us at the restaurant, but the two of us can go without Hazel. The resort has experienced sitters on staff. One of them can keep an eye on Hazel for a few hours."

"Sure, but—" Abby yawned. "Didn't I hear something about room service? We could just stay in."

"We could. But we don't want to miss tonight's reservation." Valerie handed Abby a glass of wine. "The chef is world-renowned, and she's only here one night a week. I had the pleasure of dining at her old restaurant in Florence, and it was one of the most incredible experiences I've ever had."

Abby's stomach rumbled. "That does sound pretty good."

Valerie sat down next to her, crossing one leg over the other. "How about this? We have dinner at the restaurant tonight. Then tomorrow night, I'll get the sitter to take Hazel, and we can order room service and have a night in, just the two of us?"

Abby thought for a moment. "It's a deal."

An hour later, she finished tying her hair up and stepped out of the bathroom. The restaurant had a dress code, but luckily, she'd packed a midnight blue cocktail dress and heels, which she quickly slipped into. She'd bought the dress on sale a few years ago. It was far from high fashion, but it was her favorite. She liked the way the blue complemented her hair. Not to mention the way it showed off her figure.

And the hungry way Valerie looked at her when she stepped into the living room told her that she liked it too.

Valerie rose from the couch, her eyes skimming Abby's body. "Don't you look beautiful tonight?"

Abby's cheeks grew hot. She glanced away, then stole a look at Valerie. Her outfit definitely hadn't come off the discount rack, or any rack at all. The black off-the-shoulder dress shimmered gold and silver when it caught the light, and it fit her like a second skin, flowing down her every curve, swaying as she moved. She wore a string of pearls around her neck, and her lips were a deep, dark red.

"I'm starting to think you were right," Valerie purred. "Perhaps we *should* stay in. Have some fun of our own."

"You don't want to show me off?" Abby teased.

"Oh, I do. But I'm a greedy Mistress. And I want you to myself even more." Valerie leaned in close, her lips brushing Abby's ear. "I want to fuck you in that dress until you come undone around my fingers. And then, I want to take it off you slowly, savoring every moment, before fucking you breathless again."

Abby exhaled sharply. But before either of them could say another word, there was a knock on the door.

Valerie took a step back. "But the sitter is here. So we'll have to pick this up after dinner."

She went to the door and let in the sitter, an older woman dressed in the crisp white polo shirt of the staff. Leading her into the other room where Hazel was playing quietly, Valerie rattled off a long list of instructions. She'd already had the sitter vetted and background checked, but that didn't stop her from personally making sure the woman understood her expectations.

Finally, Valerie joined Abby by the door. She took Abby's hand. And together, they left the villa.

They made their way down the winding path that led to the main resort building. The sun was setting, the darkening sky casting an orange glow over the surrounding trees. There wasn't a single soul around, the rustle of leaves and the faint whoosh of the ocean the only sounds they could hear.

As they neared the main resort building, they crossed paths with some other guests for the first time. But beyond a courteous nod or two, none of them reacted to Valerie at all. Abby wasn't surprised. Anyone who could afford to stay at the resort had to be rich, famous, or both.

They reached the garden outside the restaurant. There were a handful of guests milling about, all dressed in evening wear. Valerie exchanged polite greetings with them, her hand still clasped around Abby's.

Abby's pulse fluttered. Why did this make her heart race more than all the other things they'd done together?

Valerie squeezed her hand. "You have that look about you. Something on your mind?"

Abby shook her head. "I'm just having a nice time, that's all."

Valerie put her hands on Abby's waist, drawing her close. "That makes two of us."

Suddenly, a cacophony of clicks rattled the air, coupled with blinding flashes of light. At once, Valerie swiveled around, looking for the source.

Abby blinked, her eyes filled with stars. As her vision cleared, a security guard dressed in black sprinted over to the bushes nearby and dove headfirst into them. A second guard quickly followed. Not a moment later, both emerged, dragging a third man by his shirt.

They threw him down onto the path, ripping a camera from his hands.

"Are you all right?" Valerie said. "Abby, are you okay?"

She nodded, tearing her eyes from the scene playing out before them. Only then did she notice that Valerie had stepped forward and put her arm across Abby's body as if to shield her from the scuffle.

Valerie took her hand, leading her toward the safety of the building. "I don't believe it. We fly halfway across the world, and we still can't escape this." She opened her purse. "I need to talk to my people. I need to make sure those photos don't get out."

But before she could pull out her phone, the resort's owner appeared before her. "Ms. Kane, I am so, so sorry. I do not know how he got onto the island. Let me assure you, this kind of thing does not happen here."

Valerie crossed her arms. "And yet, it *did* happen."

He held up his hands. "I promise you, Ms. Kane, we take our guests' privacy very seriously. This breach will be rectified. The man will be taken to the mainland and charged with trespassing. Our security will ensure that any photographs he has taken are destroyed."

"Yes, they will. It's the least you can do."

He gave her a small bow. "Thank you for understanding. Please, come inside now. Dinner is on the house tonight. Drinks, too. To make up for all of this." He waved his hand toward the paparazzo, who was protesting loudly in Italian as the security guard dismantled his camera in search of the memory card.

Valerie took one last look at the scene, then led Abby into the small, intimate restaurant. Once inside, the resort owner ushered them to their seats. The candlelit table was set for two, with rose petals scattered across it.

"Here, allow me." He scrambled to pull out a chair. "The best seats in the house."

Valerie gestured for Abby to sit, waiting for her to obey before taking the seat across from her.

"Now, if there is anything at all you need, let me know," the man said.

Valerie gave him a nod. "Just give us a moment." As soon as he was gone, she turned to Abby. "Are you sure you're all right?"

"Yeah. That was just… intense, that's all." She glanced at Valerie's face. "Are you okay? It was you they wanted a photo of."

"I'm fine. It's far from the first time something like this has happened. You get used to it." Valerie took her phone from her purse. "I need to get my people on this. While I'd like to believe that security here has taken care of the photos, I need to make sure nothing gets leaked. Those photos cannot, under *any* circumstances, get out."

Would it be so bad if they did? But Abby didn't say that. Valerie had been clear from the beginning that no one could know about them. That it could ruin her career, her whole life.

Abby was Valerie's dirty little secret.

She took a sip of her water to settle her stomach. And when she looked up again, Valerie was frozen in place, her eyes fixed on her phone screen.

"Valerie?" Abby said.

She cleared her throat. "Yes. Just give me a moment to send this message and get those photos taken care of."

She began tapping away at her phone, her face stiff as stone. Was she more upset than she was letting on?

"There. It's done." Valerie put her phone away. "Now, let's try to enjoy dinner."

Abby hesitated. "Are you sure you're all right?"

"*I'm fine,*" Valerie said. "*Don't ask me again.*"

Abby's heart sank. "I'm sorry. I was just worried, that's all."

"No, *I'm* sorry." Valerie reached across the table and put her hand on Abby's. "I shouldn't have snapped at you. Perhaps this incident has me more shaken than I realized."

"It's okay. I understand."

But it wasn't only this evening that Valerie had been acting preoccupied, dismissing Abby's attempts to talk about it. Hadn't the same thing happened when they arrived at their villa in the morning? Hadn't Valerie seemed distracted all day?

Abby had put it down to her being focused on work. But that wasn't it. Something was wrong. She was sure of it.

A server came by, introducing himself before describing the evening's menu to them. It was an eight-course meal, starting with handmade wild mushroom ravioli in white truffle butter sauce, paired with prosecco.

Abby nodded along, but her mind was elsewhere. Maybe she already knew what was wrong with Valerie. Maybe it was *her*. This was the first time she and Valerie had been out in public together without Abby acting as

Hazel's nanny. Maybe Valerie was having second thoughts about the two of them.

Or maybe there was some truth to what Erin had said to her that day in the coffee shop. That whenever Abby started getting feelings for someone, she'd panic and find some reason to end things. Because that was easier than the inevitable rejection.

Abby took a deep breath. She wasn't going to let her doubts get the best of her. Not when her Mistress needed her. If there was one thing Abby could do to help, it was to take Valerie's mind off her problems, if only for a moment.

Tomorrow evening. After dinner, when we're all alone, I'm going to give her a night to remember.

I'm going to give her what she wants from me more than anything.

CHAPTER 25

Valerie set the dessert plate down on the coffee table. "That was divine."

Abby murmured in agreement as she polished off the last of her dessert, a salted caramel mille-feuille with gold leaf and raspberries. Their room service dinner was almost as delicious as dinner at the restaurant the night before. And now that dinner was over?

It was time to put her plan into action.

Her stomach swirled. Trying to seduce a woman who thrived on control? There were so many ways that could go wrong. But just this once, Abby wanted to be the one to give *her* the perfect night, instead of the other way around.

And what did Valerie take pleasure in more than anything else? Exploring her submissive's limits. With her consent, of course.

All Abby needed to do was give it.

And she wanted nothing more than to give Valerie this. After that night at Club Velvet, she was certain of one thing—Valerie would take care of her. She wouldn't let Abby get hurt. She wouldn't let a scene spin out of her control. More than that, she would grant Abby an experience so exquisite that it would be imprinted on her soul for the rest of her days, just like that night at Club Velvet.

Valerie finished the last of her wine. "The sitter has Hazel for a few more hours, so until then, we have the place to ourselves. Whatever will we do?"

Abby tucked her legs underneath herself on the couch. "Actually, I was thinking we could try something… new."

"Oh?" Valerie drew her fingertips up the side of Abby's arm. "Does this something involve you tied up on the bed in lingerie while I ravish every part of your body?"

Abby bit her lip. "It can. It's just, there's something I want to try with you. Something I've never done before."

Valerie studied Abby's face, curiosity and desire smoldering in her eyes. "Go on."

"Well…"

Abby leaned in and whispered into Valerie's ear. When it came to sex, she was far from shy, but there were still things that felt taboo to her.

She sat back on her heels, awaiting her Mistress's verdict.

"You're sure about this?" Valerie asked.

Abby nodded. "I've already prepared."

"Oh? So you've been planning this?" Valerie's voice dropped low. "That's very naughty of you."

Heat rose to Abby's skin. Valerie's lips curled up in a smile.

"All right. Have it your way." She plucked Abby's wine glass out of her hand. "Go into the bedroom and wait for me on the bed. Take that dress off first."

Abby nodded. "Yes, Madame V."

She got up from the couch and hurried into the bedroom, stripping off the loose summer dress she wore. Since they'd planned to stay in that night, she wasn't wearing a bra underneath, which Valerie must have noticed by now.

She slung the dress over the back of a nearby chair, then stretched out on the bed on her side, facing the door. Barely a minute later, Valerie stepped into the room. She was still dressed in the chic white linen minidress she'd worn all day, her lips the same delectable shade of coral red. But her hair was loose now, tumbling down her shoulders in coils and curls.

She sauntered over to the bed, hips swaying.

"My, my." Her eyes skated along Abby's body, lingering on her breasts. "Don't you look good enough to eat?" She reached down and traced a finger along Abby's collarbone and down to her chest, a fingertip brushing her nipple. "I'll give you what you want, just like I said. But first, you're going to give me what *I* want."

Abby shivered with pleasure. "Whatever you need, Madame V. I'm yours to command."

"That's right. You're my precious pet, my treasured toy to do whatever I please with. And there are so many things I want to do with you tonight."

She pinched Abby's nipple, not hard, but not gently either. Abby exhaled sharply, desire shooting through her.

Valerie let out a satisfied murmur. "Stay right there."

Abby watched from the bed as Valerie walked over to the bench at the side of the room where her suitcase sat. She unzipped it and riffled around inside before pulling something out of it.

And when she returned to the bed, she was holding a coil of thick red rope. "Lie down on your back with your hands up."

Abby lay back, bringing her hands together above her head. Slowly, Valerie wove the rope between and around Abby's wrists, binding them together, before taking the tail of the rope and wrapping it around one of the posts that made up the headboard of the bed.

She tied a final knot and gave it a firm tug. "You're not getting out of that. But I'd like to see you try."

Abby pulled at her wrists, straining to break free. But the knots held. She could barely move her arms at all. And the mattress was so soft that it swallowed up her body, holding her in place.

She was immobilized. Powerless. And Valerie didn't hesitate to take advantage of that, stripping Abby's panties from her legs while she was helpless to stop her.

Abby's breath deepened. There was nothing more exhilarating than this. Submitting to her Mistress's mercy, embracing the part of herself that craved surrender. Valerie knew what Abby could handle. She knew how to push Abby out of her comfort zone without pushing her too far. Valerie was in complete control.

Locking eyes with Abby, she drew up the hem of her dress, reaching underneath it. And slowly, she peeled her panties down her legs and dropped them on the bed next to Abby's head.

"Ever since you discovered that hidden room behind my study," she crooned, "I've been dreaming of having you on your knees before me again, worshiping me with those divine lips."

Abby inhaled softly. That moment was etched in her

mind, the taste of her Mistress burned onto her tongue. She longed to relive it.

"And while I adore having you on your knees, having you on your back is just as delicious." Valerie's gaze didn't leave Abby's as she climbed onto the bed and swung one leg over her, straddling her shoulders. "Tell me. Tell me how much you want me."

"I want you so bad," Abby whispered. "I want to serve you. I want to worship you. I *need* you, Madame V."

"Then show me," Valerie said, her voice smooth as silk. "Show me how much you want me."

She shifted up Abby's body, her knees at either side of Abby's head, and pulled her dress up around her waist. She was already wet, her glistening bronze folds tinted with a red flush.

"Worship me," Valerie proclaimed. "Worship me with your lips. Worship me with your tongue. Worship me with your everything."

Deep in Abby's core, desire stirred. But before she could say a word, Valerie lowered herself down onto her mouth, flooding Abby's head with her scent. She parted Valerie's lower lips with her tongue, sliding it greedily up and down her folds. Just the taste of her, the heat of her, drove Abby wild with lust.

She licked and sucked and kissed and stroked, worshiping Valerie like the goddess she was. Above her, Valerie gripped the headboard with both hands, rocking and rolling her hips feverishly. As Abby circled her clit with her tongue, wrapped her lips around it, Valerie shuddered and moaned, her hand falling down to grasp a fistful of Abby's hair.

"Yes…" She moved her hips faster, grinding against Abby's mouth. "Yes!"

All it took was another sweep of her tongue, and Valerie came undone. She threw back her head, a deep cry rising from her chest. Her body shuddered and quaked, her thighs gripping Abby's head as she rode her climax into infinity.

Finally, she fell back onto Abby's chest, breathing hard. "That… that was—"

Valerie dove down, pressing her lips to Abby's in a ravenous kiss. Abby dissolved into her lips, straining toward her. But with Valerie's weight on top of her, her wrists tied to the headboard above her head, she could hardly move. All she could do was channel her insatiable need through her lips.

It wasn't until Valerie broke the kiss that Abby remembered to breathe again. As she sank back into the bed, Valerie gazed down at her, eyes alight with desire.

She trailed a finger down Abby's chest, right between her breasts. "You've served your Mistress well. And now that you've given me what I want? I'm going to give you what *you* want."

CHAPTER 26

Valerie got up from the bed. "Why don't you take a moment to catch your breath while I get ready? Close your eyes."

Abby shut her eyes. She truly was everything Valerie had ever wanted in a submissive. Eager, obedient, and oh so tantalizing.

But her need to serve ran far deeper than the games they played together. Abby longed to surrender not only her body, but her mind, her heart, her *soul*. However, she feared it all the same.

Valerie understood why now. She saw the pain Abby carried, saw that behind her carefree exterior was a desire for comfort, security. But those needs had always been denied to her. So she found what she was looking for in submission, in pushing herself to her limits so that she had no choice but to be vulnerable, all while knowing that her Domme would keep her safe.

Valerie stripped off her dress and opened up her suitcase. She would give Abby what she needed. And perhaps, one day, Abby would feel secure enough to be vulnerable without needing to submit.

Valerie withdrew a strap-on from her suitcase. She liked to be prepared for anything when she traveled, and this trip was no exception. After making some adjustments, she slipped into the strap-on harness, tightening it around her hips. Then she took a bottle of lube from her suitcase and returned to the bed, placing the bottle on the nightstand.

She turned to Abby. Her eyes were closed, her hair fanned out on the pillow beneath her head like a halo of flames. Her lightly freckled skin was pale against the dark bedsheets and just as silky soft, and her breasts were flushed a rosy red, her nipples the same pink as the folds between her legs.

Valerie wanted nothing more than to devour her there and then. Instead, she told Abby to open her eyes.

Abby's cheeks glowed at the sight of Valerie's bare breasts. And when her eyes fell on the strap-on, the blush on her face deepened.

"It's, um… smaller than your other one. Not that it's a bad thing. I mean, it's still pretty big when I think about it. Maybe *too* big." She shook her head. "I don't really know. I've never done this before…"

"Abby, my pet." Valerie climbed into the bed beside her and reached out, cupping her cheek in her palm. "I need you to get out of your head. Can you do that for me?"

Abby nodded. "I'll try." But her eyes simmered with anxiety. She needed her Mistress.

And tonight, she needed a gentle hand as much as a firm one.

"Trying isn't good enough," Valerie said. "I require

your full attention. Your full *devotion*. And you can't give me that if your mind is elsewhere, can you?"

"No, Madame V."

"That's right." Valerie skimmed her fingers down the side of Abby's face. "So forget about everything else. Get out of your head. And be here with me."

She pressed her lips to Abby's in a tender kiss. And when she pulled away, there was no trace of unease in Abby's eyes. But the lust, the yearning in them, had only grown stronger.

"I'm here," Abby whispered. "I'm yours."

Heat sparked deep inside Valerie's body. She pushed it back down. She couldn't let carnal impulses distract her. She needed to be attuned to her submissive's needs at all times, but now more than ever. She was pushing Abby's limits. And with the risks involved, the heightened emotions at play, failing to meet her submissive's needs could be enough to shatter her.

But with Abby? Knowing what she needed was as natural to Valerie as breathing.

"You're mine," Valerie echoed. "You're mine."

She kissed Abby again, prying her knees apart as she slipped between her legs. She ran a hand up the inside of Abby's thigh, eliciting a shiver from her. She was already wet, the heat of her desire radiating from her skin. But that wasn't enough. Valerie had to make sure she was ready.

"Understand this. We're going to take things slow. So very, very slow." Valerie dragged her fingers up to the peak of Abby's thighs, stroking her silken folds. "I'm going to take my time, unravel you slowly, until there's nothing left but *need*."

She slid back down the bed until her head was between Abby's legs. Abby's lips parted with a soft breath. Valerie didn't give her a chance to take another before diving between her thighs.

Abby gasped, her hips rising into Valerie's mouth. Valerie drew her tongue up and down, stroking and strumming and swirling. As she pursed her lips around Abby's swollen clit, Abby's chest heaved, her hips bucking wildly.

"God, that feels…"

Her thighs clenched around Valerie's head. Valerie hooked her arms around them, pulling them back apart and holding them in place as she drove Abby closer and closer to release.

And soon, Valerie felt it—the telltale quiver, the quickening of breath, the half-whimper, half-moan. Abby was right at the edge. And that was where Valerie wanted her.

She pulled away. Abby groaned.

"Oh?" Valerie traced her fingers up the inside of Abby's thigh. "Ready to come so soon?"

Abby nodded. "Yes. Yes, Madame V."

"That's too bad. Because I can't let you come yet. I haven't given you what you want. I need to make sure you're truly ready for me first." She drew her lips up the center of Abby's stomach. "I need you delirious with lust. I need you so desperate for release that you need me more than the air you breathe. I need you so pliant and willing that your body yields to me without hesitation."

"I'm ready," Abby said, breathless. "Please, I'm *so ready*."

Valerie purred. "You know how much I love it when you beg."

She took the bottle of lube from the nightstand and

dribbled it over Abby's stomach, between her outspread thighs, letting it trickle all the way down between her ass cheeks. Valerie's fingers followed, painting a trail that spread the lube down her folds and past her entrance to the tight hole behind it. Abby murmured softly, her head falling back against the pillow.

"Looks like you *are* ready." Slipping out from between Abby's thighs, Valerie drew her onto her side and slid into place behind her. Her arms were still bound above her head, but Valerie didn't untie her. She needed Abby to relax, to let go. And the only way to make her truly let go was to take control away from her.

As she melted against Valerie's body, it became clear. Abby had reached that state of surrender.

Valerie took hold of the strap-on, coating it in the slick lube. Then, she slid it between Abby's thighs, gliding it between her lower lips and dragging it back to her rear entrance.

Abby drew in a shuddering breath. But Valerie didn't try to enter her. Instead, she reached her other hand around Abby's hip and slipped it between her legs, stroking her clit until her body relaxed again. Her fingers still between Abby's thighs, Valerie pressed the tip of the strap-on against Abby's hole.

"Is this okay?" she asked gently.

Abby nodded. "Yes, Madame V."

"That's it, my pet. Just relax."

Valerie slid the tip into her carefully until she felt an easing of pressure as she pushed past Abby's entrance. Abby's body tensed, then loosened again.

"Is this okay?" Valerie asked.

"Yes. Please, don't stop."

Slowly, Valerie eased in deeper and deeper still. And as she bottomed out, a moan fell from Abby's lips.

"Oh?" Valerie snaked her hand up to Abby's breasts, caressing her nipples in time with the hand between her legs. "You like that, do you?"

"Yes." Abby arched back against her. "God, yes."

Valerie hummed with satisfaction, sweeping her lips down the side of Abby's neck. "Do I feel good inside you?"

Valerie shifted her hips, moving inside her. Abby gasped, her whole body shaking.

Valerie stopped. "Is this okay?"

But Abby only twisted her head around, pressing her lips to Valerie's in a fiery, urgent kiss that said more than words ever could.

Valerie deepened the kiss, her arms tightening around Abby's body as she pulled her into her, her hands moving faster at Abby's breasts and between her thighs. Abby strained against her bonds, murmuring and groaning in ecstasy. Valerie ground her hips, reveling in the feel of Abby against her, the softness of her skin, the heat between her legs, savoring every sound and every quiver.

And soon, Abby's shivers turned to tremors, her moans turning to cries.

"Oh…" Her head tipped back against Valerie's shoulder. "Oh!"

A shudder rocked Abby's body as an orgasm took her, her mouth falling open in a silent cry. Her thighs clenched, her legs and feet curling as she pressed back against Valerie.

But even as her body grew slack, Valerie didn't stop moving inside her, didn't stop teasing her clit and her nipples with her fingertips. Not a second later, Abby's thighs began to shake again.

"I… I think I'm—"

Her words were cut off by a deep gasp as another orgasm rippled through her. She quaked uncontrollably, her climax stretching on and on and on, until she collapsed against Valerie's body, breathless and spent.

"Oh god." Her voice quavered as she spoke. "That was… Oh god…"

Abby trembled, heavy breaths rattling through her. She was coming down from the highest of highs. Valerie needed to catch her.

She untied Abby quickly and drew her into an embrace. "I'm here. I'm right here with you."

Abby closed her eyes and curled against her. Valerie pulled her closer, held her tighter. But her breaths didn't slow, and she didn't stop trembling.

"I've got you, my pet. I've got you." Valerie kissed her lips, her cheeks, her forehead, whispering softly. "I love you."

But if Abby heard her, she didn't say a word.

Abby lay beside Valerie under the sheets, her head on Valerie's chest. Her eyes were closed and her body was still, save for the rise and fall of her breasts. Her face wore a serene expression, one Valerie had come to relish seeing on her. It was that subspace high that erased every thought, every doubt, every worry in a submissive's mind, until all that remained was bliss.

Valerie's mind, on the other hand? It was nothing but turmoil.

I love you. Three simple words that had slipped out unbidden. It was as if someone else had said them, someone who wasn't weighed down by the pressures of a life that could fall to pieces at any moment.

Is there someone else?

Does she know the truth?

Does she know what you did to me?

Blocking Francesca had done nothing to stem the tide of messages and phone calls. Instead, she'd grown even more persistent, sending calls and texts from a dozen other numbers. One thing was clear.

Francesca wasn't going to stop.

Abby glanced up at Valerie's face. "Are you okay?"

"Of course." Valerie kissed the top of her head. "How are you feeling?"

"I feel great. That was just…" Abby shook her head. "It was so intense. I didn't know that could feel so *good*. I think you sent me to a whole different plane. I don't want to come back down to earth."

"You don't have to. Not yet. We can just lie here."

Abby let out a contented sigh, laying her head on Valerie's chest again.

"Madame V?" she said. "Can I ask you something?"

"Go ahead."

Abby hesitated. "Have you had many other subs before?"

Valerie drew her fingers gently through Abby's hair. "No, not many. There have been submissives I played with, but only casually. And there was rarely sex involved. I've only ever taken on one long-term sub. Francesca."

"Your ex-wife?"

Valerie nodded. "It's part of why we ended up together. We met when she auditioned for one of my films. She got the part, and eventually, after filming was done, we started seeing each other. It was our shared love of kink that really brought us together. I was the first woman she'd ever been with, and me being a Domme was part of why she took that chance in the first place."

At times, Valerie had wondered if that was the only reason her ex had been interested in her. To Francesca, people were nothing more than tools for her to use. And Valerie was a convenient way for her to have her sexual fantasies fulfilled.

"So what happened between you?" Abby asked. "Why did you end things with her?"

Valerie stretched out on her back. "It's a long story. Our relationship was… complicated. But it didn't start out that way. In the beginning, it was perfect. We were a Hollywood power couple living a life most people only dream of. The films we made together? Even now, I can't deny that they were brilliant. Every single one propelled us further into stardom. But there was one thing we both wanted, more than career success, more than anything else—to have children.

"Or so I thought. It wasn't until we started trying that the cracks began to show. Because the truth is, Francesca never wanted kids the same way I did. What she wanted was a carefully crafted family to show off to the cameras, children she could use as accessories, just like her designer handbags. She'd always been more concerned with her image than anything else."

Abby gave her a sympathetic look. "I know what that's like."

"But I didn't realize it at the time. I was too preoccupied with making my dream of having children a reality. We looked into adoption, but the process was long and difficult, so we turned to IVF. That was difficult too, far more difficult than we expected. And as time went on, our relationship grew strained."

There had been fights. Guilt trips. Breakdowns, accusations, manipulation. And for a while, she'd started to fall for Francesca's mind games.

For a while, she'd started to believe she was the monster Francesca made her out to be.

"Over time, it became clear to me that it wasn't working," Valerie said. "That I needed to leave her. But by then, I was so close to finally having the child that I so badly wanted, that I'd poured my everything into, that I couldn't accept it. I never considered having children by myself. I grew up in an old-fashioned household. I spent my childhood listening to my parents going on and on about the evils of single motherhood, divorce, so-called 'broken homes.' Anything other than the traditional family. I never wanted a traditional family, or a traditional marriage. But a small part of me was still hesitant to go it alone."

"It's hard to shake off the stories we're told when we're young," Abby said, echoing Valerie's words from that night after Club Velvet.

Valerie nodded. "Eventually, I realized it would be better for my future child to have just one loving mother than one who loved her and one who resented her. So I left Francesca. I tried IVF again, by myself this time. And I had Hazel."

Abby blinked. "Wait, Francesca isn't Hazel's mom?"

"Why would you think—" Valerie held back a curse. Abby had been with her the day Francesca stormed the set demanding to see her so-called wife and daughter. "No, she isn't Hazel's mom. Not biologically, not legally. Long before Hazel was born, I made sure the divorce was finalized and all ties I had with Francesca were severed permanently."

Of course, it hadn't been that simple. Francesca had refused to accept it at first. But eventually, she'd conceded, all so she could live single and free again.

However, the shine of the single life hadn't lasted. And now, she wanted Valerie back.

How far would she go to get what she wanted?

"Let me assure you, Francesca isn't part of Hazel's life, or mine." And she never would be. Valerie had to make sure of that. "But she's the last thing I want to think about right now. Not while I have you in my bed." She wrapped her arms around Abby once again. "I want to enjoy this moment with you."

"Me too." Abby nestled against her. "But there's one more thing..."

"Yes?"

"It's just, earlier you said that—" Abby glanced up at her, then looked down again. "Never mind. It's nothing."

Silence fell over them. Valerie felt a pang of guilt. She pushed it aside, glancing at the clock on the nightstand. It was getting late.

She sat up. "I should get dressed. The sitter will be back with Hazel any minute."

Abby nodded. "Right."

"Abby, I..."

Abby gazed up at her. Valerie knew what Abby wanted to ask her. She could see the uncertainty in the other woman's eyes, could feel how much she wanted Valerie to say the words she'd said in the heat of the moment again.

But she just couldn't do it.

"I want to thank you," she said. "For tonight. For this. I needed it."

Abby gave her a weak smile. "No problem. Glad I could help."

Valerie got up from the bed. "You stay here. I'll take care of things with the sitter."

Without another word, she picked up her dress, slipped it back on, and left the room.

CHAPTER 27

Abby unbuckled her seatbelt and got out of her seat, stretching her legs and looking around the cabin. They were on their way back to Los Angeles, and the private jet was no less impressive the second time around. The plush leather seats were as comfortable as her own bed, and there was an *actual* bed at the back of the plane. It even had a full-sized bathroom, with marble accents and a spacious shower. Plus, they had not one, but two flight attendants waiting on their every need, from food and drinks to fine cotton pajamas and five different kinds of pillows. It was a final taste of paradise before they returned home.

Abby wandered over to the lounge area nearby and sprawled out on the couch. When had she stopped thinking of it as *Valerie's house* and started thinking of it as *home*? Was it around the same time she'd started thinking of Valerie as her Mistress?

Her stomach fluttered. Had she only imagined what Valerie said to her the night before in the villa? After all,

Abby had been deep in subspace, her mind in a daze. No, even then, Valerie's words had been clear as day.

She glanced toward the back of the jet, where Valerie was putting Hazel down for a nap. Abby wanted to ask her if she'd meant what she said. She'd already tried. But her doubts had come flooding back, and she'd lost her nerve.

Abby steeled herself. Once they were back home, she would talk to Valerie. She would tell her how she felt.

And she'd pray that Valerie felt the same.

Valerie slid the curtain at the back of the jet closed. "Hazel is finally asleep." She took a seat next to Abby, reaching up and freeing her curls from her bun. "It's been a long few days. I'm looking forward to getting back to LA."

Abby murmured in agreement. She was exhausted.

Valerie stretched herself out on the couch. "I'll say one thing. This trip was a roaring success. The location scouts were right. The island setting is perfect. I have so many ideas for revisions to the script so we can shoot more scenes on location. I want to take full advantage of the natural beauty of the island, really give the film the sense of romance, wonder, grandeur that it needs."

Abby smiled to herself. It was reassuring to hear Valerie speaking passionately about her work again. Since the night before, she'd seemed more energized, more relaxed, less distracted.

Abby's plan had worked.

"But script revisions can wait. Until we land, work is off limits." Valerie picked up her phone and turned it off. "There. No more emails. No more messages. And no more movie talk. Let's enjoy the last of our little getaway together."

As if on cue, a flight attendant appeared in the cabin, pushing a cart with a bottle of champagne on ice and two flutes.

"Ms. Kane. Ms. Peters. The captain has informed me that our ETA is 10:25 p.m. Pacific Time." She set the champagne bucket on the table in front of them before popping the cork and pouring them each a glass. "Let me know if you need anything else."

Valerie gave her a nod of thanks. She disappeared to the back of the plane, leaving them alone again.

Valerie picked up both glasses, handing one to Abby and raising her own in the air. "To a successful trip."

They clinked their glasses together and drank. Abby savored the sweet burn, letting it spread through her body. It tasted better than any champagne she'd had before. No, anything she'd drunk before.

"Now, where were we?" Valerie traced her fingers up the side of Abby's arm. "I believe I was saying I want to enjoy the last of our little getaway together?"

Abby's breath deepened. Valerie plucked her champagne flute from her fingers and set it on the table alongside her own, then drew Abby's face to hers, kissing her soft and slow. Abby sighed into her lips. It had been less than a day since Valerie made her come so hard that her soul left her body, and twice in a row. But that didn't stop her desire reigniting.

Valerie snaked her hand up the front of Abby's chest, drawing it down to expose her bra. She slipped her hand inside the cup, brushing a thumb over her nipple. Abby bit back a gasp, glancing toward the front of the plane. The last thing she wanted was to draw the attention of the flight crew.

One hand still teasing Abby's nipple, Valerie slid her other hand down Abby's stomach, her hip, her thigh, reaching under her skirt. She skated it up to where Abby's legs met, fingertips grazing her inner thighs.

Abby trembled, parting her knees wide as Valerie ran a finger up and down, pushing the fabric of her panties between her lower lips.

She stroked Abby's clit with a fingertip. "It doesn't take much to get you wet, does it?"

Abby didn't dare answer her. She could feel a moan building in her chest, and she couldn't risk opening her mouth and letting it out.

Valerie's lips brushed her cheek as she whispered into her ear. "Take off your panties."

Abby didn't need to be told twice. She lifted her hips, pulling her panties down her legs.

But as Abby pushed them aside with her foot, Valerie held out her hand. "Give them to me."

Heat rose to Abby's face. "You want..."

But she wasn't one to question Madame V's orders. She picked up the panties and held them out to Valerie, her cheeks burning. She'd dressed for comfort for the flight, and the pink cotton panties she'd chosen were no exception. The fabric was worn thin, and the lace trim was stretched out. They were the furthest thing from sexy. She hadn't expected anyone to see them, let alone take them from her.

But Valerie didn't seem to mind. She took the panties, slipping them into the pocket of her linen pantsuit jacket.

"You can have them back when we get home. If I'm feeling generous."

Abby's face burned even hotter. "Are you serious? We don't get home for another ten hours!"

"Twelve, actually. And maybe when we get home, I'll let you come."

Abby groaned. Valerie had gotten her all worked up, and now she was leaving her hanging.

"Don't pout, my pet. Once we get home, I'll make it worth your while. But until then…" Valerie reached over to the table and refilled their glasses. "How about some more champagne?"

With a sigh, Abby took the flute from her and tossed the entire glass back.

It was going to be a long flight.

Twelve hours later, they were sitting in the back of a car, crawling along in the Los Angeles traffic.

"I need to turn my phone on," Valerie said. "God knows Alex has tried to call me a dozen times."

Abby yawned. How could Valerie possibly be thinking about work right now? Surely, she was as exhausted as Abby was.

Valerie reached into her purse and took out her phone. As soon as she turned it on, an endless stream of notifications erupted from it. She scrolled through them, her brows drawn together in concentration, then concern.

She cursed under her breath, then again, louder.

"What's the matter?" Abby asked.

Valerie's voice shook slightly as she spoke. "There's a photo. A photo of the two of us."

Abby's stomach dropped. "What? How? I thought you took care of it."

"I did. This wasn't the paparazzo. It was a guest at the resort. Some social media model, who apparently has no respect for the privacy of such places. She took a photo of us at the restaurant and shared it on her profile." Valerie shook her head. "I can't believe this."

Abby peered at Valerie's screen. On it was a photo of the two of them in the restaurant, leaning towards each other across the small table, Valerie's hand on hers in an unmistakably intimate way. It looked as if they were about to kiss.

"This is a *disaster*," Valerie said.

"Hey, it's going to be okay—"

"You don't understand. You couldn't *possibly* understand!" Valerie shook her head again. "I need to call my publicist. I need to fix this before it's too late."

She dialed a number on her phone. A few seconds later, the call connected. Abby was close enough to hear a woman's voice on the other end of the line.

"Valerie," she said. "You're back. You got my message?"

"Yes. Tell me, what's the damage?"

"Nothing so far. I had legal get in touch with the model. She's taken the photo down. It only got a thousand views or so."

Abby's mouth fell open. *A thousand views? A thousand people saw the photo?*

"I'll have my team keep an eye out in case someone reposts it," the woman continued. "But as of a few hours ago, it's gone."

"Thank you," Valerie said. "Be sure to keep me posted."

She hung up the phone. Abby let out a breath. The photo had been taken down.

So why didn't Valerie seem relieved?

The rest of the car ride passed in silence, tension hanging in the air. Abby didn't try to reassure Valerie again. This was something she couldn't fix.

When they finally arrived back home, Valerie got out of the car and unbuckled Hazel from her car seat, holding her tightly as she hurried toward the house. Abby followed, a sick feeling in her stomach.

They made their way inside. The driver set their bags inside the door, then disappeared with a tip of his hat. It wasn't until he was gone that Valerie addressed Abby.

"Here, take Hazel up to bed." She handed the sleeping toddler over. "I need to—"

Valerie froze in place, then turned slowly, her eyes fixing on something in the living room.

Abby frowned. "What's the matter?" She followed the path of Valerie's eyes.

And her heart jumped out of her throat.

Sitting on the couch, a glass of wine in her hand, was a woman dressed in a black trench coat and heels, with long dark hair and olive skin. And while Abby had only met her once before, she knew the woman's face. Everyone did.

Francesca rose to her feet, her ruby-red lips curling up into a smile as she spoke with a deep, sultry voice.

"Hello, Val."

CHAPTER 28

Valerie's blood froze in her veins. Francesca was here, in her *home*.

And so were Hazel and Abby.

She spoke calmly, her eyes never leaving Francesca's. "Abby, take Hazel to her room and stay there." She needed to get them out of harm's way.

"Uh, okay." Abby glanced between Valerie and Francesca. "Do you want me to—"

"Go," Valerie said. "*Now.*"

Abby obeyed. It wasn't until they were safely upstairs that Valerie addressed Francesca.

"What are you doing in my house?" she snapped.

"What do you think?" Francesca set her half-drunk glass of wine on the coffee table and sauntered over to where Valerie stood. "I'm here to talk. And there's plenty we need to talk about."

"This is…" She shook her head. "How the hell did you get in here?"

"I had to get a little creative. The security system was

the biggest obstacle, but it wasn't hard to get around. You're really still using that old password you use for everything?"

Valerie stifled a curse. She should have been more careful. But she'd never have guessed that Francesca would break into her house. And she'd never told Francesca any of her passwords in the first place, not even when they were married.

Had she been spying on Valerie back then, too?

Francesca stepped toward her, closing the distance that remained between them. "I finally have you alone. It's just you and me now. So let's talk, honestly. No more lies. Just the truth."

"I have *nothing* to say to you."

"Yes, you do. You see, you haven't answered my question. I asked you if there was someone else. I'm still waiting for an answer."

Valerie crossed her arms. "I don't owe you an answer. We're *done*. I've told you that."

"We're *not* done. We'll never, ever be done. Don't you see, Val? We're meant to be together, always. I know it. You know it. Even Hollywood knows it. The movies we made together—they were magic. It just goes to show that our love was meant to be. Sure, we've had our ups and downs, but we got through them. We can get through this too, together. We can be a family again. You, me, Hazel, all of us. Isn't that what you always wanted?"

"This is absurd. Can't you hear yourself? You're being completely irrational."

Francesca's eyes darkened. "You need to stop saying that. You don't want to piss me off. I know things about you, Val. And if those things got out, they could destroy you."

"No, Francesca. I'm done with your games. I'm done with your threats. I know what you're doing. You're trying to paint me as some kind of monster, trying to guilt me, blackmail me, into taking you back. But your bullshit doesn't work on me."

"Maybe it doesn't work on you. Everyone else, on the other hand? What would they think if they knew who you really are? What would they think if they knew all the things you did to me? All the ways you *hurt* me."

Valerie's hands curled into fists, her fingernails digging into her palms. "I never did anything to hurt you. Everything we did, you wanted."

"That's what abusers always say, isn't it?"

"I won't let you twist the truth. I never, ever did a single thing with you without your explicit consent. And I never, ever abused you. Yes, for a while you had me convinced that I did. I let you get into my head, let you manipulate me. But I'm stronger than that. I'm stronger than you. So go ahead. Tell everyone whatever you want. No one will believe you."

"Oh, Valerie." Francesca shook her head. "After all this time, you still don't understand how things work. Who do you think everyone will believe? Beloved Hollywood darling Francesca Moreno? Or the ice-cold bitch producer who half of the industry wishes they could take down?" Her voice dropped low. "I know how to work an audience, darling. The media, the people, they love me. They'll believe whatever I tell them."

Valerie scoffed. "They won't believe your empty

words. Not without proof. Your accusations are baseless. They'll see that."

A slight smirk crossed Francesca's lips. "I wouldn't be so sure about that."

Valerie's skin prickled. Something was wrong.

"Do you remember the first time it happened? That night at the hotel after the premiere? We'd been dating for what, three months? We were in bed together, things were getting hot and heavy, and you suggested we make things interesting." Francesca's voice grew wistful. "That was the first time you tied me up. You were careful not to leave any marks on my wrists since those would be hard to hide. But the marks from the flogger, the paddle? Those were in places that were easy to cover up, so you didn't hold back there."

"What's your point?" Valerie snapped.

"That night, I took photos of the marks you left on me. A memento of the experience that I could look back on and remember. I did the same thing the time after that. And the time after that. And every other time, too. I photographed every bruise, every mark, that you ever left on me. And I kept them all as a record—no, a tribute—to the love we shared."

Valerie's whole body tensed. She'd always been able to tell when Francesca was lying.

And right now? She wasn't bluffing. She was telling the truth.

How many photos did she have? Hundreds, maybe even more. They'd been together for years. And Francesca had always loved when Valerie would leave imprints on her skin. She'd begged for them. They'd fought about it more than once because Valerie had refused to go to the extremes Francesca wanted.

But that didn't matter. Not when Francesca had tons of photos, tons of evidence against Valerie.

"But that love?" Francesca said. "It was all a lie. You were just using me for your sick, sadistic pleasures."

Valerie shook her head. "That isn't true. None of this is true."

"Then prove it. Prove that you loved me. Give me, give *us*, a second chance."

"I can't, Fran. I *won't*."

Francesca shrugged. "Then I have no choice. I'll release those photos. I'll tell everyone about how you took advantage of me, how you took pleasure in hurting me. How you're no different from all those men in Hollywood who use their wealth and status to prey on young women. That's what you've always feared the most, isn't it? Facing the fact that you're no better than *them*? Having everyone find out that the great and virtuous Valerie Kane is just another lecherous Hollywood executive, using her power to exploit young women who have no choice but to go along with whatever she wants?"

Dread flooded Valerie's body. But she couldn't panic. She needed to defuse the situation.

"Just think about this," she said. "Please."

"Oh, I've had more than enough time to think. You've been dodging my calls for months now. I'm done thinking."

"What do you think this will achieve? You want to punish me for refusing to take you back? Is that it?"

"I'm not trying to punish you. I just need you to understand how this feels. I need you to know what it feels like to have your life, your heart, everything you have, ripped to *shreds*. There's nothing you care about more than your precious career, your reputation. And with just a few calls, I could end it."

"You don't have to do this. Why are you doing this?"

For a moment, Francesca was silent. And for a moment, it seemed like Valerie had finally gotten through to her.

Then, something snapped behind her eyes.

"Because I know, Val."

"You know? You know what?"

"I know about your fucking nanny."

Valerie's stomach turned to ice. "What are you talking about?"

"Oh, please. You never were a good liar. That's why you chose a life behind the camera, not in front of it." Francesca pulled out her phone. "But I don't need you to confirm it. I have the evidence right here."

She held her phone up to Valerie. On it was the photo of her and Abby at the restaurant, taken from a social media post.

Valerie held back a curse. The post had barely been up for an hour. The only way for Francesca to have seen it was if she'd been stalking the internet for anything to do with Valerie.

She was obsessed. *Dangerously* obsessed.

"Now," Francesca said. "I'm going to give you one last chance to tell me the truth. *Is there someone else?*"

"Just listen to me. There's no one else. No one."

Francesca nodded toward her phone. "And this?"

"It's just a photo. You of all people can understand how misleading photos can be. We've both had it happen before. We've been snapped by the paparazzi at the wrong time, the wrong place, had a photo twisted to look like something it's not."

Francesca scoffed. "You expect me to believe this isn't exactly what it looks like?"

"Yes. Look, here's what happened. I was in Italy scouting a location for a film, and I took my nanny with me to look after Hazel. I treated her to dinner at a restaurant as a thank you. That's all this was."

Valerie held her gaze. Francesca couldn't know the truth. She'd already vowed to destroy the thing Valerie cared about the most.

But Francesca had gotten it wrong. There were two things Valerie cared about more than her career. Her daughter.

And Abby.

And if Francesca knew that? She would destroy Abby too.

She stepped toward Valerie until their bodies were almost touching. "There's nothing between you? Then what's this?"

Before Valerie could stop her, Francesca reached down and tugged at the piece of lace sticking out of Valerie's jacket, pulling Abby's panties from her pocket.

"Well then." Francesca held the panties up, dangling them from a finger. "Aren't these... cute?"

Valerie snatched the panties from her. "Give them back."

"Why so possessive? They're clearly not yours. Black lace is more your style." Her eyes skimmed up Valerie's body. "That can only mean one thing. They're hers, aren't they? That fucking nanny? What's her name again? Abby?

Yes, Abigail Peters. And she's only 23. That's a little young for you, don't you think?"

Valerie's jaw stiffened. The only way Francesca could know so much about Abby was if she'd gone digging. It was worse than she'd feared.

Abby was already in Francesca's crosshairs.

Valerie needed a way out of this. A way that wouldn't lead to Francesca destroying her life, along with Abby's.

"All right," she said. "You want the truth? Yes, Abby and I are… involved. But it's just sex, nothing more. I'm sure you can understand that."

"Oh, do I ever." Francesca chuckled softly. "I haven't exactly been celibate since we ended things. But no other woman has ever compared to you. That's how I knew I had to get you back." She took Valerie's hand. "So you mean what you said? About you and your nanny? You're not in love with her?"

"No," Valerie said. "It's just a fling. It means nothing to me. *She* means nothing to me."

A smile spread across Francesca's lips. "Then she won't be a problem for us."

A shiver rolled down Valerie's spine. Something wasn't right.

She turned slowly. Her heart sank.

Standing at the bottom of the stairs, her face pale and twisted with pain, was Abby.

CHAPTER 29

"She means nothing to me."

The words pierced through Abby's chest as she stood frozen in place. There Valerie was, Abby's panties in her hand, standing close enough to her ex-wife to kiss her, denying that she ever loved Abby.

Denying that she felt anything for her.

Denying *her*.

Francesca said something Abby didn't hear. Valerie turned toward the stairs. She called out Abby's name.

But Abby couldn't face her. She couldn't face the humiliation.

So she turned and ran up the stairs and into her bedroom, shutting the door behind her.

She took a deep breath, then another, then another. She needed to get out of there. Her suitcase was still downstairs, so she grabbed her duffel bag from under the bed and went around the room, throwing everything she could get a hold of into it, her vision blurry with tears.

She means nothing to me. She means nothing to me. She

means nothing to me. Those words echoed over and over in her mind, drowning out everything else. But Abby couldn't fall apart. She needed to keep herself together until she could leave.

There was a knock on her door.

"Abby, can I come in?" Valerie asked. "I need to talk to you."

Abby just kept stuffing things into her bag. Clothes. Shoes. Books.

"I'm coming in, all right?"

Valerie opened the door and stepped into the room. Abby didn't look at her. She *couldn't* look at her.

"Francesca is gone, okay?" Valerie said. "Now, let me explain—"

"Explain what?" Abby snapped. "I heard what you said. You made yourself very clear."

"No, I… This isn't what you think. Francesca, she was saying these things, these *awful* things. I couldn't let her know about us."

Abby scoffed, her back to Valerie. "She can't know about us. *No one* can know about us. That's what you've been saying all along. You've always treated me like your dirty little secret. One that could ruin your image, your career, your entire life. You wanted me, but you never wanted to *be with* me, not really."

"Abby—"

"I'm such an *idiot.*" She snatched a jacket off the arm of the chair and shoved it into her bag. "This whole time, I thought I meant something to you. And despite everything, I hoped that would be enough for things to finally change. For you to want something more with me." Her voice quivered. "But that was never going to happen. Because I'm nothing to you. I never have been."

"Just listen to me, please."

Abby shook her head. "I've heard enough."

She zipped up her duffel bag and slung it over her shoulder. And without giving Valerie another look, she marched out of the room. She left the house.

And she didn't look back.

Abby knocked on the door to her old apartment. It was past midnight, and Erin was probably fast asleep. But she had nowhere else to go.

Abby slumped down onto the floor next to the door and leaned back against the wall. She was all alone. Just like she'd always been.

The door opened and Erin appeared, a light robe wrapped around her. It took her a moment to notice Abby sitting next to the door.

"What are you—" Erin blinked. "Abby, what's wrong? What happened? Talk to me!"

Abby's shoulders slumped. Did she really look so pathetic? "Can... can I stay with you?"

"Yeah, of course." Erin lowered herself to the ground next to her. "Of course you can."

"Thanks. I know Dan is living here now too, but I couldn't think of anywhere else to go. I promise it'll only be for a couple of days. Just until I can find something else."

"Abby, stop." Her friend put her hand on her shoulder. "You can stay as long as you like. We got rid of the bed when we turned your old bedroom into an office for Dan, but we still have the couch. I'll make it up for you, okay?"

Abby nodded.

"Now, do you want to talk about what happened?"

"It's… It's Valerie, she—"

She swallowed and told Erin everything. About how Valerie had never really wanted to be with her. About how the minute Francesca had shown up, Valerie had pushed Abby aside.

About how Valerie had said she meant nothing to her.

Abby shouldn't have been surprised. It wasn't the first time she'd been tossed aside by someone she thought cared about her. Her mom. Her stepdad.

And now, Valerie.

"I couldn't stay there," she said. "But I feel awful about leaving. I abandoned Hazel. I didn't want to, not again. But I just couldn't be there anymore."

"I'm sure Hazel will be okay. You need to take care of you. And if you won't, I will." Erin squeezed Abby's shoulder. "Come on, let's go inside. I'll make you a drink and we can snuggle up on the couch together like we used to."

Abby shook her head. "I don't want to bother you. I'll just crash on the couch. You can go back to sleep. Dan is probably waiting for you."

"I don't think he's even noticed I'm gone. He could sleep through an earthquake. Besides, you need me. You've put up with me crying over Dan since middle school. I'm just returning the favor."

Abby shook her head. "This isn't anything like you and Dan. You two are in love. I'm just an idiot who thought I was."

"Hey, stop beating yourself up. So you fell for the

wrong person. It happens. But I promise it'll get better." Erin stood up and held out her hand. "Come on."

Erin pulled her to her feet. Abby followed her inside. And she was back in her old apartment with her best friend, just like before.

But things would never go back to the way they were. Because Valerie had swept into her life. Abby had trusted her with her everything.

And now, there was a hole where her heart had once been.

CHAPTER 30

"It's okay, Hazel." Valerie bounced the crying toddler up and down on her hip. "It's all right."

But Hazel's cries only grew louder. "I want Abby!"

"I know, sweetie. I know."

Valerie's phone began to ring. She carried Hazel over to the kitchen counter where she'd left it. Was Abby finally returning her calls?

But it was just Alex calling her, and for the third time that day. She'd told him in the morning that she wouldn't be going into work, which had sent him into a panic. She'd missed deadlines, meetings, important calls. But with Abby gone, she had no choice but to stay home and look after Hazel.

No, that wasn't true. She'd stayed home because she was barely able to hold herself together. If it wasn't for Hazel, would she have even gotten out of bed that morning?

She silenced the call, shifting Hazel to her other hip as she opened the fridge door. "Are you hungry? Let's get you a snack."

"No!" Hazel screwed her eyes shut and began to scream. "No, no, no!"

"It's okay. It's okay." Valerie shut the fridge, then headed into the living room, where Hazel's toys were strewn haphazardly about. "Let's play a game instead."

"I don't wanna play!" Hazel wailed. "I want Abby!"

"*I know,*" Valerie snapped. "But Abby isn't here!"

Hazel began to wail even louder.

Valerie cursed internally. She'd vowed long ago to never yell at her child in anger. She'd never once snapped at Hazel until now.

"Sweetie, I'm sorry," she said gently. "I shouldn't have raised my voice at you. Mommy is just tired."

They both were. Valerie hadn't slept at all the night before, and that was on top of the jet lag.

She kissed Hazel on the forehead, holding her tightly, rocking her back and forth. Finally, her cries grew silent and her tears dried.

Hazel rubbed her eyes with her fists, sniffling quietly. "I want Abby."

"I know," Valerie said. "So do I."

"Where is she?"

"I don't know, sweetie. I wish I did."

Since Abby stormed out of the house the night before, Valerie hadn't heard from her at all. She'd left her car behind, disappearing into the night with her duffel bag and suitcase, her bedroom littered with remnants of her. Valerie didn't know where she'd gone, or if she had somewhere to stay, or if she was safe at all. She had no way of finding out if Abby was all right.

But how could she be all right after hearing what Valerie had said?

Something squeezed inside her chest. She'd never meant for this to happen. She'd never meant to hurt her. But she'd hurt Abby worse than she ever thought she could.

Her phone rang again. This time, it wasn't Alex. But it wasn't Abby either.

It was Francesca.

Her stomach tightened. Before leaving her house the night before, Francesca had told her she'd give her some time to "consider her offer." But Valerie had been too preoccupied to think about anything Francesca had said. And now, her words, her threats, were a crushing weight on Valerie's chest, and she could barely breathe—

She closed her eyes and drew in a deep, calming breath. Then, she picked up her phone, silenced Francesca's call, and dialed Simone's number. It was the middle of the afternoon, and Simone was undoubtedly busy with work. But there was no denying it. Valerie couldn't deal with this alone.

Simone picked up after a few rings. "Val, you're back. How was the trip?"

The trip. The wonderful trip, where, for the first time, it had felt like Abby was truly hers.

Now, it seemed like a distant memory.

"Are you there?" Simone asked. "Valerie, what's going on?"

"It's Francesca," she said. "She broke into my house last night, and Abby was here, and now she's gone, and I can't reach her, and everything is falling apart—"

"Val, just breathe. Is Francesca gone? Are you and Hazel safe?"

"Yes. But Abby, I don't know where she is."

"Where are you right now?" Simone asked.

"I'm at home with Hazel."

"All right. Just give me half an hour and I'll come over. I'll be there soon. We'll figure this out."

Valerie hung up the phone and sat down on the living room rug, setting Hazel down next to her. "It's okay, sweetie. Everything is going to be okay."

The doorbell rang. Hazel sprang to her feet. "Abby's here!"

Valerie reached for her. "Wait, that's not—"

But she was already halfway to the front door.

Valerie followed, not bothering to tell her not to run. Joining Hazel by the door, she opened it up to find Simone on her doorstep.

But not only Simone. Jade, Elle, and Olivia were standing there too.

Hazel pouted and ran behind Valerie's back, peering out from behind her leg. "You're not Abby."

Valerie placed a reassuring hand on her daughter's head. "What are you all doing here?"

Simone gave her an apologetic look. "I filled them in on the situation. I hope I didn't overstep, but it sounded like an all-hands-on-deck situation."

"This is…" Valerie shook her head. "I don't know what Simone told you, but you didn't all need to drop everything to come here."

"Of course we did," Elle said. "You're always there for us when we need you. We're simply returning the favor."

"Well?" Olivia crossed her arms. "Are you going to let us in?"

"All right," Valerie said. "Come in."

They entered the house and made their way to the living room, stepping around the toys and stray toddler clothes strewn across the floor. The house was in such disarray that it was as if Abby had been gone for weeks.

Elle and Olivia took a seat on the couch. Simone nodded to Jade, who stepped forward.

"I can take Hazel for you if you'd like," she said. "That way, you can all talk privately."

Valerie nodded. "I'd appreciate that." She hadn't known Jade for long, but if Simone trusted her, Valerie could trust her with her daughter for a short while. "Hazel, why don't you go show Auntie Jade your toy room? If you ask her nicely, she might read you a book."

Jade held her hand out to Hazel. "I can't wait to see your room. Can you take me there?"

Hazel glanced at her warily, then took her hand. "Okay. I wanna read the penguin book."

She led Jade to the stairs, chattering animatedly about her books. It seemed like only yesterday that she'd been unable to say a single word, let alone have a conversation with someone she'd never met. The once-shy toddler was finally coming out of her shell. Was Abby to thank for that?

Valerie sank down onto the couch across from the others. She needed to fix things with Abby. But how could she when Francesca was hell-bent on destroying everything she held dear? She'd already begun ruining Valerie's life by making sure Abby heard her say all those awful things about her. She would never let Valerie know peace.

And if she knew how much Valerie cared about Abby, she'd never let her know peace either.

Simone sat down next to her. "Now, tell us what happened. In detail, this time. Francesca broke into your house?"

"Yes, last night," Valerie said. "We got back from the airport, and she was inside waiting for me. She's been harassing me for months now, and things have been escalating. I should have done something about it sooner, but I never thought she'd go this far."

She told them everything, going all the way back to the beginning when they were still married. And for the first time, she spoke about the full extent of her ex-wife's behavior.

"She threatened me back then too, when I first told her I wanted a divorce. But I never told anyone. I was ashamed. She made me feel like I had reason to be. Like I was this monster, and she was the victim. It wasn't until after I left her that I saw it was the other way around. But that's why I never dealt with her. We'd been married for years. She knew my darkest secrets, my deepest fears. And that gave her power over me, power I was afraid she would use. And now she's threatening to do just that."

Valerie told them about the photos Francesca had taken. She told them about Francesca's jealousy, about how she'd lied to protect Abby. She told them how Abby had overheard her lies, and it had crushed her.

And now, she was gone.

Valerie held her head in her hands. "Everything has gone so wrong. I don't know what to do."

"That's why we're here," Simone said. "You don't need to figure this out on your own. First things first, you need to deal with Francesca. Rather, you need to have your lawyers deal with her. Call them. And call the police. She's been harassing you, stalking you, and she broke into your home. You want her out of your life? You need to throw the full force of the law at her before she can so much as think about releasing those photos."

Valerie nodded. "I'll talk to my lawyers today, and to the police. I hope it's enough to stop her from acting on her threats."

"It will be," Olivia said. "And if it isn't, I'll lend you my PR expertise and make any false accusations go away."

"Thank you. I appreciate it."

"All right," Simone said. "Once you've dealt with Francesca, how are you going to get Abby back?"

Valerie shook her head. "I don't know. She won't even talk to me. She's not answering her phone. I tried messaging her too, but she wouldn't reply."

"There must be some other way. She's been living with you, working for you, all this time. Don't you have her details? An address, emergency contacts?"

"Yes, somewhere. But I can't take advantage of the fact that I'm her boss to track her down and show up at her doorstep. That would make me no better than Francesca."

"Valerie," Elle said. "I say this with love, but you need to realize it's okay to break the rules once in a while. All this happened because you were too stubborn to make Abby yours for good. Why? Because it's against the rules. Francesca certainly wasn't playing by the rules when she drove a wedge between the two of you. So if you want to fix the mess she caused, you have to be willing to get your hands dirty."

"Elle has a point," Olivia said. "You need to do whatever it takes to find this woman. You're obviously in love with her, and she obviously has feelings for you. Find her.

Apologize. Explain what happened. And tell her how you feel. If she feels the same way, she'll understand."

"You're right." Valerie closed her eyes for a moment. "You're right. I need to get her back."

"And how are you going to do that?" Simone asked.

"I have a few ideas. But first, I need to handle Francesca."

Simone nodded. "If you need someone to look after Hazel while you do, we're here. We can all pitch in."

Valerie steeled herself. She was going to deal with Francesca once and for all. Then, she was going to tell Abby how she felt.

She couldn't let the woman she loved slip through her fingers.

CHAPTER 31

Abby lay stretched across the couch, a book in her hand. She'd been staring at the same page for the past ten minutes. There were so many things she was supposed to be doing. Finding a place to live, to start with. While Erin had told her she could stay as long as she needed, the apartment was barely big enough for two people, let alone three.

But what really made living with Erin and Dan intolerable was the way they kept tip-toeing around her. It was as if they thought she was so heartbroken that seeing them act like the lovey-dovey couple they were would break her. Being treated like she was fragile? That was so much worse.

She needed to find her own place. Not to mention, a job and a car. But she couldn't bring herself to do anything. She was too numb.

She let out a heavy sigh. She wasn't really numb, but she wished she was. Because no matter how hard she tried, she couldn't stop the churning in her stomach and the stabbing in her chest that she'd felt every moment since she'd walked away from Valerie.

Maybe I should have listened to her. Maybe I should have given her a chance...

She shook her head. There was no way she could ever forget what Valerie had said. Before that night, the most humiliating moment of her life had been her sixteenth birthday, when her stepdad had finally snapped and told her he wished she'd never been born.

But what Valerie had done? That had been worse. And there was no taking it back.

The front door opened. Abby sat up. It was too early for Erin to be home from work. Or had Abby wasted another day on the couch without realizing it?

Erin stepped into the living room, shutting the door behind her. "Good, you're here."

Where else would I be? But Abby didn't say that.

Erin sat down on the arm of the couch. "So, uh, heard from Valerie?"

Abby shrugged. "Not for a few days. She kept trying to call me at first, but I guess she gave up."

"Right. Well, you see, she actually called me."

Abby blinked. "*What?*"

"You put me down as your emergency contact when she hired you, remember? Anyway, she just wanted to know if you're okay. She's really worried about you. You should talk to her. Or at least listen to what she has to say."

"What's the point?" Abby muttered. "There's nothing she can say that can undo what she did."

"Maybe not. But aren't you being a little harsh with her? She made a mistake. She's only human. And she wants to apologize, make it up to you. Shouldn't you at least give her that chance? You want to be with her, don't you?"

Abby shook her head. "*She* doesn't want to be with me. She said so herself. I was never more than a fling to her." An image flashed across her mind. Of Valerie standing before her ex-wife in her living room, Abby's panties in her hand, denying that there was anything between them. "She made her choice. It wasn't me."

Erin let out an exasperated sigh. "For god's sake Abby. You need to snap out of it. Valerie is out there fighting for you right now, and you're just going to sit there making excuses?"

Abby scowled. "I'm not... Wait, what did you say? Valerie is *what?*"

"Uh, about that. So when she called me, she wanted to —" The doorbell rang. Erin jumped up from her seat. "Let me get that. I think it's for you, though."

"For me? Erin, what's going on? *What did you do?*"

But her friend was already walking to the door.

She opened it up, revealing a familiar man dressed in a suit and cap. Valerie's driver. He was a man of few words, so Abby had only spoken to him a couple of times.

He gave Erin a polite nod. "I'm looking for Abby Peters."

"She's right here." Erin turned to her. "Well? What are you waiting for?"

Abby sighed and dragged herself off the couch, joining Erin at the door. "Valerie sent you, didn't she?"

He nodded. "Ms. Kane would like to meet with you. I'm here to take you to her, if you agree to it. She's waiting for you."

Abby shook her head. "No. Absolutely not."

Erin grabbed Abby's arm and gave the man an apologetic look. "Can you give us a minute, please?"

The man nodded.

Erin shut the door and turned to Abby. "So, I may have told Valerie you were staying with me."

"Of course you did."

"And she may have told me to expect this."

Abby crossed her arms.

"You have to go, Abby. Look, I know how badly you're hurting. And I know that facing her seems daunting right now, but would she go through all this trouble if she didn't care about you?"

Abby hesitated. Maybe Erin was right. Maybe she needed to give Valerie a chance.

Maybe she was worth fighting for.

"All right," Abby said. "I'll go."

Erin smiled and threw her arms around Abby, squeezing her tight before breaking away again. "I'll tell the driver you'll be out in twenty minutes. You go get ready. You're not meeting Valerie looking like *that*."

"What's wrong with..." Abby looked down at her clothes. She was wearing the same oversized t-shirt and old sweatpants she'd slept in. "Yeah, I'll go change. And fix my hair." She couldn't remember the last time she brushed it.

"Just make it quick," Erin said. "Valerie is waiting."

Half an hour later, Abby sat in the backseat of a car making its way through the streets of Los Angeles. She'd asked the driver where they were going before getting in, but he replied that he'd been instructed not to tell her. That almost made her turn around and head right back up to the apartment, but Erin had practically shoved her into the car.

She stared out the window, nerves dancing in her stomach. It didn't help that they were barely moving. She'd lived in Los Angeles her entire life, but tonight, the crawling pace of the traffic only added to her anxiety. She'd already put the privacy screen up. The last thing she needed was for the driver to notice that she was a mess.

She settled into her seat. She'd lost track of what part of the city they were in, but the streets were lined with designer boutiques, high-end bars, and fine-dining restaurants that Abby could never afford. Not even on the salary Valerie had been paying her.

Finally, they pulled up to the curb. They'd arrived.

The driver got out of the car and opened the door for her. As she stepped out onto the sidewalk, he gestured toward the restaurant in front of them. "Ms. Kane is inside."

Abby thanked him, turning toward the restaurant. The sign above the door was written in French, and it looked even more expensive than the restaurant Valerie had taken her to at the resort in Italy.

That night had been a disaster. So had the night of her sixteenth birthday dinner. Every time she set foot in a fancy restaurant, it turned her life upside down in the worst possible way.

But she'd come so far already. She couldn't turn back now.

She marched to the doors and stepped inside. At once,

she was greeted by the maître d'. "Good evening, Ms. Peters. Let me show you to your table. Ms. Kane is waiting for you."

How did he know who she was? She was too nervous to ask. Instead, she followed him through the restaurant, trying not to think about how out of place she felt among such luxurious surroundings. Crystal chandeliers hung overhead, the tables set with fine china and artful floral arrangements on top of crisp white tablecloths. A jazz quartet played in the corner, and the guests wore cocktail dresses and suits, along with the waitstaff. While Abby had traded her t-shirt and sweats for a comfortable sundress, she was *not* dressed for a place as upscale as this.

They reached a quiet part of the restaurant towards the back. And seated at a table that overlooked the entire room was Valerie.

Abby's heart stopped. Just the sight of Valerie took her breath away. And when her eyes met Abby's, it took all her willpower to keep herself from crumbling.

"Abby." Valerie rose to her feet. "I'm so glad you came."

Abby mumbled a hello as the maître d' pulled out a chair for her. It wasn't until she was seated that Valerie sat down again, giving him a nod of dismissal.

"I asked them to give us some time so we can talk without interruption," she said.

Abby didn't say anything. There were too many thoughts, too many feelings, racing through her mind.

Valerie folded her hands on the table before her. "Thank you for coming here tonight. And thank you for giving me a chance to explain myself. Because I need you to know the truth. About Francesca. About everything

I've been dealing with. And most importantly, how I feel about you."

Abby's stomach flipped.

"I told you about Francesca. About how our relationship grew strained over time. That was… an understatement. I won't go into detail, but the things she did and said weren't pretty. I never told anyone how bad it had gotten because I didn't want to admit it myself. And when we got divorced, I put it all behind me. I thought it was over."

Valerie shook her head. "But my peace didn't last. A few months back, she started calling me, messaging me, telling me she missed me, telling me she wanted me back, trying to reinsert herself into my life. And when that didn't work, she doubled down, showing up at my job, at Club Velvet. But I ignored her in the hope that she'd eventually go away. I know that I should have done something about it, but I was afraid of what she was capable of. Especially when the threats began."

A knot formed in Abby's chest. "What kind of threats?"

"She threatened to expose me, to show the world what a violent, abusive monster I am. Her accusations are false. I never laid a hand on her in any way that wasn't consensual. If anything, it was Francesca who tried to push our agreed-upon boundaries, but I always shut her down. We did everything the right way. We were always safe. But I have no way of proving that. She has photos she took when we were together, of bruises, marks, and more, and she threatened to use them, twist them, to fit her false narrative. It would be enough to destroy my career. No, to destroy me entirely."

"Oh my god. Valerie, I had no idea she was like that."

"I couldn't believe it myself. I never thought she'd go so far. It wasn't until she broke into the house the night we got back from Italy that she told me about the photos and her plan to release them. She tried to use them to blackmail me into being with her again. It made me realize how serious the situation was, how dangerous *she* was. And when she started asking about you, I knew I couldn't let her get you in her crosshairs. So I lied to her. I told her that there was nothing between us. That..."

"That I meant nothing to you."

Valerie winced. "I said that to protect you, but it was a mistake. I know I hurt you. And not just that night. There were so many things I did and said..." Her voice faltered. "All this time, I've been so wrapped up in my own problems that I didn't think about how much my actions were hurting you. But I see now. I know that every time I said we had to keep things between us secret, it cut you deep. I know that refusing to tell you that I love you was a knife in your heart. I know that denying you meant anything to me only buried that knife deeper.

"Saying those words? It was the hardest thing I've ever done. Because even if you didn't hear me say them, it tore me apart to deny that I loved you. I *do* love you, Abby. More than I could ever possibly express."

Abby's heart skipped. Those were the words she'd been waiting to hear for so long. But could she truly believe them?

Valerie held up her hand. "You don't need to say anything. Just listen. Because I need to tell you how I feel. Ever since we met, I've been so deeply drawn to you that I feel it in my soul. You light up my life, my heart, in a way no one else ever has or ever could. And when I look at you, every part of me longs to make you mine. I love you, Abby. That's why I'm asking you to come back to me. Not as my nanny. But as my submissive, my girlfriend, my partner."

She reached to the side, placing her hand on a black velvet jewelry box that was sitting on the table.

"I had this made just for you." Valerie slid the box toward her. "Open it."

Abby picked up the box. It was square and flat, and bigger than her hand.

Tentatively, she opened it up. Inside was a collar made of soft leather in a deep, rich crimson, so dark that it was almost black. It was accented with gold and had a trio of rubies embedded at the front. A small gold lock hung from the buckle at the back, and dangling beneath the rubies was a tiny golden charm engraved with the words, *Owned with love by Madame V.*

"I once told you that when I give you a real collar, it will be a collar that's worthy of you," Valerie said. "A collar you can wear proudly to show the world you're mine. The truth is, there's nothing I can give you, nothing I can say, that could ever convey how precious you are to me. But this is a token of that. A token of my love for you. And if you accept it, I'll make sure to show you how much I cherish you each and every day."

Valerie reached across the table and put a hand on hers. Abby's pulse quickened.

"So, Abby. Will you do me the honor of becoming mine?"

"I..." Abby looked down at the collar, then back up at her Mistress. "Yes, I will. I love you too."

Valerie leaned across the table, cupping Abby's cheek in her hand. "You have no idea how happy that makes me."

Valerie pressed her lips to hers in a tender, aching kiss. Abby sighed into her lips, warmth spreading through her. This was what she'd always wanted. Someone to love, to serve, to devote herself to in all the ways she craved. Someone who would always take care of her, always be there for her.

Someone she belonged to.

"I knew it!"

The screech hit Abby like a slap. She broke away and turned her head to see Francesca marching toward them.

"I knew it!" She smacked the table with her palms, wild eyes fixed on Valerie. "I knew you were lying. You never—"

Her eyes fell on the collar in the box in front of Abby, her face contorting with shock, then anger.

"You... you... I don't believe this." She looked at Abby, then back at Valerie, her eyes darkening. "I'm going to show everyone those photos. I'm going to tell everyone what you—"

"Ma'am, I'm going to need you to come with us."

Francesca flinched, looking over her shoulder. Behind her stood two security guards, their thick arms folded across their massive chests.

"What the hell is this?" She turned back to Valerie. "You need to tell them to leave, Val. I'm just trying to talk to you."

"I'm afraid I can't do that." Valerie took Abby's hand across the table. "They're here because I told security to keep an eye out for you. That I filed a restraining order against you, which you're currently in violation of. So either you let these fine gentlemen escort you out, or we wait here for the police to arrive and escort you out in handcuffs. Imagine the headlines. *Hollywood darling Francesca Moreno arrested*. The gossip sites will go wild."

Francesca opened her mouth, then shut it again, looking around the room. A few tables away, a pair of young women had their phones pointed surreptitiously at the scene playing out before them. And they weren't the only ones.

Francesca glanced at the two men, then back at Valerie. And without another word, she turned and walked away, the security guards following closely behind her.

It was only once she was out the door that Abby remembered to breathe.

"Wow," she said. "You really weren't kidding about her. I can't believe she showed up here. Has she been following you?"

"It appears so," Valerie said.

"I'm just glad she left without you needing to call the police."

"Oh, I'm still calling the police. She's not going to get away with this, or anything else she's done. My lawyers are confident that the break-in and the pattern of harassment are enough to get her charged. And now that she's violated the restraining order, it will speed up the process considerably." Valerie's hands curled into fists. "I'm going to make sure those charges stick. And I'm going to make sure she understands that I will *not* let her hurt me or anyone I love ever again."

Abby put her hand on Valerie's. "Are you okay?"

"I've never been better. And that's the truth. I'll never

hide how I feel from you again. And I'll never, ever let anything or anyone get in the way of us again."

Smiling, Abby leaned across the table and planted a gentle kiss on Valerie's lips. And when she broke away, Valerie was smiling too.

"You know what? All of a sudden, I'm not hungry." Valerie's eyes flicked to the box on the table. "How about I take you home so I can put this collar around your beautiful neck with all the ceremony the occasion demands?"

"I would love that," Abby said.

CHAPTER 32

Abby stepped through the front door of Valerie's house. She'd lived in a dozen different places throughout her life. The homes she'd grown up in. Apartments she'd shared with roommates. The houses of families she'd nannied for. None of them had ever felt like home.

But this? This felt like home.

Valerie took her hand, drawing her toward the stairs. Were they going up to Valerie's bedroom so she could collar her and claim her on her bed after marking Abby as her own?

But instead of going up the stairs, Valerie led her past them to the study and punched a code into the keypad next to the door, unlocking it. Then she drew Abby inside, all the way to the bookcase at the back of the room.

"Why don't you do the honors?" she said. "You remember which book it is, don't you?"

Abby nodded. Then, pulse racing, she reached for the vintage copy of *Wuthering Heights* and pulled.

The bookcase slid to the side, revealing the room beyond. Just like the first time, it was filled with all kinds of kinky toys and gear.

Just like the first time, it took Abby's breath away.

Valerie drew her into the room. "When I had the plans for this house made, this was one of the first rooms I designed. I wanted somewhere that was mine and mine alone, a place I could come to simply *be*."

She looked around the room, her eyes growing wistful.

"I once told you that I don't bring anyone in here who hasn't earned it. That wasn't a lie. But it wasn't the whole truth either." She returned her gaze to Abby, eyes glimmering under the soft lights. "The truth is, I've never brought *anyone* back here. I always hoped that one day I'd find someone to share my haven with, but it never happened. Not until you."

Abby's chest fluttered. "I'm honored that you'd bring me here. Honored that you chose me." She got down on her knees. "I love you. And I swear to you, I'll always be yours. I'll serve you. I'll belong to you. Now, and forever."

She bowed her head and rested her hands on her thighs. This was her place. Not only here, in this house. But here, on her knees, at Valerie's feet.

And there was nowhere she'd rather be.

Valerie placed a hand on Abby's shoulder, her fingers soft on her skin. "It's time."

Valerie disappeared from view before returning to stand in front of her. Abby kept her head bowed, peering up from under her eyelashes. Valerie was holding the black velvet box in her hand, the box containing the collar.

At last, the moment Abby had never dared to dream of had come.

"You've sworn yourself to me," Valerie said. "To serve me, to belong to me, and no one else. And now, I swear myself to you. From this moment on, you are under my care, my protection. I will do everything in my power to keep you safe, to make you happy. I will look after you. I will be there for you. Now and forever."

Valerie circled behind her, sweeping Abby's hair to the side. "With this collar, I bind you to me. Let it symbolize my ownership of you, my devotion to you, and your devotion to me. Let it represent the love we share in all its beautiful forms."

With deft fingers, Valerie slid the collar around Abby's neck and buckled it closed before circling back around her.

"Rise," she commanded.

Abby rose to her feet. Valerie drew a hand up the front of Abby's throat, tilting her head up to examine the collar.

"A collar worthy of the woman I call my own." Her eyes met Abby's, her voice a velvet whisper. "The woman who holds my heart."

She pressed her lips to Abby's, a passionate, possessive kiss that sent desire rippling through her. Abby wrapped her arms around Valerie's neck, her lips parting Valerie's as she deepened the kiss, pushing back against her urgently. Valerie slid her hands down Abby's body, grasping, groping, caressing, her touch as hungry as her kiss.

A murmur rose from Abby's chest. Valerie drew her lips down Abby's neck, kissing and sucking and biting as she reached for the hem of her dress. Not a second later, she had it over Abby's head and on the floor, along with her own dress. Abby's bra soon followed, then her panties, leaving her in nothing but the red leather collar around her neck.

She drew Valerie into her again, need smoldering inside her. Their lips still locked, Valerie pushed her backward, pinning her to the wall behind her.

Abby gasped, her legs threatening to collapse from underneath her. Valerie purred into her lips, slipping her thigh between Abby's legs. Abby ground her hips against her, heat sparking in her core.

"Do you remember the day I caught you snooping in here?" Valerie slid her hand down the inside of Abby's arm, pushing it against the wall. "The entire time, all I could think about was how much I wanted to do *this*."

She seized Abby's wrist, dragging it up the wall beside her. Abby trembled. But before she could say a word, she felt Valerie wrap something around her wrist.

Huh? She looked up, just in time to see Valerie fastening the cuff shut. It was made of the same red leather as her collar. But unlike the collar, it had a gold chain trailing from it.

And the other end of the chain was attached to the wall.

Abby turned her head to the other side, looking up. Sure enough, there was another cuff chained to the wall, waiting for her other wrist. She looked down. There were two longer, thicker cuffs at ankle height on either side of her. Had they been there all along?

Her heart thumped. And when she looked at her Mistress again, Valerie's lips were curled up in a smile.

"When I had your collar made, I had these cuffs made, too." She took Abby's free hand and drew it up to the other cuff, buckling it around her wrist. "I've always loved a matching set."

Ordering Abby to spread her feet wide, Valerie fastened the cuffs around her ankles. All four were spaced far enough apart that her arms and legs weren't strained, but she could barely move them. And she definitely couldn't close her legs.

"Since the day I caught you in here, every time I came into my study, I was distracted by thoughts of this. Of having you here in this hidden room, strung up for my pleasure, subject to my every whim. And this?" Valerie trailed her fingers up the side of Abby's thigh, all the way to her breast. "This is so much sweeter than I imagined."

A whimper spilled from Abby's lips. But that didn't stop Valerie. She knew that Abby's whimpers meant *yes*. She knew that Abby's gasps meant *don't stop,* that her pleas meant *more*. She knew what Abby craved.

Valerie drew her hand up to Abby's collar, tracing her fingertips over the trio of rubies embedded in it. "They say redheads shouldn't wear red. But we've already broken all the rules. What's one more?" She slipped a finger into the ring at the front, pulling firmly. "You look delectable with my collar around your neck."

Abby quivered. Valerie gave the collar another tug. Then, she stepped to the side and opened up a nearby cabinet.

Abby bit back a groan. She needed Valerie, *now*. But cuffed to the wall, she was powerless to do anything but pull and squirm in her restraints as she awaited her Mistress's mercy.

But Valerie didn't make her wait long. Shutting the

cabinet, she returned to stand before Abby, a red leather blindfold in her hand.

"The final piece of the set," she said. "Close your eyes."

Abby shut her eyes. Valerie slipped the blindfold over her head. She heard the click of Valerie's heels on the marble floors as she retreated.

Then, she heard nothing at all.

Her pulse surged, anxiety and adrenaline rushing through her. She took a deep breath, letting the thrill overtake her. Embracing it. Surrendering to it. As the silence stretched out, her mind calmed, her worldly concerns crumbling to dust, leaving only the exquisite ache of desire.

Valerie's hand touched her cheek. "Are you still with me, my pet?"

Abby nodded. She hadn't heard Valerie return. What had she been doing?

She pressed her body to Abby's, skin against skin, bare breasts against hers. Valerie was naked now. And there was something hard pressing against Abby's stomach.

She bit her lip. She didn't need her sight to know what that was.

"Tonight calls for something different." Valerie drew the strap-on down to where Abby's thighs met and slipped it between them, her warm breath whispering along Abby's cheek. "I slipped a little something special into my harness. Something that goes inside me, too."

Abby let out a soft breath. That meant Valerie would feel everything she felt. The idea alone sent heat pulsing between her thighs.

Valerie slid the tip back and forth, skating it over Abby's folds, teasing her entrance. "What better way to claim you as my own than to make you come apart with me inside you and my name on your lips?"

A shiver trickled through her, the throbbing between her legs deepening. "God, yes. *Please—*"

But she didn't get to say another word before Valerie buried herself inside her, filling her completely. Abby gasped, her body stiffening, then loosening, pleasure swelling inside her. And as Valerie began to thrust, that pleasure rolled through her from head to toe.

"Oh, god. Oh, god!"

She squeezed her eyes shut under the blindfold. She was hurtling quickly to the edge, her body obeying the command in Valerie's voice, in her lips as they kissed her neck, in her powerful thrusts and unbridled moans. *Yield to me. Yield to me. Yield to me.*

"Valerie…" Abby's head tipped back against the wall. "Oh, Valerie."

"That's right, my pet." Valerie hooked a finger into the ring at the front of Abby's collar, pulling hard as she growled into her ear. "You're *mine.*"

She slammed her other hand into the wall beside Abby's head, bracing herself as she moved inside her, faster, harder, deeper, reaching depths of Abby's being that had never been touched before. Abby quivered and moaned, pleasure rising within her.

"Oh!" She writhed against the wall desperately. "Can I come for you?"

"No, my pet. Come *with* me."

Valerie thrust into her harder, her chest heaving with heavy breaths. Abby bit down on the inside of her cheek, holding back the tidal wave inside her until Valerie began to tremble. Only then did Abby give in, letting her pleasure build and build until it reached a crescendo.

And then, the climax, an eruption that rose from deep in her core and spread through her whole body. She shuddered and shook, waves of ecstasy ripping through her, unrelenting. At the same time, Valerie quaked against her, hips arching, breasts hitching against Abby's, as she cried out in release.

But the only sound that fell from Abby's lips was her Mistress's name. *Valerie. Valerie. Valerie.* A cry. A prayer. A plea.

And as she tumbled into the sweet oblivion of surrender, she knew that Valerie would always be there to answer that prayer.

CHAPTER 33

When Valerie awoke the next morning, she was alone in her bed.

Closing her eyes, she rolled over and drew in a deep breath, savoring Abby's lingering scent, her warmth, on the sheets beside her. There was only one thing sweeter than this. And that was having Abby in her arms.

Valerie slipped on a light silk dressing gown and made her way downstairs. It didn't take her long to find Abby. She was in the kitchen, nursing a cup of coffee.

Her face lit up as Valerie entered the room. "You're awake."

Valerie planted a kiss on her lips. "Good morning to you too."

"Here, I made you coffee."

Abby picked up a mug of steaming black coffee from the kitchen counter and handed it to her. Valerie sipped it slowly, letting its warmth revitalize her.

She glanced at the clock. It was past 9 a.m. "Looks like I slept in."

"I thought about waking you up, but you looked so peaceful," Abby said. "I didn't want to disturb you."

"I'm glad you didn't. I needed that. It's been years since I've slept in."

And not only because she had a two-year-old. There was always something that needed doing, some emergency to deal with, some fire to put out.

Not this morning. Valerie didn't have to look at her phone to know she had countless messages and emails waiting for her. But they didn't matter. Not right now.

All that mattered was the woman standing before her.

A pink flush bloomed on Abby's cheeks. "Why are you looking at me like that?"

"No reason." Valerie drew her arms around Abby's waist. "I'm just happy the woman I love is finally *mine*."

She pressed her lips to Abby's in a deep, demanding kiss. Abby melted into her body, her lips growing hungrier and hungrier—

The doorbell chimed. Valerie broke away.

"That must be Simone and Jade with Hazel." She set her coffee cup down on the counter. "I'll get it."

She made her way to the front door. As soon as she opened it, Hazel flung herself at her.

"Mommy!" She threw her arms around Valerie's legs, holding her tightly. "I missed you."

"I missed you too, sweetie." Valerie scooped Hazel up in her arms before greeting Simone and Jade. "Why don't you come in?"

They stepped inside. As she shut the door, Hazel leaped from her arms and ran into the living room. Valerie followed, Simone and Jade behind her.

"Thank you again for taking Hazel for the night," she said. "I tried to find a sitter, but—"

Simone held up her hand. "We're happy to help."

"I appreciate it," Valerie said. "I hope she wasn't too much trouble."

"Not at all," Simone replied. "We had a lovely time. It helps that Hazel took a liking to Jade after the other day."

"Hey, she took a liking to you too. You were great with her." Jade slipped her arm into Simone's. "You'd make an incredible mom, you know?"

Simone shook her head. "I never imagined I'd want kids. Everything I went through growing up put me off having children for good, I thought. But after spending time with Hazel, I'm starting to reconsider."

Valerie didn't miss the way Jade perked up at Simone's words. "I think you'd make a good mom too."

Abby chose that moment to emerge from the kitchen, coffee cup in hand. "Hi."

A blush rose up her face. Was she embarrassed that she'd been caught the morning after? Or was it because the first time she met Simone and Jade, Valerie had been groping her like a horny teenager in the middle of the club?

But before anyone could say another word, Hazel squealed with delight.

"Abby!" The toddler raced over to her. "You're back!"

Abby lifted Hazel high into the air before pulling her into a hug.

"That's right," she said. "I'm back. And I'm not going anywhere."

The night before, she and Valerie had stayed up until the early hours of the morning, talking about what would happen next. While they didn't yet know exactly what their life together would look like, Valerie had made one thing clear.

Abby was hers. And Valerie was never letting go of her again.

"I'm glad you two worked things out," Simone said. "By the way, did you hear the news?"

"What news?" Valerie hadn't looked at her phone since the evening before.

"It's Francesca. She was arrested at her home last night."

"Last night? That was fast." Valerie grabbed her phone from the coffee table. She had a dozen missed calls and messages from her lawyer, her assistant, and her publicist.

But instead of reading them, she searched Francesca's name online. The very first headline?

Francesca Moreno arrested on charges of stalking and harassment against ex-wife Valerie Kane.

She clicked the link. At the top of the page was a slideshow of pictures, starting with a series of photos of Francesca being escorted through the restaurant by security and ending with a grainy shot of her being taken from her home in handcuffs. There was even a video of her at the restaurant, yelling inaudibly at Valerie.

She studied the video. It showed Abby sitting across from Valerie, her face fully visible. It was only a matter of time before speculation and rumors about their relation-ship began. They'd have to go public with it sooner rather than later.

But that didn't bother Valerie. Not anymore. She didn't care if anyone thought her relationship with Abby was wrong. She knew in her heart that the love they shared was right.

She skimmed the rest of the article. Francesca was being held pending charges of stalking, harassment, and breaking-and-entering. On top of that, she'd been unable to post bail, so she had no choice but to remain in police custody.

Valerie scoffed in disbelief. How was it possible that Francesca couldn't afford bail? The money she'd made from her acting career was enough to last a lifetime, several lifetimes, even. Had she frittered it all away, not realizing that one day, her work would dry up? Hollywood was a fickle mistress. And now that Francesca's star had dimmed, she'd lost it all. Her fame. Her money. Everything.

That was why she'd been so desperate to get Valerie back. She had nothing left.

But Francesca wasn't her problem any longer. And she never would be again.

Abby slipped a hand into hers. "Are you okay?"

"I'm wonderful." Valerie slipped her phone into her pocket and gave Abby's hand a squeeze. "Francesca is finally facing consequences for her actions. She's out of my life for good. And now, I can dedicate myself to building a new life with you."

Abby smiled. And in that moment, Valerie vowed to do whatever it took to protect that smile for the rest of her days.

Simone cleared her throat. "That's our cue to leave."

"Are you sure?" Valerie said. "You're welcome to stay awhile."

Simone shook her head. "Thank you, but we need to

get going. We're meeting with Ashton to work out the details of her investment in the club."

Abby's eyes widened. "You mean, *the* Ashton? From the real estate mogul family?"

Valerie nodded. "She wants to invest in Club Velvet. It's certainly unexpected, but her interest is genuine. It's not a done deal yet, so we'd appreciate your discretion."

"Yes, of course," Abby said.

Simone put a hand on Jade's back. "We'll get out of your hair."

They said their goodbyes, but not before Hazel made them promise to come back and visit soon. And as Valerie shut the front door, she let out a contented sigh. It was just the three of them now. Her, and the two people she loved the most in the world.

But as she swept Hazel into her arms again, Abby's face paled.

"Crap." She began looking around the room. "Where'd I put my phone?"

"What's the matter?" Valerie asked.

"I was supposed to message Erin last night. I promised her I'd check in after meeting with you. She must be so worried, especially after I didn't come home—"

Valerie held up a hand. "No need to panic. She already knows you stayed over."

"What? How?"

"She messaged me last night while you were in the shower. She has my number from when I called her. Rest assured, I told her that you're fine and you're with me."

"Oh." The color returned to Abby's face. "Thanks. I just completely forgot."

"Not a problem." Valerie shifted Hazel to her other hip. "She really cares about you, you know?"

"I do. She's a good friend."

"I'd love to meet her one day."

"She'd love to meet *you*. Seriously, she's a little obsessed with you. If she wasn't straight, I'd be worried."

"Even if she wasn't straight, you wouldn't need to worry. You're the only woman I'll ever want." Valerie cradled Abby's face in her palm, stroking her cheek with her thumb. "Now, why don't we all have some breakfast?"

Abby nodded. "I'll whip something up. Eggs for Hazel, and toast for you?"

Valerie shook her head. "Let me take care of it this morning. After all, you and Hazel have some catching up to do."

"We sure do." Abby took Hazel from her again, holding her close. "I've missed you so much."

Valerie's chest filled with warmth, a smile pulling at her lips as she went into the kitchen to make breakfast for her family.

Abby threw her hands up. "Where the hell is it?"

She opened each drawer of her dresser, one by one. *Nothing.* Then she went over to Valerie's dresser and opened all of her drawers too.

But her collar was nowhere to be found.

Abby cursed. She couldn't have lost it. She'd kept it in the same place for years, in its box in the top drawer of her dresser, stashed safely away until the next time she had the chance to wear it.

But lately, she'd only gotten to wear it for brief play sessions at home. She and Valerie had been far too busy for anything more than that. Hazel had just started kindergarten, and it had taken her some time to adjust. On top of that, *The Resort* had premiered a couple of weeks before, and as Valerie had predicted, the film was a hit. She had her hands full with publicity and interviews.

And so was Abby. They'd gone public with their relationship years ago, but with the success of *The Resort*, Valerie had been thrust even further into the spotlight.

Everyone wanted to know about the woman behind the powerhouse that was Valerie Kane. The attention had felt awkward at first, but Abby had gotten used to it. Having Valerie by her side made it easy.

But her time in the spotlight hadn't been without its problems. All the publicity had drawn the attention of her mom and stepdad, who were suddenly very interested in being a part of her life again. Abby had used the opportunity to reconnect with her brothers, who were old enough now to understand why she'd left home. But after years of silence from her mom and stepdad, she wasn't interested in rekindling her relationship with them. They were only interested in her girlfriend's fame, not to mention her money.

Abby didn't need them. She already had a family, in Valerie, and Hazel, and Erin, and all Valerie's friends, who, over time, had become her friends too.

And that was what tonight was about. Escaping the spotlight and all the pressures that came with it to spend time with their friends in the sanctuary they'd built together. Valerie had left to take Hazel to the sitter's house half an hour ago. And when she came back, they were going to Club Velvet.

Which was why Abby *needed* her collar.

She groaned. "Where is it?"

"Looking for something?"

Abby glanced at the door to the bedroom. Valerie had returned.

"You're back." Abby began riffling around in her night-stand. "I can't find my collar. I don't know where I put it, but it's not here. I need it for—"

"Abby, stop," Valerie said. *"Breathe.* You haven't lost your collar. I have it right here."

"You do?" Relief washed over her. She turned to see Valerie holding the black velvet box in her hands. "Oh, thank god."

But as she reached out to grab it, Valerie moved it behind her back. "I took your collar to the jeweler. It needed some modifications."

Abby frowned. "Was there something wrong with it?"

"No, not really. I simply wanted to make a few small improvements."

"Oh. You didn't have to. Not that I don't appreciate it," Abby added quickly. "But it was perfect the way it was."

"It was *almost* perfect. I'm sure you'll like it even more now. Would you like to see it?"

Abby nodded. She needed to know why Valerie was acting so strange.

Valerie held the box out in front of her and opened it up. "What do you think?"

Abby peered down at the collar. It looked the same as it had before, but with one difference. The trio of rubies at the front?

They'd been replaced with three massive diamonds, which sparkled and shimmered every color of the rainbow.

"This is..." Abby's hand flew to her chest. "These diamonds, they're stunning."

"That's not all. Look closer."

Abby examined the collar again. Her heart stopped.

Dangling from the collar, right next to the tag that read *Owned with love by Madame V,* was a gold diamond ring.

Abby's lips parted in a silent gasp. She looked up to find Valerie gazing back at her, her eyes sparkling brighter than the diamonds on the ring.

"When I first gave this collar to you, it was to mark you as my treasured submissive," she said. "But that isn't enough for me. Not anymore. Because what I want to give you, what you truly deserve, is a collar worthy of my wife."

Abby's breath caught in her chest. "Do you mean…?"

"Yes, I do." Valerie got down on one knee. "Abigail Peters. My love. My life. My everything. Will you do me the honor of marrying me?"

Abby's heart soared. "Yes, Valerie. Yes."

She fell to her knees and threw her arms around Valerie's neck, kissing her until she was breathless and dizzy. Then she kept on kissing her until Valerie broke away, forcing her to come up for air.

She took Abby's hand and drew her to her feet. "Allow me."

Carefully, she removed the diamond ring from the collar and slipped it onto Abby's finger.

"A perfect fit." She took both of Abby's hands in hers. "And this is only the beginning. I don't just want you to be my wife. I want you to be Hazel's mom, too."

Abby blinked. "What do you mean?"

"I want you to adopt her. And so does she. I asked her how she feels about it, and she could barely contain her excitement. I wasn't surprised. She loves you to death, and she already calls you Mom half the time. But I've been holding off on having a proper conversation with her about it until today so she wouldn't spoil the surprise. It isn't easy to get a five-year-old to keep a secret. Especially one as talkative as Hazel."

Abby stared at her. "That's why you insisted on taking her to the sitter yourself."

Valerie nodded. "So, what do you say? Would you like to become Hazel's mother?"

"Valerie…" Abby's voice quivered as she spoke. "Of course. It would mean the world to me."

Valerie smiled. "It will mean the world to me, and Hazel too. You're already our family. This just makes it official."

She kissed Abby again. This time, the kiss was soft and slow and sweet. But it was no less possessive, no less intoxicating.

Valerie drew back. "How about we head to Club Velvet and share the good news? I made sure everyone is coming tonight so we can all celebrate together."

"That sounds wonderful," Abby said. "Let's go."

"Aren't you forgetting something?"

"What do you… Oh!" Her hand flew to her neck. "My collar."

"Let me put it on for you."

Valerie took the collar from the box. Abby held her hair out of the way as Valerie slipped the collar around her neck and buckled it closed.

"There," Valerie said. "Why don't you take a look?"

She guided Abby over to the full-length mirror in the corner and slipped behind her.

"Finally." Drawing her in close, Valerie reached around her to trace her fingertips over the collar, her eyes locking with Abby's through the mirror. "A collar that truly shows everyone how precious you are to me."

Abby reached up, her hand joining Valerie's at her neck. There was a comfort, a familiarity, in the collar's soft leather, the shining gold accents, the way it fit snugly around her neck. But the diamonds transformed it into something new, something different, something unknown, just like their future together.

That future stretched out in the mirror before them.

And it was beautiful.

ABOUT THE AUTHOR

Anna Stone is the author of lesbian romance bestsellers Being Hers, Tangled Vows, and more. Her sizzling sapphic romances feature strong, passionate women who love women. In every one of her books, you'll find off-the-charts spice and a guaranteed happily ever after. Anna lives in Australia with her fiancée and their two cats. When she isn't writing, she can usually be found with a coffee in one hand and a book in the other.

Visit **annastoneauthor.com** to find out more about her books and to sign up for her newsletter.

9 781922 685278